THE LOST

THE LOST

KIM PRITEKEL

SAPPHIRE BOOKS

SALINAS, CALIFORNIA

This and other Sapphire Books titles can be
found at
www.sapphirebooks.com

Kim Pritekel Books

Standalones
1049 Club
After Shadow
Blinded
Connection
Control – with Alex Ross
Damaged
Shadow Box
Swann Song
The Gift
The Plan
Wild – with Alex Ross
Unbroken
Unmasked Desire
Zero Ward

Dance with Me Series
Curtain Call
Encore Performance

The Traveler Series
The Traveler: The Hunted
The Traveler: The Hunter

The Wynter Series
Finding Faith
Taking Liberty
Justice Won
Keeping Hope
Showing Mercy
Having Honor

The Destiny Series
She Who Would be King
Daughter of Ankou
Doors
She Who Dreams
Shadows
She Who Would be Queen

Destiny Series – Ancients:
The Lost

Prologue

Lacedaemon, Greece—75 CE

Bampás?" Kazia called out, dark eyebrows furrowed in irritation as she scanned the wall where the tools were hung. Again. "It is not here!"

"What do you mean, 'it is not here'?" Eugene bellowed, startling his daughter, as he was no longer back at the forge where she'd left him, but standing mere feet behind her in the supply room.

The fifteen-year-old looked at him. "I mean what I said," she growled, her irritation growing with his sudden presence.

She hated when he did that. She tugged nervously on the fabric of her chiton, adjusting the lightweight fabric garment that draped over her body, fastened at both shoulders.

He scanned the wall where all his tools and their accessories hung in neat rows from the hooks and shelves he'd made for them. Sure enough, there was a blank spot for what he'd sent her to fetch. Turning away, he reached down into the large pocket of the leather blacksmith's apron he wore and fished something out.

Kazia crossed powerful arms over her chest, head slightly cocked to the side and dark eyebrow arched as she waited for an apology. Of course, none was forthcoming, even as he stared stupidly at the very tool he'd sent her in to get. At one time, not too terribly long ago, he would have taken her into a playful headlock in lieu of verbalizing his folly, and the two would have gone back to work.

At one time, and that time was no longer.

A man raised with six brothers and then his years in the Hoplite infantry, her father was a physical man, lover of all things sports and physical activity. Initially, he'd been delighted to find that his daughter had been blessed by Kratos with almost divine strength, stamina, and an almost instant ability to gain muscle, all while remaining everything that a little girl—and now, a young woman—should be biologically, all of which Eugene had done his level best to ignore.

In fact, Kazia had been told her entire life that she was incredibly beautiful with her long, dark brown, nearly black hair and so-called soulful hazel eyes. She had developed womanly curves in all the right places where men liked them, and frankly she found it an impediment to life, not a benefit.

She cared absolutely nothing about any of that. Her life was her father's blacksmith's shop and learning the trade. She was already a skilled smith and, in her opinion, her technique and creativity were growing superior to her father's. She'd never tell him that, though. The two had a complicated relationship as it was.

Her parents had been older when she'd been born, and her mother, Maia—eight months in her grave—had been overjoyed to finally be blessed. After years of unanswered prayers and offerings to the goddess Demeter, their family had expanded. Though Kazia had never been told this, she knew that her father had been disappointed that she wasn't a boy. His one shot at fatherhood wasted, no doubt, in his mind.

Like most of the male persuasion, he was a proud man, though his pride went far beyond the average.

His fell right over the cliff into narcissism and, at times, a darkness that used to really bother Kazia's mother. Maia had been a wonderful woman, very small in stature but huge in heart.

Kazia often wondered how such a magnificent creature had ended up with Eugene, but it had been so for many years before her birth. As she'd grown larger and stronger—nearly the height of her father by the time she was twelve—she'd appointed herself as her mother's personal protector. If it had been a bad day at the shop, Kazia put herself in the line of his attacks, more than once literally shoving her mother behind her.

Physical abuse hadn't been an everyday occurrence by any stretch, but when it happened, Eugene's already dark eyes would turn nearly black. Kazia and her mother had always referred to it as "the storm." His entire countenance would change, and the father and husband they both knew, already a difficult man, would vanish. In his place was a man impossible to please, no matter if it was in word or action. By that point, he was looking for a fight in any and everything either of them did.

Kazia would often provoke him so he'd literally take it out on her. However, the last time it had happened had been when she was fourteen. She'd beaten him to a bloody pulp during one of his rages. He'd never touched her again, nor even tried with Maia. But, that had also been when their physical play had stopped, too.

No, Kazia wasn't the son he'd wanted, but she could keep up with any boy, let alone her father. They'd wrestled in the courtyard of their little villa, ironically sounding like a couple of giggling little girls in their play. They wouldn't stop until they were both panting from exertion, hair plastered to their heads with sweat. Usually, one or both were also bleeding from somewhere, be it from an errant elbow or a bad scrape to the knee when taken down by the other.

Once her mother grew sick and died, their relationship changed yet again. He no longer pounded her on the back at the end of a long day for a job well done. He was moody and seemingly indifferent. He did, however, still allow his customers who had commissioned weapons to come in and try their luck against Kazia.

Like pretty much everything that required physicality, Kazia had an innate mastery of bladed weapons as well. So, it had begun when she was twelve. A customer had come in to commission a xiphos be made for his young son as a gift. Though he had been a bit too young yet to fulfill his duty with the Hoplites, the man wanted the boy to have an edge and learn how to fight.

Kazia's ears had perked up at this, of course. She'd offered to be a sparring partner for the boy, not much older than she was. By year's end, she'd been pitted up against teenaged boys and then, eventually, grown men. It had become a gimmick for Eugene's business, bringing in customers just to see the Freak of Lacedaemon pummel her opponents.

Bets were made and so was money, so Eugene not only let it continue, but *insisted* that it did. For her part, Kazia was fine with it. She was able to get some of her aggression out in her growing hurt, long turned to anger, toward her father and his indifferent attitude toward her as a daughter. But also, to learn. She had no idea what would happen, but she could feel those storms brewing again, and she wanted to be ready.

❧ ❧ ❧ ❧

It was a particularly sunny day. She would always remember that. Kazia and her father were out in town to get some supplies, but first, as always, he wanted to make his offerings at the Temple of Ares. The God of War, a deity her father had always worshipped, she'd been told. Ares was not a very popular god, as he represented the darker aspects of warfare, but somehow it made sense for Kazia's father.

He never let her go in with him for reasons she didn't understand. His response, when she'd bothered to ask for one, had always been, "This is not for you." That had made no sense to her, considering he had her sword fighting on the regular with men and used to wrestle with her until one or both of them were bleeding.

But, like so many things, her father was a man of contradictions and, often, hypocrisy. So, while he was in the temple doing whatever it was he did, Kazia walked over to a stone bench near a water fountain and sat down. Looking around, she watched people going about their business in singles, pairs, or groups.

Nothing remarkable about any of them until she saw a woman who seemed to have just…*appeared*. Kazia started at her very sudden presence. No doubt she'd stepped out from one of the surrounding buildings or temples unnoticed. But, something about her felt so strange to Kazia.

What got her the most, however, was how utterly stunning she was. She wore similar dress of every other woman around, including Kazia herself, but there was something about her. Her hair was midnight black, even darker than Kazia's own hair, long and twisted into braids atop her head, again, like the other women around them.

She looked to be somewhere in her twenties and was utterly breathtaking. Kazia had never seen anything like her before, and her eyes... They were a very light blue, bordering on silver, and they were looking right at her. A wide pathway lay between them, the woman disappearing and coming back into view as people strolled by.

Kazia was riveted to the spot. The woman's chin was raised just a bit in a posture of almost challenge. With the combination of the paleness of her skin and chiseled femininity of her features, it almost looked as though she'd been sculpted by the finest of artists with light blue sapphires added for her eyes.

If Kazia hadn't known that the woman hadn't been standing there mere moments before, she honestly would have thought she wasn't real. She was too...*perfect.* Something about her was unlike any of these other people wandering about, none of which seemed to notice her.

"Ready?"

Startled, she turned to see her father walking over toward her. Nodding, she quickly turned to see the woman was gone, though she did notice an elderly man now standing in the exact spot she had been.

Shaking the image out of her mind, Kazia pushed to her feet. She glanced one more time, the old man looking back at her before he turned and walked away.

"Coming?" Eugene asked, already taken several steps away, irritation in his voice.

Nodding again, she joined him as they headed

back toward their villa. Imaginary or not, she couldn't get the woman's face out of her mind's eye. There was no way she was real, she reasoned. She had to come from Kazia's own feverish imagination. Or perhaps one of the gods had planted it for some reason?

She doubted that one very much. Though she'd never, ever said the words aloud, she didn't worship the Greek gods. She didn't worship *any* god. Though she'd been raised in the practice of prayer and offerings, she just couldn't wrap her mind around it. Her mother had been very connected to the Greek gods, but Kazia felt nothing.

"When we get home," he said, pulling her from her musings once again. "I need you to go to the shop. Linus will be by to pick up his order."

Kazia nodded dutifully. "All right."

⁂

Using the key Eugene had given her, Kazia let herself into the shop. Though the sun had gone to sleep for the night, Apollo hadn't relinquished the heat left behind. She wanted a cool bath and bed. The shop was, as expected, dark and quiet. It was a simple space: the showroom, where she was now; a doorway leading to the room where all the tools and raw material was kept; then in back, the forge.

Sitting atop the counter was the wrapped package that would be picked up by a regular customer. He was a farrier, so was back often for shoes for this or that animal with this or that dimensions. A nice enough guy, though Kazia felt his eyes on her a little longer than she'd like. At fifteen pushing sixteen, Kazia was well in range to be married or certainly spoken for.

She'd never so much as kissed a boy, let alone let one near enough to whisper sweet nothings in her ear. She'd gut him first. Amusing herself at that thought, she blew out little puffs of air from expanded cheeks, like a little chipmunk, to amuse herself as she wandered around the shop by the light of the oil lamp she'd lit upon entering the space.

She stopped, hand resting on the wood slab of the counter, when she heard something from the supply room. Glancing that way, she looked into the darkness beyond the open door. She heard nothing else but decided to check. A few years ago, a man had broken in, and the last thing she needed was for it to have happened again and she not check it out. Her father would skin her alive for that one.

She headed in that direction when the door to the shop opened. Of course she hadn't locked it, as their customer needed to get in. But when she turned to see if Linus had finally shown up, it was not the farrier who was looking back at her. She barely had time to register that when she was hit in the back of the head with something very hard.

Crying out in pain and surprise, she was nearly knocked to the floor. Something told her that if she went down, she wouldn't be getting back up. Instead, she turned and let her instincts take over. With an inhuman growl, she turned to face whoever had hit her and used her shoulder to plow into a midsection.

The ferocity of her attack sent the assailant wheeling backward and into the wall of her father's hung tools. A horrible clatter met the person upon contact. Kazia just barely managed to move away to prevent planting her head into the wall along with him. The person, who looked to be the size of a man, went down.

She just barely noticed that when she ducked as she whirled around, sending out a sandaled foot to wipe the legs out from beneath the charging man. He managed to grab her as he went down, pulling her down with him. The two sounded like rutting bears as they fought on the floor, him to keep hold of her and her to get the hell away from him.

With a solid kick to his groin, she scrambled away and toward a blacksmith's hammer she saw on the ground that had fallen with the first man. Her heart was racing, and she was doing her best to keep her breathing under control so she didn't hyperventilate herself into an unconsciousness that she knew she'd never wake from.

Suddenly, a third man was there. He grabbed her under the arms and yanked her up like she was a rag doll. He wrapped powerful arms around her, hands clasped just below her breasts as he held her back against his body. She kicked her legs out like a bucking bronco, but he refused to release her, even as he staggered back a few steps.

A fourth man stepped into view, just in time for her to deliver powerful kicks to his face. His head whipped back with the action, and he was sent back into the now empty tool wall. Coughing and still clearly in pain, the man from the floor that had taken the kick to the groin slowly got to his feet. She couldn't see much of his face, but she could see his eyes, and they were filled with a fiery hatred.

Walking over to Kazia, who was still held in what amounted to a bear hug from behind, he was careful to avoid her legs. With teeth bared, he delivered a devastating punch to her gut, Kazia unable to double over as her body wanted because of the hold she was in. She absolutely could not breathe nor catch a breath.

He spat a word at her, but she didn't understand the language, never having heard the word before. With a snarl, he delivered a backhand to her right cheek, her eye feeling like it was about to explode. She tasted blood in her mouth as she'd bit her tongue. For a moment, she was worried she'd bitten it off.

Kazia had little time to worry about that as the two other men had gathered themselves from the beating they'd taken and were making their way over to them. Frantic now, Kazia screamed, kicked, tried to slam her head back into the man behind her, anything.

She did manage one last kick to the first man's chest, sending him flying back again before the man behind her had his arm wrapped around her throat. Like a boa constrictor, it tightened more and more until it squeezed the air, and the consciousness, out of her.

❧❧❧❧

Kazia had no idea how long it had been—minutes, hours, days?—when she regained consciousness. She was in a cage secured in the back of a wagon. Her entire body hurt, and the jostling of the horses and roadway beneath the wheels wasn't helping. Her head hurt so badly she felt like she'd throw up.

Looking around, she tried to peer through the bars of her cage beyond the wagon's high walls. There was very little she could see except that it was daytime. She had to assume that, bare minimum, she'd been out cold all night.

Groaning, she brought her hand to her face.

She hissed in pain instantly, the flesh of her right eye swollen to the point that she couldn't even open it. She had dried blood on her chin, and everything just *hurt*. She was still in her clothes, and though they looked to be splattered with dried blood, they didn't seem to be torn or have been removed in any way.

"Hello?" she called out, eyes squeezing shut as the pain intensified. This time, she did throw up.

"You are awake," someone called back to her.

Spitting out the remnants of her sickness to the floor of the cage, she groaned and sat back against the bars on the opposite side from the smelly mess. She didn't recognize the voice, but he was speaking her language, unlike what she remembered of the men the night before. His words were accented, however.

"Who are you?" she asked. "Where are you taking me?" she managed, her voice weaker than it had been.

"I am Consus," the man called back, his voice distant and just barely heard above the horses' hooves. It sounded like he may be speaking from the wagon's driver's seat. "I am taking you to Rome."

Chapter One

Roman Province of Britannia: Three years later

Standing her post, Kazia was nearly statue-still as she stood in the middle of the little town that had sprung up over the years near the garrison. She'd been stationed there for the better part of a year, and admittedly it was nice to stay in one place for a bit. The town was filled with all sorts of permanent buildings and some tents for merchants to peddle their wares. One guy was even selling out of a wagon.

There was everything from various foods to fabrics to weapons and goods sold at the blacksmith's shop. This, of course, was what always had Kazia's attention. She'd wandered in a few times during her time off.

Most of her comrades went to the public baths, but for her that wasn't exactly an option. Well, that is, not in groups with them. She went on her own and did her level best to avoid being seen by any of them if they were there at the same time.

The irony was, it was a known fact that Kazia was a woman, something she didn't try to hide, at the advice of one of the few early on who had been sympathetic to her situation: taken and forced into service for new recruits to the Roman army to wage their skills against.

When many of them ended up stabbed, cut, bruised, and humiliated, she'd been pitted up against trained warriors. When they, too, ended up stabbed, cut, bruised, and humiliated, Kazia had been given a uniform and, grudgingly, respect.

Three years later, here she stood. Though she had essentially become one of the "boys," she still didn't put herself in situations that reminded them that she was, in fact, *not* one of the boys, such as by going to the bathhouses when they were there.

The one and only time thus far in her military career that one of her fellow men-in-arms tried to exploit the fact that she was a woman, he'd been left standing there with his own severed penis still held in his hand. The only reason she hadn't been executed there on the spot was because she was a much better soldier than he was, and they were headed to a very difficult campaign.

Needless to say, word had spread like wildfire, and she'd been left alone. She said little, as she had not much to say, but also because it was another reminder that she was a woman, as she had the voice of one, lower timbre or not. So, she chose to remain quiet, observe, and learn. Because of this, she'd earned her nickname—Exspiravit—or, the Ghost.

In her full uniform, including her galea, she observed. She was grateful for the helmet, as the rain was beginning to come down harder from the drizzle it had been off and on. It kept her hair out of her eyes, at least. She noticed many of the merchants were beginning to close up shop, wares beginning to get wet as the rain leaked in through spaces in the roofs.

If this rain got very bad, no doubt tomorrow they'd be ordered to go and help patch or rebuild. The men at the garrison had a bit of a symbiotic relationship with the villagers around the fort. The soldiers offered safety and a good revenue source to the people. In turn, the villagers offered goods and, most importantly, women.

Over her time in the Roman army, Kazia had awoken many, many times to the quiet sounds of her fellow soldiers rutting in the darkness with each other, a practice not only supported but highly encouraged. Common wisdom was, a man was far more likely to fight to the death for a man he had a sexual relationship with than one he played a dice game with.

Stunned the first time she'd seen it, and honestly had thought the man was being raped. Not so. She'd learned a very valuable lesson that night: It was very possible for two men to engage in very consensual carnal pleasure with each other. But she'd also learned that given the choice, most of the men would prefer the pleasurable company of a woman, so when that was available, everyone seemed to benefit.

Kazia certainly had not found her very own "rutting buddy," though many over the years had made it clear they were willing if she was. She was disgusted by the whole thing, even if she did have genuine fondness for many of the men she served with. She saw them as colleagues, some as brothers, but none as any sort of sexual or love-of-the-heart kind of partner. That had eluded her completely.

Perhaps she wasn't built for that? Wasn't meant for that? After all, she was built far more like a man and could compete with them, even as she clearly had the woman's figure to make many a man watch her come and then go. Skin deep, she thought. In fact, she was surrounded by what most women would see as the embodiment of Adonis every single day. Her heart felt nothing for them in that way.

Nothing.

Perhaps they'd been right back in Greece all

along. Perhaps she *was* the Freak of Lacedaemon, after all.

Kazia tossed all that out of her mind as she realized someone was speaking to her. Focusing on her current situation, she saw that a young woman had approached her. From the expectant look on her face, it seemed she had said something and was awaiting a response.

"Forgive me," Kazia said. Her Brittonic wasn't terrible, but she wouldn't call herself fluent. She'd learned enough over the past year to communicate with the locals. She understood it better than she spoke it, generally. "What?"

"The rain is coming down harder," the woman said, indicating the weeping skies above. She had her hands wrapped around Kazia's forearm. "Come."

Kazia allowed herself to be tugged into a nearby shop, which wasn't much more than a three-sided building with a roof and heavy canvas that was flopped down over the open front and tied down to "lock" it. The two stood there side by side as the rain turned into a deluge. It was nearly deafening as it pounded down upon the roofs of the shops and pelted the leaves on the endless trees in the wooded land nearby.

Kazia glanced at her, noting she was a small woman, but then that wasn't hard next to her own unusual height and size. Her long brown hair was a bit stringy at the moment from the rain.

Kazia felt bad, as no doubt that had been from her running out to grab Kazia. What she wanted to know was, how on earth had the woman touched her, let alone grabbed her arm, without losing a hand? Troubling, and something that Kazia needed to work on.

As the rain grew heavier, she realized the woman's wares—weaved baskets, which were displayed closer to the open front—were beginning to get wet. Quickly, she set about to grab as many as she could to move them deeper into the store. The woman let out a little frantic cry when she realized what was happening, and she too began to gather her merchandise.

Together, they got everything moved, only one or two of the baskets getting irredeemably soaked. She could see the distress on the young woman's face. No doubt if she hadn't been worried about Kazia, she could have saved her own wares.

"How much do these cost?" Kazia asked, indicating the two destroyed baskets.

The young woman, who was hugging herself, looked up at the soldier and gave her a price. Nodding in acknowledgment, Kazia considered what money she had buried back at the garrison. She had enough to cover both and felt the obligation to.

"Tomorrow," she said. "I am off duty. I will buy them both."

The woman looked at her, dark brown eyes wide in surprise. She shook her head vigorously. "No. You do not need to—"

"I do," Kazia argued. She indicated the rain outside, which was beginning to slow a bit. "Because of me you weren't here to grab your baskets."

The indecision in the woman's eyes was clear. She needed the money; that was very plain to see in her distress at destroyed wares. But, no doubt she was nervous about dealing with one of the soldiers on such a matter. Sadly, not all of the men were known for their integrity. Many took great advantage of their position.

Kazia remembered her father, who, despite

what kind of husband and father he'd been, had been a very honorable man of business. Extending a hand, she waited until the woman met her gaze again after looking down at that strong, tanned hand.

"Shake on it?" Kazia offered.

Still hugging herself, the woman unwrapped one of her arms and placed a smaller, soft hand in Kazia's. She gave the warrior a very uncertain smile but accepted the gentle yet firm grip and shook on a promise to be kept.

Her duty finished, Kazia headed back through the western gate, an imposing structure of two towers on either side of the massive double wooden doors. The fort was a sight to behold, with massive walls made of stone bricks surrounding it in a rectangular shape with rounded corners. A western and northern gate provided entry or exit.

Inside the secure walls were avenues between the rows of buildings, which housed the cohort of soldiers, grain and supplies, the latrines, and the grand house of the Prefect and his family. He was not only commander of the unit but acted as mayor of the town that had sprouted up around the fort.

Stables, a hospital, and a large hall for the men to gather and eat their meals in also filled the space, amongst other auxiliary buildings.

Not caring about any of that in the moment, Kazia headed to the row where her barracks was located. She passed door after door after door until she reached hers. Inside each of those doors was the exact same thing: bunk beds for eight men, and a wood-fed stove for warmth and to cook meals upon its hearth.

It was her night to cook, so she was glad she got there before her peers. They all took turns, which made for nice camaraderie, as well provided a little feel of home to come back to a cooked meal. Some of the guys weren't half bad at it. Kazia…it was not one of her best skills.

Entering their room, she reached up and removed her galea, tucking the helmet beneath her arm as she walked to her bunk, which was beneath Janius, a good man if not for his ever-fragrant habit of nighttime flatulence.

Setting the metal helmet on her own bunk, she removed her gladius and the scabbard the deadly sharp short sword was tucked into, tossing it to the bed. Next came the layers of her uniform. The metal outer components of her lorica lightly clinked together as she unbuckled the armor and rested it on the bed. Next came her beltea, the apron of leather strips that were weighted down by metal tips and hung all around her hips to just below mid-thigh.

This left her in her tunica, the red, woolen tunic that went under it all. It, too, was tossed onto the bed. Her groan was nearly obscene as she unwrapped her breasts, a must since the uniform wasn't made with room for those. She didn't have much time to relish the freedom, though, so went to her own personal trunk and grabbed casual clothing to tug on so she could get dinner started.

Later that night, after everyone had returned to the barracks, eaten, and had a pretty good night, Kazia lay in her bunk. Her hands were tucked beneath her head as she listened to a couple of the guys chatting while a few others were playing board games. She loved a good game of Ludus Duodecim Scriptorum, which was what they were playing. It was a game similar to backgammon.

Her mind went back to her day and what she needed to do tomorrow. She thought of the young woman in the basket shop. She'd been so kind to pull Kazia in from the storm. A small smile found its way to her lips at that. Yes, the soldiers and villagers overall had a good relationship, but mostly the soldiers were left alone, nobody wanting to bring personal attention upon them.

In thinking back, she'd guess the woman wasn't much older than Kazia's eighteen, almost nineteen years. Perhaps a year or two older. She'd been lovely in her own plain way. Nothing remarkable per se about her features individually, but put them all together, and she had a very sweet face. Clearly, she had a kind heart also.

Was she married? There living with her parents? A woman wouldn't be there alone, but Kazia didn't remember seeing her before. Not that that was incredibly unusual because she didn't pay much mind to the villagers unless she was dealing with them for a specific reason in a specific moment.

She'd unburied her stash of money before her barracks mates had arrived and counted out what she'd promised for the two destroyed baskets. The look of distress on the lovely young woman's face haunted her. She hoped that she wouldn't be beaten or punished in some way for what truly had been out of her control. That had been the look in her eyes: fear and concern.

As Kazia stared up at the underside of Janius's bunk, she almost wished she could head out right now and take the coins to her home. *Here you go,* she'd say.

Just like I promised. She wanted to see relief in her eyes, to know that Kazia had made it all better.

Rolling her eyes at that, the legionary turned to her left side, watching her comrades play their game. They were so intense about it, she thought. Competitive about everything, those two, both on the training field and in their late-night passion.

Niklos and Titus were two of a rare handful she'd seen over the years who seemed to truly love each other as a man loves a woman. It wasn't just about sex for them, but much more.

Kazia had wondered what it would feel like to have someone look at her the way Niklos looked at Titus, who seemed to be the more dominant of the couple. There was always adoration, desire, and love in his deep blue eyes for the other man, who seemed to feel the same.

In previous years, when Kazia had heard the moaning and grunting start, she'd just roll her eyes and wait for it to be over so she could go back to sleep. But with those two, she felt more often than not that she and the other five men were interrupting something beautiful. What was that like?

Letting out a long sigh, she turned over to her back again. Maybe someday she'd know.

❧❧❧❧❧

She was dressed in uniform, though she had her galea tucked under her arm. Kazia wasn't on duty, but she rarely ever left the garrison out of uniform in case she was needed. As she made her way through the rows of little buildings and tents, she ran her hand through her short, dark hair.

About three months into her enslavement with the Romans, one of the recruits she'd walloped had been so angry at her that for punishment he had literally sat on her while using his military-issued pugio to cut off her hair. She'd been thrilled and had thanked him.

Ever since, she'd kept it very short, just like her cohorts. It made zero sense to wrestle with long hair or try to stuff it into her helmet. Plus, it was quite the chore getting blood and gore out of it.

Reaching the basket shop, Kazia saw the woman she'd dealt with the day before. She was dressed in a similar plain dress, her long dark hair pulled atop her head today, however. She was helping another customer, so Kazia wandered while she waited.

She walked over to a huge basket with a lid, which she pulled out of the top. Looking down into the cavernous depths, she was amused, thinking her mother could have hidden her entire body into such a thing.

"Looking for something to store your belongings when not in uniform?"

Kazia's head whipped up to see the young shopkeep standing a couple feet away. Smiling, Kazia shook her head and replaced the lid.

"No, I was actually just thinking that my Mamá could have used this to play hide-n-seek," Kazia said.

The woman smiled. "Well, if she is anywhere near my size, trust me, she can."

"She was," Kazia said softly. "Actually."

"My apologies," the woman said, giving her a contrite smile. "She's with Ankou?"

Kazia just stared at her for a moment. "Uh," she said. "Well, to Hades, if that's what Ankou is here."

The woman's smile was sweet. "I'm sorry for

your loss."

Kazia gave her a nod. "Thank you." Feeling very uncomfortable at such a personal topic, she raised her hand and opened her fingers. The necessary coins sat in her palm. "For the baskets."

The woman looked down at them, then her gaze flicked up to meet Kazia's. Shaking her head, she reached up and closed Kazia's fingers. "No. I cannot let you pay for something that I had to throw away."

Using her other hand, Kazia took the young woman's hand and turned it palm up before dropping the coins onto it. "A promise is a promise, kyria," she said.

The woman looked down at the coins then, as if coming to some sort of decision in her mind, and nodded as she closed her fist around the money.

"All right." She met Kazia's eyes again. Just for a brief second that same distress from the previous day filled their brown depths, then it was gone. "Thank you. Truly." She stuck her other hand out, as Kazia had done the previous day.

Looking down at it, Kazia met her gaze, her larger hand wrapping around it. "Deal closed," she said.

The woman smiled, nodding. "Aye." They shook hands and then released. She played with the coins, dropping them from one hand to the other. "I had heard there was a woman legionary here," she said conversationally. "I didn't think it could be true."

Kazia shrugged, holding her galea up to emphasize her claim. "True it is."

"I've never heard of such a thing before I got here." Her smile was bright, making her more relaxed countenance quite beautiful. "You must be very good."

Kazia nodded, proud of the fact. "I am."

"Well," the woman said, glancing over when two women entered her shop. She started to move to head toward them, not taking her gaze off Kazia. "If I have need of a personal warrior, I know who to call for." She stopped, eyebrows falling. "Well, no. I have no name to call."

Chuckling, the warrior answered. "Kazia."

"Kazia," the woman said softly, as if testing it on her tongue. "You are Greek." She began to move toward her customers again. "I'm Ione." With that, she turned to help the women.

Chapter Two

As predicted, the following day was soldiers working with villagers to repair storm-damaged businesses and homes. After the initial storm that afternoon, another had washed through overnight, taking some buildings down completely. The garrison had fared well, though some of the men were dealing with a few leaks that had sprung in a couple buildings.

The sounds of hammering and instructions shouted back and forth filled the air, as well as the voices of the village women, who helped by running parts and tools back and forth as well as delivering water to those hard at work. Kazia was on the crew working on the roads, part of which had been washed out. They were crucial to getting supplies in and troops out.

"Kazia, push that rubble over this way," one of the men called out to her.

Glancing toward him, she nodded acknowledgment before she used her shovel to do as asked. Powerful arms were put to use to shove large amounts of crushed rock and small stones from the pile dumped before her from the wagon it had been shoveled into for transport to the road location.

Briefly glancing up, Kazia saw a few women headed their way, two carrying wooden buckets and one a large burlap sack. One of the women was Ione, the other two also village women come to offer refreshment. She returned her focus back to what she was doing as the women were still further down the way, starting with the men working at the beginning of the project and making their way down the line.

Hearing giggling, Kazia glanced over again to see one of the soldiers talking with two of the women—Ione and the one holding the burlap sack, which she now realized was filled with small loaves of bread that she was handing out to the workers. Ione's bucket held water and a drinking ladle.

The woman with the sack and the soldier seemed to be the ones doing the talking, or, more accurately, flirting. He seemed to be trying to bring Ione in on whatever they were talking about, but she simply smiled politely at him, looking as though she were ready to move on down the row of soldiers.

Kazia didn't know the soldier, but in a garrison filled with more than four thousand of them… She kept an ear on the situation, however, as she could tell some of those around her were doing. For one, they needed to get the project done, but for two, it had been made quite clear by their superiors that the soldiers were to leave the village women alone unless her business *was* men.

Apparently, a few years before, a soldier had begun messing around with a married woman and it had gotten ugly—and deadly. Now, their Prefect wanted no part of that. Kazia had actually been surprised by the edict, as she'd been under supervisors who felt it was the Roman army's gods-given right to take what they wanted. Sadly, that was the norm, or simply to turn a blind eye.

But here, she was greatly pleased that the iron fist was swift when it came to punishing the men who colored outside of the lines. So now, the soldier was beginning to garner the attention of those around him.

A centurion was posted to watch each group, and if his attention was grabbed, it would not be good for the young soldier. Though he wasn't harassing the young woman nor intimidating her, as she was clearly receptive, he was choosing his flirting over his duty.

Kazia glanced to a man nearby who called the soldier's name, warning in his voice. The man, apparently named Leo, glanced over at him. A look of irritation entered his brown eyes before he looked away and turned his back to the two women, getting back to work. The one woman looked slightly disappointed, but Ione looked relieved as the two young women moved on.

Being where she'd been over the last three years with the Roman army, the hardest part of it had been seeing how the so-called conquered were treated at times. She hated it, especially for the women. Kazia had no issue going up against an armed man, an equal in a foreign military campaign. She'd slice them open all day long then eat dinner and sleep soundly that night.

But when it came to the average citizen just trying to survive, Kazia saw her mother. She saw the others from back home, good people doing the best they could for their families and themselves. The day she'd first seen Ione, a young Celt showing kindness to her "conqueror" and essentially keeper, had touched Kazia.

One of the reasons she'd gone back to pay for those ruined baskets. One human being to another, Celt or Greek, soldier or simple villager. At the end of the day, weren't they all the same? Kill with a gladius or kill with kindness. Some days Kazia got confused about which end of the spectrum she belonged or deserved to be on.

"Kazia?"

Pulled from her somewhat morose thoughts, the soldier looked up to see that Ione and her companion had reached her. Ione gave her a shy smile as she held up the ladle filled with water.

"Drink?" she offered.

Nodding, Kazia took it from her and held it by the long handle as she brought the cup portion to her lips. Her eyes closed as the cool water entered her mouth and then her system as she swallowed it down. She kept them closed as her body relished the relief for a moment before opening them and looking down into Ione's pleased-looking smile.

"Thank you, kyria," she said, easing the ladle back into the water in the bucket.

The young shopkeep's head tilted slightly. "You called me that yesterday, too. What does that mean?"

Kazia had to think for a moment. What had she said? Then it hit her. "Kyria?" At the young woman's nod, she explained. "It is meant as respect to a woman where I come from."

Ione seemed to consider that, and then the softest, most lovely smile spread across her face. "I understand," she said. She met Kazia's gaze for a moment, then with a small nod of deference to her position, moved on.

Kazia watched her go, eyes dropping to notice a shapely behind caressed in the material of her skirts as she walked, then quickly looked away. She felt guilty for noticing and then more so for staring. As a woman, it wasn't her place nor her right.

She had endless respect for other women, knowing what they had to go through, and to stare at them, she felt, was so utterly disrespectful. Didn't that make her no better than the men who ogled and exploited them? Abused and used them? As penance, she gave the other young woman a polite smile and shake of her head at the offer of food.

෴ ෴ ෴ ෴

Though it was not her turn to cook, it *was* her turn to hunt. Quiver upon her back and bow in hand, Kazia was making her way into the woods. She was concentrating on everything she heard, both to detect her prey but also to listen for other humans. It wouldn't do to accidentally kill someone.

Stopping by a large tree, she leaned against it and closed her eyes, listening. She heard the expected sounds: birds up high in the branches, insects and their mating calls, and little critters scurrying. She heard movement off to her right, and it sounded like something large enough to be substantial yet something she could carry back on her own.

Opening her eyes, she looked in that general direction as with very slow movements she reached behind her to ease an arrow out of her quiver. She stopped when she heard grunting off to the left, perhaps fifty yards away. Another grunt and then what sounded like a chopping sound. The creature off to the right scurried away.

Cursing under her breath, Kazia looked back to her left. It was a woman's voice, and it sounded as if she were chopping at foliage or something. She either needed to find another position or help this woman to get her gone, as she'd scare away anything Kazia could take back to the barracks for dinner.

With an irritated sigh, she pushed away from the

tree and headed in the direction of the woman. More grunts and more chopping sounds helped her find her way in the dense forest. Finally, she broke through some trees, quickly raising her hands in supplication when she was met with an angry-looking Ione holding an axe in a defensive position toward her.

She was in her usual peasant dress, and her dark hair was pulled up again, though it had largely come loose from its updo and hung in her face, some strands stuck in tear streaks. Instantly, Kazia was concerned.

"Just me, kyria," she said, her voice calm, as she'd clearly startled the smaller woman.

Looking away, a panting Ione lowered the axe, which was far too heavy for her. "Sorry," she muttered. "Thought I was alone."

"As did I," Kazia said softly, hoping for the small smile which she did receive.

Her gaze fell to the rather paltry pile of small branches and sticks the other woman had managed to cut, her eyes flicking back to Ione.

"Gathering wood?" she asked, not wanting to assume, as for all she knew, the village woman was simply getting out some frustration. Ione wouldn't look at her but nodded. "Can I help?" Kazia asked, as it seemed the young Celt was upset.

Clearing her throat, Ione rested the head of the cutting tool on the ground as she took one of her hands from the long wood handle to brush her hair out of her face. "No need, but thank you."

Kazia's knee-jerk reaction was to respect her wishes and leave her be to find another place to hunt, but her gut told her to stay. She felt awkward, not entirely sure what to say.

Clearing her throat, she finally managed, "Please

let me help."

Ione glanced over at her, her normally warm brown eyes guarded. "Why?"

Fantastic question. "Well," Kazia said, nodding toward the small pile. "The cold weather is upon us, kyria, and that will do little to keep your fires warm."

"Aye," Ione conceded. "But that still doesn't answer why you'd help."

"Then," Kazia drawled, attempting to put a tone of amusement in her voice. "How about I need to get dinner and this will take a long time and scare away any prospects." She indicated first her bow and then the tiny pile of progress of Ione's efforts at their feet.

Kazia nearly panicked when the tears started anew, the other woman burying her face in her hands. Clearly that had been the wrong tactic, and her attempt at humor had flopped horribly. For a moment, she looked around as if for inspiration of what to do for the crying woman. A memory surfaced of holding her mother, many years ago, after one of her father's outbursts. She'd been eight years old.

"I am sorry," Kazia murmured, stepping over to the other woman.

She set her bow down before gently easing the axe away from Ione and leaning its handle against the tree Ione had been hacking at. Ione was initially stiff as Kazia enfolded her in her arms, but then she leaned against her, the tears still coming.

As she held her, Kazia began to understand that the upset wasn't about her own poor attempt at humor, but whatever had happened before Ione had come out here. The smaller woman's head tucked beneath Kazia's chin, she held her tightly against her. She had to admit, it felt good to have that human contact, even as it was given in comfort.

Finally, the tears began to slow and then stop. Ione stayed huddled against Kazia for a moment longer before she eased away from her. Turning her back to Kazia, she seemed to be using the sleeve of her dress to wipe at her eyes and face.

"My apologies, Kazia." Ione sniffled, using her hands to brush her hair back from her face, the updo all but destroyed.

"Do not be." Kazia stood where she was, not reaching out to touch her again but wasn't about to leave her in her upset. Though the tears had stopped, she could feel it coming off the smaller woman in waves. "Are you all right?" she asked gently.

One more sniffle and Ione finally turned to face her. She took a deep, cleansing breath and let it out as she nodded with a shrug. "My husband can be a bit…" She paused, as if to consider the word to use. "Abrupt, I suppose."

Kazia felt her stomach drop at those words, the mention of a husband, and she honestly had no idea why. It made her feel deeply uncomfortable. Pushing that aside, she focused on the current situation. "Did he hurt you?"

Ione shook her head, looking down at her feet. "He was wounded a couple years ago where we used to live." Her gaze flicked up to Kazia, who stood a few feet away. "He can no longer work or do much of anything." She shrugged, hugging herself. "We came here hoping that perhaps with the fort," she said, nodding in the general direction of the garrison, "I could make us money selling my baskets."

"Have you?"

Another shrug as Ione looked back down to the

forest floor. "It's been a difficult situation, Kazia," she admitted quietly. "But," she blew out, "life is hard for all of us." She gave her a brave smile, though Kazia noticed it didn't reach her lovely brown eyes. "We all do the best we can."

"We do."

Kazia stepped over to the tree and took hold of the axe. She raised her eyebrows in question. At Ione's nod, she looked around for a better target to get the most wood without having to cut down the entire tree, then got to work.

Thirty very sweaty minutes later, Kazia had a huge pile at her feet, large branches she'd been able to cut down then cut into manageable sized logs to carry. She rested the axe head on the ground, leaning the handle against her leg, before running a hand through her short hair, which was plastered to her head from her exertions.

Looking to Ione, who had stayed far out of the way, she saw her eyes were huge as she eyed the wood. That wide gaze flicked up to meet Kazia's eyes.

"Thank you," she whispered, awe in her voice.

Kazia nodded. "Of course."

Leaning the axe handle against an adjacent tree, Kazia walked over to where her bow and quiver had been set, as well as her rucksack, which would hold her dinner once she finally got to hunt for it. She shoved as many logs into that sack as would fit, then began to gather the rest in her arms.

Ione stepped up to her. "You can load my arms, Kazia," she said. "I want to help."

Looking around, Kazia nodded toward her bow. "Grab that?"

Ione jumped into action, grabbing the quiver

and hitching the arrows over her shoulder by the strap before grabbing the bow. "Now what?"

Kazia smiled, amused by the woman's eagerness to do whatever was asked of her. "I can get this," she said, indicating the last of the logs she was piling into her arms. "Can you get the axe?" Nodding, Ione did as asked, dutifully walking with Kazia as the two headed toward town.

Kazia's chin was raised slightly to see over the tall stack she held. She felt so much anger toward this little man Ione was married to. What sort of man sent his wife out to do such a chore? And, her bitter thoughts added, a woman who had worked all day to help those rebuilding after the storm.

"Does he work at the shop, your husband?" she asked.

Ione shook her head. "He doesn't walk very well," she explained.

Kazia's eyebrows furrowed. "Could he not sit on the stool and help customers?" she pushed.

When there was no response, she bit her tongue to stop herself from saying anything more. She could feel that anger and upset building again in the woman walking beside her, and she certainly didn't want to add to it. Again.

"How did you, a woman, end up in the Roman army?" Ione asked.

Kazia snorted. "I was volunteered." She smiled at the wide brown eyes that earned her. She shrugged very carefully, so as not to cause a log avalanche. "It's been three years now, and it is what I know, kyria."

"Do you like it?"

Kazia knew she had to be very careful in how she responded, should she be overheard. "Duty is an honor," she said simply. To her, that wasn't entirely untrue, she just would prefer her duty not be to the Roman Empire and all it stood for.

Ione was quiet for a moment before she spoke. "I have seen many soldiers, Kazia. Both living here and where we used to, foe and countrymen," she added. "I've not seen anything quite like you, though."

Kazia chuckled, shaking her head. "I would assume not."

Ione smiled. "No, I don't mean just the fact that you're a female." She placed her hand on Kazia's shoulder. "Stop here." Kazia instantly stopped and looked to her for instructions. Ione nodded toward the tree line and town beyond. "My husband would be… *upset* if he saw you helping me."

Nodding, Kazia eased her burden down to the forest floor before kneeling on one knee to unpack her sack as well. She glanced up at Ione. "You can make several trips to carry these, then?" she asked.

Nodding, Ione leaned the axe against a tree as she removed the quiver from her shoulder. "Aye. But…it's more about who you are as a person," she continued her earlier statement. "You have this incredible sense of…"

Ione shrugged, almost as though trying to decide what she wanted to say. Her gaze followed Kazia as she pushed to her feet, taking the quiver and bow from the smaller woman.

"Goodness, I guess," she said. "Duty, aye, I can see that." She smiled, head slightly cocked to the side as she studied Kazia's deeply tanned face. "It's more than that, though." She leaned up and left a soft kiss on Kazia's cheek. "Makes me feel safer to know you're here, looking out for us."

Kazia honestly had no idea what to say, and she knew she was about fifteen shades of shy right then. She rubbed the back of her heated neck with a hand.

"Well," she said after a moment. "I can load your arms, if you wish." She nodded down at the wood.

"No." Ione wrapped her fingers around Kazia's much larger hand. "You've done enough." She smiled and playfully shook the hand before releasing it. "Go get dinner." With that, Ione turned away and to the little piles Kazia had made for her to easily scoop up to carry home.

Chapter Three

Resting her head back against the tiled wall behind her, Kazia closed her eyes. It felt so good, the warm water and steam wafting up all around her naked body, which was dipped below the water to just above her breasts. She'd already washed her body and hair, which was slicked back from her face, and was just now sitting and absorbing the warmth before heading out into the cold night.

She preferred to go to the public bathhouses late, when typically only the men went and most women were at home dealing with children or expectant husbands. The bathhouse was separated by gender, so she all but had the women's side to herself, which was the point. Her preference in all honesty was to grab a bath in the wild—river, lake, whatever.

When she and her legion were on the march on a campaign, that's what they did. It was easier to be off by herself than feeling captive and a bit trapped in a building like the baths. She could more than take care of herself, but she hated being stared at. So for the time being, she was going to enjoy the quiet relaxation.

The room she was in had high ceilings to allow the steam to move up and off the bathers. The fully tiled bath was rectangular in shape, she sitting along one of the shorter sides. There was walking space along the outside edge of the baths, also tiled. A door extended from the large room which led to the changing room for the women to dress or undress, and then the door to the front where a coin was paid to use the baths and enter or leave.

Kazia had seen many, many public baths in her life, both back home in Greece, then in Rome and in her travels in the army. Some were simple like this one, while others were extravagant and, in her opinion, quite ostentatious.

Opening her eyes, though they were hooded from her relaxed state of mind, she looked around the empty space in the water. She wondered what it would be like to sit there with the bath filled with other women, all talking amongst themselves, and to her as well. What would it be like for them not to give her the side-eye, not sure what to make of her? A woman, very clearly, but a woman unlike them, also very clearly.

Kazia had met a woman once, the wife of a senator back in Rome. She'd been a sweet woman, if not a bit dangerous in her beauty and flirtatious nature.

She'd told Kazia that it wasn't so much Kazia's physicality. Certainly, she was larger and taller, well-muscled in a way that women weren't, but mostly it was her bearing that made her seem so very different from her other female counterparts.

She'd said Kazia had a "way about her" that either garnered her attention or confused people and made them shy away in uncertainty. She'd then told her something that had confused Kazia, and still did to this very day.

"My darling Kazia, either women will run to you to be protected or they'll run to you to be conquered." She'd given her a little smile then that had sent a thrill down Kazia's spine. "Either way," she concluded. "Enjoy the ride."

Kazia was pulled from her thoughts when she heard a noise from the changing room. A moment later, to her absolute shock, Ione stepped through the door. Kazia felt the very sudden need to cover herself, but there really wasn't anything to cover herself with. She just had to suck it up. And, while she was doing that, she had to do everything in her power to not look at the woman who was making her way to the stairs to enter the baths, very naked.

Kazia kept her eyes lowered to her own legs, which shimmered beneath the surface of the water, lit by the myriad oil lamps and candles that burned and were placed around the baths. She heard the sound of Ione's body submerging beneath the warmth and moving, likely to get settled, she figured.

"I'm sorry," Ione said quietly once the water stilled. "I didn't know anyone was in here, Kazia."

Glancing up and over to her, Kazia had to force her eyes to not take in the pale skin of delicate shoulders and throat, let alone anything else. She gave her a smile.

"You do not need to apologize, kyria." She indicated the large, empty space around them. "Public place."

Ione nodded, her gaze focusing on her hands, which played with the water. "I always come in to bathe before I go home," she explained quietly, still not looking over at Kazia. "I clean things up here and they let me bathe as part of my pay." She smiled. "Well, that *is* my pay." She spared a very shy glance over at her. "The time I have alone for a moment."

"Oh, I am so sorry—" Kazia sat forward, intending to leave.

"No!"

Kazia stopped, standing in the water now, which reached to her waist. She turned and looked over at the other woman who was looking at her, a look of—what was it?—on her face. Panic? Upset? But then, her eyes dropped and took in Kazia's upper body, all bared to her intense gaze.

From her expression, Ione seemed to be drinking in what she saw: powerful shoulders and arms, then a flat, muscular stomach, before her eyes eased up to take in Kazia's breasts, small but full with her dark nipples rigid and with water dripping off them, as well as the rest of her upper body

Feeling like a deer caught in torchlight, Kazia had no idea what to do or say. She'd never seen that look on a woman's face before, certainly not aimed at her. Her entire body began to heat up, as though the water she stood in were growing hotter.

After a moment that seemed like a lifetime, Ione looked away, though it seemed she was extremely moved by what she'd seen, though in what way, Kazia had no idea. Was she disgusted? No idea what to do, Kazia stood there, that deer ready to bound off back into the forest at any moment.

"Don't go," Ione finally said.

Kazia slowly lowered herself back into the water, so grateful for the hidden depths once more. They were quiet for a moment, sitting more than ten feet apart. Finally, Ione seemed to pull herself out of wherever she'd gone in her mind and looked over at Kazia.

"Can I tell you something?" she asked, her voice soft.

Kazia nodded. "Of course you can."

"I once saw a carving, it was of Macha. She's our Goddess of War," she explained. "Big, strong." She smiled shyly. "She'd have to be. But, when I just looked at you," she continued, her voice almost sounding like that of a little girl in awe. "I thought I was looking at the goddess, come to earth." There was so much wonder in her big, brown eyes as well as her tone. "I have truly never seen anything so beautiful, Kazia."

Those sweet words hit Kazia like a hammer in the gut. She couldn't speak, could hardly breathe. She could only sit there and stare at Ione, mouth open a bit in her stunned shock. It took a full fifteen seconds for her to be able to gather her wits about her. Finally, she swallowed.

"Um," she managed. "I do not know what to say. Nobody has ever said anything like that to me before."

"Then they're fools," Ione said. "Because you are exquisite." She slowly shook her head. "Never forget that." The air got heavy between them for a moment before Ione suddenly grabbed a bar of soap that was in a nearby soap dish, left for the bathers to use while in the baths. She held it out toward Kazia. "Will you wash my back?"

Heart in her throat, Kazia nodded and moved through the water to sit near the other woman, who was turning to expose her back to her. The shopkeep gathered all her hair to one side of her neck and down her front.

Kazia had taken the soap and was lathering it between her hands, the white froth pale against the tanned skin. Her gaze went to the creaminess before her. Setting the soap aside back into the dish, she eased her hands over the softness of Ione's back. She'd never touched another woman like this before, not even her own mother.

She smiled at the little moan of pleasure she got as

she performed her task, making sure to get every inch, and even gently massaging the muscle that connected her neck to her shoulders.

"Feels good," Ione murmured, words muffled as she effectively spoke into her own upper chest.

"You work hard," Kazia said. "I know how a long day can be on the body."

They were quiet for a moment as she grabbed more soap, using the lathering for Ione's arms, massaging the muscles in her shoulders and arms as she went. This earned her a flat-out groan, which sent little butterflies batting at Kazia's insides in places that almost made her gasp.

"You're never allowed to stop," Ione murmured.

Kazia smiled. "Did you get the wood home okay?" she asked, though it had been weeks since that night, the last time they'd seen each other.

"Aye," Ione said with a little nod. She snorted. "My husband looked at me, stunned. He was being such a bully that night, I think he sent me out to do the impossible to punish me."

Kazia grinned despite herself. "We showed him."

A bark of laughter escaped Ione's lips. Her head lifted and she glanced at Kazia over her shoulder, a saucy little look in those brown eyes.

"Oh, *we* did." She turned back facing front, still chuckling. "He didn't talk to me for two glorious days. I think he was far more angry that I proved him wrong than whatever he was angry at me for initially."

Feeling quite smug, Kazia dipped her hands into the water before using them to cup warm water to let flow down over Ione's shoulders and back. Another groan as Ione's head fell once more.

"If you ever decide to leave the army," the

merchant muttered, "I know of another occupation for you."

"To bathe basket makers?" Kazia teased. She grinned at the snort that earned her.

"Exactly." She turned around when Kazia finished. "Would you stay?" she asked shyly. "While I finish?"

Kazia nodded. "I will."

Staying put, Kazia watched as Ione took the bar of soap and moved out more toward the center where it was a bit deeper. She carefully bent backward and used the hand that wasn't holding the soap to push her hair back into the water away from her face. As she did this, her breasts broke the surface, the skin as pale as her back.

Kazia didn't want to look, but she couldn't look away. The nipples were small and rigid, a dusky rose. The breasts themselves looked to be a bit larger than Kazia's. She felt an ache deep between her legs that nearly took her breath away. She'd never felt such a thing before, and then a moment later she realized that Ione had stood back erect, and she was looking at Kazia.

Feeling deeply ashamed at being caught looking, Kazia quickly averted her eyes, little pricks stinging against their backs. She felt like she was about to cry. When she heard her name, she had to swallow the emotion down. She was so confused. Again, her name. Looking up, she saw that Ione still stood where she'd been but was now using the soap lather she'd created in her hands to wash her hair.

"It's okay," Ione assured softly, her gaze kind, understanding. She gave her a sweet smile. "I looked at you," she reminded, just before putting her head back once more to rinse the soap from her hair.

This time, Kazia looked away.

❧❧❧❧

Titus was off on duty, so Kazia sat across from Niklos as the two played a game of Ludus Duodecim Scriptorum. Her gaze flicked up to study his face as he contemplated his next move.

Like her, he hailed from Greece, though his mother had been Roman. When his parents had died, his grandfather had whisked him off to Rome. From there, he'd joined the army.

"Niklos, can I ask you something?" she asked in their native tongue, as she wanted to ask him some private questions.

His dark eyes spared a glance up at her before returning his focus to the board. "Sure."

"Was Titus your first?"

His gaze flicked back up to hers briefly, but he didn't look entirely surprised at the question. "No," he said. "First in love, yes."

Kazia nodded, watching him make his move before it was her turn. "How did you know?" she asked. "That it was not girls for you?"

He shrugged a shoulder, surreptitiously looking around to make sure the other guys weren't paying attention to them, regardless of their speaking Greek. They were not.

"I tried," he said, a boyish grin on his face, shaking his head. "No offense, my friend, but no."

Kazia's grin was wide. "None taken." She looked into his eyes. "I feel the same, hmm?"

Niklos studied her for a long time, then nodded,

watching as she made her move in the game. "I figured as much. You try it with a girl?" he asked just loud enough for her to hear.

The very thought of that sent a little thrill through her body that almost made her shiver. She was ashamed, yet again, when Ione's face popped before her mind's eye.

Clearing her throat, she shrugged. "I do not think anyone would want that with me, Niklos."

His eyebrows drew. "Why?" He reached over and punched her playfully in the shoulder. "You would be surprised, my friend. There are many who are curious just because you are a Roman soldier." He winked. "Virile."

She rolled her eyes. "It is your turn."

He grinned. "And, perhaps it is yours, too."

❧❧❧❧

Later that night, Kazia lay in bed staring up at the underside of Janius's bunk, as always. Her mind went back to her talk with Niklos. It was the first time she'd ever spoken to him about his relationship with Titus. It was the first time she'd asked questions about that sort of relationship, and it was the first time she'd been asked questions about herself.

It had also been the first time she'd admitted aloud that she was not attracted to men. Now what? And, why was he not surprised? Shouldn't he have been stunned, disgusted, offended, and turned her in? Granted, the latter could still happen, though she didn't believe he would. She had done nothing wrong, hadn't acted on anything, and it was his word against hers that the conversation had ever happened. Right?

Her mind went to the baths a handful of nights ago when she and Ione had spent that time together. She enjoyed being around her. It hadn't happened again. As tempted as she'd been, Kazia had not returned at that same time. She tried to tell herself it was because she had duties back in the fort.

She was being a coward, and she knew it. Yes, Ione had been so sweet to her, so understanding at catching Kazia looking at her body, but as she'd said, she'd looked at Kazia's, too. She'd commented on it. But, no doubt that was a onetime thing, a free pass, as it were. Kazia didn't trust herself to not do it again.

There were two reasons why Kazia had not been thrown out of the military or put in horrendous situations: she was better than most of the men, and she did absolutely *nothing* to get into trouble or catch unwanted attention. She was Exspiravit, after all. If she did something that displeased or frightened Ione, that could all be gone in the blink of an eye.

She may not have wanted to be part of the Roman army, but she was, and it was all she had. Kazia had nothing that belonged to her except the pride of being one of the best legionaries there was. Without that pride, she had nothing. She owned nothing. She *was* nothing. So, she'd stayed away from a young woman that was far too tempting in ways Kazia truly didn't understand.

Never had she felt an urge to be around someone before. Never had she felt an urge to touch someone before. The day in the woods, when Ione had been so upset at the treatment of her husband's bullish ways, Ione had let her hold her. She'd let her comfort her, and she'd trusted her.

The night at the baths, again, she'd trusted

Kazia to touch her. She'd literally turned her back to her, trusting she'd not hurt her. And she'd let Kazia look upon her nakedness with such understanding of Kazia's curiosity. If she'd known how it had made Kazia feel, made her body burn in ways it never had before, would she still have trusted her?

Certainly not.

Women were affectionate with each other. Kazia had seen it her entire life, with her female peers when she'd been a child in Greece. Even then, though, they'd stayed away from her, instinctually, perhaps. Did they know something Kazia did not? Did they sense, even as children, that someday when they were all women, their peer would want to see their breasts? Would wonder how they felt, how their nipples felt?

Yes, she thought. After all, she *was* the Freak of Lacedaemon. Ione was a very sweet woman, and she seemed to be lonely. Kazia understood this all too well. But she also needed to understand that she needed to stay on guard, never mistaking the smaller woman's open and kind nature as anything more than that—an open and kind nature. From a very lonely woman.

"Do not be stupid," Kazia whispered to herself. "Do not."

Chapter Four

Kazia nodded greeting to a man who was passing her as he left a shop. He braced a heavy bag of feed upon his shoulder with his hand. He returned the nod and hurried on his way. In uniform, as always, she wasn't wearing her helmet as it was her day off. She decided to get some fresh air in the cool day and wander.

Her cloak was clasped at her throat, covering her armor. In some ways, she felt like an ordinary citizen for a moment. She wandered the avenues that separated the rows of buildings, though they weren't as uniformly placed as those in the garrison. As she looked around, she smiled inwardly, pretty sure whoever had planned this out had been drunk on good ale at the time.

Heading out on her day off on what amounted to a patrol was not at all unusual for Kazia. Essentially, she had nothing else to do, so just continued her duty. But today, she was admittedly not just making sure the peace was being kept. Though she hadn't been to that part of town just yet, she was loath to admit that she wanted a glimpse of someone, a certain basket maker.

So, she began to make her way in that general direction, keeping a keen eye on the goings-on. It was midmorning, and people were going about their business, be it running shops or shopping. It was bitterly cold, every breath a white puff of steam commingling in the fresh air with the not-so-fresh scents of the village.

Her heart began to race when she spotted the

shop that sold fabric, knowing that Ione's basket shop was on the other side.

Taking a deep breath, she forced herself to pass the fabric shop and finally arrive at the place she'd wanted to go all morning. She was surprised, however, when she reached it to see that the person behind the counter was not Ione, but a man.

Literally starting, Kazia stared for a moment. He was alone in the structure, pale, his hair long and stringy. He looked as though he hadn't bathed in a month. He sat on the stool behind the counter and just glared off into space, as if angry at a time and place where nobody else could join him, or she wagered, wanted to.

Something told her this was Ione's husband, which made her stomach roil for reasons she didn't understand. Well, other than he seemed like a rather useless individual. Standing there, she tried to decide what to do. She could just turn and leave, which is what she should do, or she could ask after Ione.

"What?"

Kazia's gaze focused on the man once more and the word barked at her. She gave him a nod of deference. "Just looking, kyrie," she said.

"You have questions, too bad. My wife will be back later," he muttered. "Come back then."

Nodding again, she turned and walked away. Suspicions validated, it certainly made her feel better to know that Ione was all right, at least. She walked back the way she'd come, trying to decide where she wanted to go. Probably best to just go back to the barracks. Perhaps she could mend her tunica that needed a patch.

She ran a hand through her hair, feeling

something she'd so rarely felt in her life: lonely. That was, lonely because she had something specific in mind she craved and she couldn't have it, even though she wasn't entirely sure what *it* was. She just knew smiling brown eyes were part of it.

Reaching the end of the row, her gaze turned in the direction of the western gate, which would take her home. No idea how long she'd stood there, she turned and walked in the opposite direction.

Never an indecisive person, Kazia felt out of sorts and not herself. She realized she was headed in the direction of the river, and she was fine with that. It would be cold over there, but maybe that's what she needed—a little cold air, or even some cold water, to knock her out of this stupor. Then, she could head back to barracks, and she'd be fine.

She made her way toward the water, which would be just off to the right, the woods straight ahead and to her left. The town and garrison was all behind her. She began to mutter a little Greek lullaby her mother used to sing to her when she'd been really little, one she often sang in her head on a long march.

When you had to cover twenty miles in five hours, you had to keep your mind busy so you wouldn't pay attention to how your body began to hurt. So, the lullaby was not only comforting, but a great distraction.

Movement off to the left caught her eye, and she realized that it was Ione. She was just barely inside the tree line, though was hidden enough that Kazia couldn't tell what she was doing. It had been a quick movement between an open space in the trees that allowed her to see that it was the other woman at all.

Stopping her momentum, Kazia stood there yet again trying to decide what to do. Chewing on her bottom lip, she decided to go left. She made a quick bird call whistle to alert Ione that she wasn't alone, a dark head popping up in surprise. Kazia was still several yards from her, as she didn't want the poor thing to be frightened that someone was almost on top of her before she knew they were there.

Instantly, a smile came to Ione's lovely face. "Good morrow."

Kazia gave her a nod of respect. "Kaliméra," she answered in kind in her native tongue, returning the smile. She saw that Ione had a couple burlap sacks, one already half filled and resting on the ground. "What are you doing?"

Ione took in the bags before she met Kazia's curious gaze. "I am gathering materials to make baskets." Her hands went to her hips, and she eyed Kazia. "For some reason, I've had a small army come through my shop and nearly buy out my inventory."

"Hmm," Kazia said, sounding mystified.

"Indeed," Ione grumbled. She cocked her head to the side. "I had no idea the Roman army had such need for baskets."

Kazia nodded sagely. "We will no longer be using the sarcina to carry our belongings on the move," she explained. "We will now be using baskets."

Ione's giggle made Kazia smile   despite herself. "You lie."

Ione walked over to her and took Kazia's arms, holding them out a bit so she could step her smaller body inside the space she'd made.

Stiff from surprise for a moment, Kazia encircled the smaller body that leaned against her. She'd never known anyone who liked to hug as much as Ione did, and as much as it threw her off, it was...nice.

"I feel so safe with you," Ione murmured, her arms wrapped around a trim waist beneath Kazia's cloak and head tucked beneath Kazia's chin.

Kazia held her a bit tighter. "You are safe with me," she assured.

She gave her a tight squeeze then released her, noting they weren't fully hidden by the trees. The last thing they needed was for a villager to mistake Kazia at a glance for one of her male counterparts. They could both be killed for adultery.

She gave her a bright smile. "Can I help?" She smirked. "Since you are convinced it is my fault you need more baskets."

"Aye," Ione said, excitement in her voice. "You can."

"All right. What do I need to do?"

"Well, I'm gathering vines," Ione explained, sparing a glance to her. "I use them with straw to make them." She indicated the tree nearby where she'd been working, cutting the vine off that had grown up around the trunk.

Nodding, Kazia pulled out her knife and worked on the vines higher overhead that Ione would never be able to reach. They worked in companionable silence for a while, both making good headway on their task. Finally, the smaller woman spoke.

"How did you know I was out here?"

"I didn't," Kazia admitted. "I saw you were not at your shop, so was I headed to the river."

Ione was quiet for a moment then said, "Was Ronal still there? I had a man coming in today to pick up the baskets his wife had bought yesterday, so someone had to be there."

"Your husband?" At Ione's nod, Kazia said, "He

was."

Ione didn't look at her as she asked, voice quiet. "So, you met him?" She almost sounded ashamed.

"Very briefly." Kazia studied the other woman for a moment before returning her attention to her task. "How long have you been married to him?"

Ione's heavy sigh came out in a white puff as she carefully peeled the vine she'd just cut off the tree from its cling to the bark. "Seven years."

Kazia's eyebrows shot up. "But you look so young."

"Yet, I feel so old," Ione murmured. She grabbed the sack that was already partially filled and placed the vine inside. "I was promised to him when I was nine years old, then we were married when I was fifteen."

Sadly, Kazia knew this was not uncommon. She wasn't sure what to say. "Very young," was all she managed.

Ione nodded. "Aye." She glanced over at Kazia, who worked to peel the vine she'd cut free from the cold bark of the tree. "Have you been married?"

Shaking her head, Kazia smirked. "Can you imagine?" She met Ione's gaze. "What sort of man would marry me?" She chuckled. "I think I frighten them."

"One fortunate enough to," Ione said quietly. "But…" She shook her head. "I don't see it." She smiled. "Have you ever been in love?"

Kazia shook her head. "I have known very little love, Ione," she said softly, shrugging as she continued to work. "I loved my mother very much, but that is about all."

"Not your father?"

Kazia said nothing for a long moment before she

said, "I learned a lot from him."

"But," Ione hedged. "Not love?"

Kazia shook her head. She paused when she felt a touch to her arm. Looking down, she saw Ione had moved to stand next to her, her cold fingers wrapped around Kazia's forearm.

"Why is it," Ione said, her voice soft and filled with sadness. "That fathers can be so harsh?" Her fingers began to stroke the inside of the arm she held. Kazia tried to ignore the sensations that was sending throughout her body. "Or, is it men who are harsh?"

Kazia studied her for a long time, so much going through her mind. Yes, at just how lovely Ione was, but for the first time since she'd known her, she saw such a profound loneliness, not just in her eyes but seemingly all around her. It was strange, the same loneliness Kazia had been feeling when she'd stumbled upon her not an hour before.

"I have known some good men in the army," Kazia said. "Also, some not so good ones. As you said, harsh, sometimes cruel. I do not understand it."

Ione looked up into her eyes. "You are not harsh or cruel."

Kazia smiled. "I am not a man."

The shopkeep met her smile with a small one of her own. "No, you are not." Her fingers continued to stroke Kazia's arm, moving up to trail over a defined bicep. "Why have you not been back to the baths?"

Trying to calm her racing heartbeat, Kazia raised her other arm, pretending to sniff at her armpit. Looking back to the smaller woman who grinned up at her, she raised a questioning eyebrow.

"No," Ione murmured. "Not saying that, silly." She kept her eyes on her fingers as she added, "I enjoyed talking to you there that night." She shrugged a shoulder shyly. "Spending time with you." Her gaze flicked up to Kazia's. "I don't really have time to have friendships here, Kazia. The baths are my only free time really." She let out a steam-coated breath as she looked out at the day. "My only time to be me."

Oh, how much Kazia understood those words. And, after the brief meeting of the man Ione had been forced to marry and now support, she understood all the more. Though their circumstances were different, yet again her mother came to mind. Clearing her throat, she spoke, her voice soft and as understanding as she could make it.

"I will be there."

❧❧❧❧

It was nearly a complete repeat of the first time several nights before. Kazia relaxed after bathing herself, alone in the baths. She watched as the shadows danced upon the walls, sent from the candlelight. Many of the candles had already burned out, leaving pockets of deeper shadow. She glanced to her right when she heard movement in the changing room.

A moment later, Ione appeared. The first time, Kazia had the element of surprise to explain her nervousness. This time, it was the fact that the younger woman was making her way to the water, naked and beautiful, and she had no idea what to do with that information. So, she swept her eyes away, giving her companion the privacy and respect she deserved.

She heard Ione enter the water and then the quiet splashing as she moved her way over to her. Heart racing and stomach flip-flopping, Kazia finally garnered the courage to glance over at her, sure to keep her focus strictly on the neck up. Ione's smile was wide, her dark eyes looking happy.

"You're here."

"As promised, kyria."

"How about," Ione said softly, reaching to the closest soap dish and grabbing the soap. "You call me by my name?"

Confused at the request, Kazia took the soap that was extended to her.

"As opposed to being so polite," Ione suggested, giving her a glance before turning her back to the warrior.

Amused, Kazia nodded, even if the other woman couldn't see it. "All right. Ione."

"Was that so hard?" Ione teased, pulling her hair around one side and out of the way.

"Maybe," Kazia teased in return. As she'd done the last time, she lathered her hands and began to work it over the expanse of Ione's back. "Your skin is very soft."

"I like how you touch me," Ione said, words muffled into her own upper chest. "You're so gentle."

"I like touching you," Kazia admitted, her words not much more than a whisper.

She felt ashamed but couldn't stop her ministrations even if she wanted to, which she did not. Her hands smoothed down the softness of Ione's arms, her breath catching as the backs of the fingers of her left hand accidentally brushed against the rounded side of a breast as they made their way back up the insides.

Sensation shot through her like a spear, landing low in her belly. She heard Ione's soft gasp at the contact. "My apologies, kyria," she managed.

Kazia felt dread in her gut when the other woman moved away from her. She fully expected her to move to another part of the baths or leave altogether. Instead, she turned and faced Kazia, moving closer to her. There was a fire in her eyes that Kazia had never seen before, and she honestly couldn't tell what she was feeling. Was she angry at her? Was that the look she was giving her?

Ione moved in the water until she was straddling Kazia's lap, facing her. Barely able to breathe, Kazia could only stare at her. Saying nothing, Ione took Kazia's hands, which still held the soap, and worked the soap until lather began to build once more, giving Kazia the idea. Taking a deep breath, Kazia continued the process as Ione removed her hands, resting them on Kazia's shoulders.

Swallowing again, Kazia blindly reached under Ione's outstretched arm to place the soap in the dish before returning her focus to her task. She had been so careful to not look, but now she had little choice, and it seemed that was exactly what Ione wanted her to do. Ione's breasts were so beautiful, the creamy fullness calling to her like a Siren's song.

Knowing that there was more to be washed than just her breasts, Kazia started at her shoulders. She loved the contrast of her deeply tanned hands with the pale flesh she was washing, almost caressing. It was being offered, so clearly Ione wanted to be touched, and Kazia allowed herself to do so. She was mesmerized.

As her hands moved over delicate collarbones and to her upper chest, Kazia was surprised to feel Ione's own hands on the move. Gentle fingertips traced over the musculature of the warrior's shoulders, following the definition down to her biceps, the muscle working beneath the skin as Kazia's hands worked.

Her gaze moved up to see that Ione's own eyes seemed to be locked on something. A glance down showed Kazia that it was Kazia's breasts. This almost made her gasp as her nipples tightened under the intense scrutiny, even as her own hands neared Ione's breasts. Kazia's fingers brushed along the rounded sides, her lips opening a bit at the incredible feeling of the firm yet soft flesh, slick from the water and lather.

Never feeling any other than her own, she was transfixed. And, when she heard the soft sigh escape Ione's lips, she wanted to hear that again. Taking a deep breath for courage, she moved her hands over to cup the breasts in her palms. Her own sigh escaped at the feel of rigid nipples tickling her palms.

Ione's eyes closed and full lips fell open. Her hands stilled on Kazia's biceps, fingers squeezing, almost like a pulse. Kazia gently squeezed the breasts in her hands in the same slow rhythm. Ione arched her back a bit, pushing herself more fully into Kazia's hands as her eyes opened, staring into the warrior's.

Kazia's breathing hitched, her body reacting and responding to what she was seeing in Ione's eyes. Her gaze fell to lips that looked so soft. As if of its own accord, Kazia's tongue slipped out to run along her own bottom lip. It was like her body knew and understood something her brain did not.

Her eyes left that mouth and went back to Ione's when she felt a hand moving into her hair. Like they were being pulled together, Kazia could no more keep herself from leaning in than the sun could stop rising.

"You about done, lass?"

With a loud gasp, Ione pushed away from Kazia and to the middle of the water at the sudden voice from inside the women's changing room. "Aye!" she called out. "Finishing my bath."

Kazia reached behind her and grabbed the bar of soap, tossing it to Ione, who caught it and quickly turned away to do just that.

Chapter Five

Given her marching orders, Kazia would be joining the crew to extend the roads, as a small unit was set to leave in the coming weeks. But before she joined them, Kazia left the garrison early. She'd been such a mixture of feelings overnight. She'd been a ball of almost childish excitement at what she'd been shown, given permission to see and touch.

In twenty minutes in the baths, Ione had opened up a whole new world to her, and she wasn't entirely sure that's what Ione's intention had been. Well, that was part of the other reason for what had kept her awake, what *had* been Ione's intentions? Had it been seduction? Had it been just a moment between friends that had gotten out of hand? *In* hand? She almost giggled at that last thought as she made her way through the early morning.

Her palms still tingled with the phantom feeling of hard nipples tickling them. She'd had a dream, in the bit of sleep she'd gotten, that she and Ione had been lying on a bed together. They'd been naked and, with the same trusting eyes as she'd looked at her in the baths, Ione had placed Kazia's hand upon her breast.

No doubt it was a onetime thing and could never happen again, for so many reasons. One of which, again, was that she didn't know what Ione's intentions had been. She was on her way to the basket shop now to see her. She needed to see her, but she also wanted to apologize. Maybe she'd taken things too far. Whether she was ever allowed to touch the beautiful young woman again or not, she cherished their growing friendship.

As Ione had said herself, she had little time for friendship. It wasn't so much the lack of time for Kazia as lack of women willing to give her that gift. If nothing else, she didn't want to lose that.

Kazia nodded a greeting to the legionary that was patrolling the market as she headed past the fabric shop and to the basket shop. She had to force herself to remain essentially expressionless, as her want was to break into a great big smile. Ione did that for her, a smaller version of the one spreading inside Kazia.

She walked over to the woman who sat upon a stool weaving a basket with the very vines they'd gathered the day before. She wore fingerless hand coverings, as it was terribly cold but certainly not safe to have a flame of any sort nearby for warmth.

A quick glance to her stall's newcomer, Ione finished what she was doing then set it aside before sliding off the stool and walking the few feet over to Kazia.

"How are you?" she asked softly. Her voice was friendly for certain, but there was something else in her tone as well.

"I am well," Kazia assured. "You?"

"I am well also." Ione's eyes were all over Kazia's face, as if drinking her in. "I wondered if you might help me with something?" she asked, voice projecting in the early morning. "A bit heavy for me."

Confused at the very swift turn in tone, Kazia nodded. She surreptitiously looked around to see if someone had walked by or entered the shop, but they seemed to be alone. Ione pulled back a small curtained-off area she had at the back, nodding that Kazia should follow her.

On the other side was a pot, clearly used to relieve herself during a very long day manning the shop and not being able to leave, as well as some supplies and a small bit of food, again for a long day.

Kazia was barely able to take it all in when Ione's hand was at the back of her head, pulling it down. Stunned, it took her a moment to realize what she was feeling was the softness of Ione's lips against her own. Her arms went around the smaller woman as she responded, following the lead of the other woman, as she had no clue what was expected of her.

Ione's hand moved from the back of her head into her hair. The first touch of Ione's tongue startled Kazia and, as she began to pull away, Ione held her fast. There was a lot of strength in that little body. She relaxed, understanding that Ione had done that on purpose, and when she responded, the pleasurable sigh she earned made her relax. She wasn't doing anything wrong. In fact, it was amazing.

She held the warm body tighter against her own and brushed the backs of her fingers down a soft cheek. Finally, Ione slowed the kiss and, after several soft kisses to her lips, pulled away. She looked up into Kazia's eyes, peace in her own.

"I wanted to do that last night, but obviously we got interrupted."

Nodding, Kazia returned her smile. Her entire body felt so warm, almost as though she'd been given a wonderful hug from the inside. "And," she said with a small chuckle. "Here I had come by before we head out to apologize."

"For what?" Ione asked, looking confused as she held Kazia's hands in her own. "And, where are you going?"

"We're working on the roads today," Kazia explained. "I need to go. I do not think I will be back in time tonight for the baths, but I wanted…" She had no idea what she was going to say, so lost in brown eyes. She smiled instead, feeling like a silly schoolboy. "Well, I must go."

Ione nodded before she leaned up and left a very soft, very loving kiss to her lips. "Be careful," she whispered against them. "And," she added, moving away. "You have nothing to apologize for, Kazia," she assured. "I wanted you to touch me." She gave her a small smile. "I want you to touch me again." With a last stolen kiss, she pushed the curtain aside and headed back to the shop proper and her stool.

Kazia stood there for a moment, trying to get her bearings. Finally, she did and followed. "Good luck with your baskets today, kyria," she said, nodding at the one Ione was getting back to.

"Thank you," the little shopkeep said, a twinkle in her eyes. "And, thank you for your help."

Kazia smirked and nodded before she wiped her face of expression as she prepared to leave. "Anytime."

❧❧❧❧

Of the fifty soldiers that had been sent out on road building duty, twenty of them—including Kazia—were digging the deep trenches that would run along either side of the road so the constant rains could slide off the stones and into them so as not to flood or wash out the road during a normal storm. It was backbreaking work, but it had to be done.

The mindless work allowed Kazia's thoughts

to go back to that morning. A small smile graced her lips, which still felt the ghostly touch against them. If kissing was so wonderful, what must sex be like? Two men could have sex, and now she knew that two women could kiss, so surely they could have sex as well. How did that work?

With men, it was obvious: the penis. It seemed to be the central theme of sexual intercourse, right? So, then with two women—

"Did you hear that?"

Pulled out of her musings, Kazia looked to the man closest to her, He had stopped mid-shovel, head lifted as he looked around. She, too, began to take in their surroundings. They were in an open area five miles east of the garrison. An area that was a well-worn path by both human and beast, the Romans were paving it, adding it to the hundreds of thousands of miles of roads that spiderwebbed across the empire.

"Prohibere!" the centurion supervising called out, a hand held out to halt work. He sat upon his horse, looking around as if he, too, had heard something.

The air was growing heavy, something in the day not right. Kazia could feel her heart beginning to race and the blood pounding in her neck as expectation began to spread over her like a heavy blanket. Even the songs and chatter of birds in nearby trees had stopped, seeming to silence themselves in preparation.

As if a human storm thundered down upon them, roaring emanated from the trees long before its source was seen. Men, hundreds of them, stormed out of the woods carrying swords, axes, and anything else that would work as a weapon. Kazia barely swung the shovel she'd been using in time to whack one in the head before he was upon her.

With his body flying past her, she swung again, using the edged side of the tool to slice into a man's gut, the shovel head becoming stuck as it sliced through his innards. With gritted teeth, she used all her body weight with the long handle to send him flying, shovel still sticking out of him.

Shovel gone, she grabbed her nearby scutum with one hand, to block an incoming blow and propel the Brittani warrior while she pulled her gladius free of its scabbard. He tried to push back on her shield, but got it rammed into his face for his troubles. Before he could rid himself of the blow with a shake of his head, she'd reached around the side of the curved shield to run him through.

He hadn't even hit the ground yet before Kazia used a powerful kick to send another fighter backward and out of her personal space. A slash with the deadly sharp blade and his ruined throat was a fount of blood. She nearly tripped over his body as she was engaged in a clash of blades by a man who was nearly half a foot taller than she was, and Kazia was nearly as tall as any man.

With gritted teeth she kept up, using her shield and her entire body weight to push him off her and get some distance before he was back on her like a mosquito. She could tell she wasn't going to out-blade him, as he was on her swing for swing, blow for blow. She allowed him to get closer in, watching carefully until he was in position.

With a grunt of exertion, she rammed the top edge of her scutum up under his chin as hard as she could. His head flew up and blood immediately began to pour out of his mouth, as well as half of his tongue, which he'd bitten off. He began to scream in agony, though not for long as she slashed his throat so deep, his head nearly rolled off his shoulders.

As the next Celt came at her, she could taste blood on her lips and could feel it on her face. She had to wipe her hand and blade on the garment of a dead man in order to get a better hold on the grip after she'd killed yet another combatant.

It was then that she smelled fire. Chest heaving as she was panting from her exertions, she looked back the way they'd come. Black, billowing smoke filled the air above the treetops.

She took on another fighter, using her shield to deflect his axe before she was able to use her blade to slice his hand off, the axe falling to the ground with his screams. Gutting him, she turned away when she noticed something.

A hundred yards away, not in the trees but near them, she saw a figure. By its size, it looked to be male, as it sat upon a horse, black as night. He sat there watching, a dark brown cloak pulled around his body and draping over the horse's rump. The hood was pulled up, leaving only the man's mouth and chin visible.

She had no idea who he was, but she knew he was watching her, could literally *feel* his gaze on her. He smiled, big and broad, before raising a hand to his forehead and pulling it away in a strange gesture. With that, he turned the steed around and…vanished.

Kazia cried out as intense pain shot from her left bicep to her shoulder. Baring her teeth, she turned to see a man standing thirty feet away, his slingshot in his hand and reloading. Without taking her eyes off him, she reached into her belt and grabbed her dagger. With almost inhuman speed, she tossed it up and caught it by the tip of the blade before she sent it flying, end over end, until it buried itself in the man's throat.

Looking at her with wide, shocked eyes, the stone he'd just placed into the weapon's cup fell harmlessly to the ground before his body did. She ran over to him and grabbed the blade before she whirled around, using it to slice a fighter's belly open. It wasn't enough to kill him initially, but she knew it hurt like hell and he was bleeding terribly, eventually to death if it wasn't stemmed.

Raising her left hand that still held the shield, she backhanded him with it, sending him to the ground. Knowing he was out of commission, Kazia turned back toward the garrison and the village.

The smoke had gotten worse, blacker and more dense. And, as the fighting was dying down where she was—each of the fifty Roman soldiers easily taking out two or three men each—they'd dispatched the horde.

It seemed they were a group of Celtic warriors that had not been from the village at the garrison. Still, she could hear the sound of fighting at home, even from this distance. Clearly, the horde had attacked there as well.

She heard their unit commander's horse plow through the carnage then past her, the rider waving her unit to head home. Pugio tucked away and gladius sheathed, Kazia took off at a dead run. She blocked out any pain, blocked out the miles, blocked out the blood she had to keep blinking out of her right eye from a wound sustained. She had a mission and an order, and she was going to get there.

She saw Ione's face in her mind's eye, and in that moment, it wasn't the commander's order that sent her sprinting, it was her intention of finding Ione and protecting her. The scenery blew by her unnoticed. The man speeding on his horse now far back behind her, unnoticed. The fact that she was alone, any of her unit long gone in her dust, unnoticed.

Powerful thighs propelled her, her body becoming a well-oiled machine meant for movement and exertion. Her lungs didn't burn, her feet covered in caliga sandals didn't even register the strain nor the heat through the thick leather soles from her inhuman speed.

The smoke was getting thicker the closer she got, the air harder to breathe. It was also louder. The clashing of blades, screaming of women and men and explosion of oil reserves filled the air. She slowed as she got closer for fear she'd overshoot the entire town.

One such explosion sent Kazia off her feet as she entered the town proper. She grunted as her head hit the ground, even protected by her helmet, her shield going flying. She lay there for a moment, dazed, before she gathered herself up and, noting her shield had landed in the middle of a burning building, she left it and ran farther in.

The soldiers were running from the garrison like ants from an anthill. The sheer number of the Brittani was mind-boggling. They seemed to have split themselves into three groups; one group had gone after the soldiers in the road crew while a second had gone after the soldiers and the garrison and the third was slaughtering the villagers. That was where Kazia headed.

Fires were burning out of control everywhere she looked, her lungs seizing with the thick smoke. Coughing, she drew her sword and went hunting. Every Brittani fighter she came to she gutted, throwing their bodies aside as she looked for the next.

One man was in the process of trying to pull one of the village women's dress off her body, his intent *very* clear. She grabbed him by his long, stringy hair, the man howling in pain. His howls got even worse when he landed ten feet away in one of the many fires, his severed penis, which had been erect and ready to go, next to him.

"Are you all right?" Kazia yelled to the horrified woman. She stared up at her blankly with wide, traumatized eyes. Kazia had no time to stay with her, so she threw the remnants of her garment at her before she ran on.

She was frantically looking for Ione. There were so many fires and so much destruction already, it was hard to tell what was what. Off to the right she saw what looked to be a large basket lying atop the rubble from what looked to be a collapsed building. Knowing it was a long shot, Kazia ran over to it, plowing over anything and anyone in her way.

She saw two of her fellow soldiers just off to the left from the area where she saw the basket. One was kneeling next to the other, who lay on the ground. He wasn't dead but looked to be dazed and wounded. The kneeling man looked to be trying to make sure he was all right. Kazia's gaze was pulled from this when she heard a woman screaming behind her aways.

Whirling around, she saw one of the fighters, his arm moving like a piston into a huddled figure, the one that had been screaming. With one final loud gasp, the screaming stopped and so did his arm. Kazia realized he'd just stabbed the woman, likely to death. She also realized that the woman he'd just stabbed, likely to death, was a woman with long, dark hair.

An animalistic roar exploded out of Kazia as she bounded over there and grabbed him. His wide blue eyes nearly bulged out of his head when he saw her, which made her wonder for just a second what had he seen upon her face. He still held his knife, the long blade covered in the woman's blood, as was his hand and forearm.

The smell of fresh urine filled Kazia's nostrils as she grabbed him by the neck with her bare hands and twisted. The most horrible crack rent the air, and suddenly she was looking at the back of his head, even as the front of his body still faced her. The head flopped downward, the forehead bumping against his own upper back.

Kazia grabbed the man's shoulders and, as if lifting nothing more than a child's toy, flung him like so much garbage. His body landed with a disgusting, wet flop. Still panting from her rage and exertion, Kazia dropped to her knees, her gladius clinking to the ground next to her. Sending up a prayer to anyone who would listen, she carefully gathered the body of the woman.

There was so much blood that the color of her garment was no longer visible. The body was limp as she cradled it up into her lap. With gentle, bloodstained fingers, Kazia brushed the mass of hair back. A loud keening sound left her lips when she saw the pale face, sweet brown eyes heavily hooded and staring off into a place where Kazia could not join her.

Cradling her head to her chest, Kazia's own head flew back, and the keening turned to a guttural cry that erupted from her very soul until her voice went hoarse. With little mewls, she buried her face into thick, dark hair, which now smelled of smoke and blood, and rocked Ione's body. The tears rolling down her cheeks left trails through the blood, dirt, and soot.

"I am sorry," she whimpered. "I am so sorry."

"Forget about her, she's dead!"

Kazia's head whipped up, glaring at whoever *dared* interrupt. When she saw that it was the soldier who had been kneeling over the prone man, her rage bubbled up again. With deceptive gentleness that belied the murder in her eyes, she lay Ione's body to the ground. Never taking her eyes off him, she grabbed her sword and pushed to her feet.

"You could have saved her," she growled. "You could have saved her!"

"My job is to save my men," the soldier yelled. "Not some village whore!"

With murderous rage, Kazia charged him, sending the razor-sharp edge of her gladius through his neck and not stopping as the headless body fell to the ground. The other soldier, who had raised himself to a knee from the ground, looked at her with wide, terrified eyes. Her blade coming down was the last thing he saw.

Chapter Six

Head resting back against the bars, Kazia tried to focus on something—*anything*—other than the fact that her stomach was threatening to revolt. It didn't help that the pot she'd been given to do her business in was sitting not four feet away from her. She'd done her best to not eat or drink much so her body wouldn't have much to expel—from either end. Her lack of appetite had helped with that, to be sure.

Even still, the stench of three-day old urine wasn't helping the seasickness, as that was the last time the pot had been gathered and emptied by one of the crew. She'd never done well when she'd been on a ship. Her stomach became her biggest enemy every time. She had no idea where she was going, no doubt to an outpost somewhere for a general to handle her execution.

After the battle was over and the smoke had cleared, so many dead had been left behind—villagers, the enemy, and Roman legions, alike. She'd been dragged in front of the commander.

"Strip," he'd said, standing five feet away, hands tucked behind his back.

Without comment or question, Kazia had done as ordered. Her uniform had lovingly been removed, as it had every time she'd removed it, and placed on the floor at her feet. It was torn and bloodstained, but she'd still handled it with care. Her galea had been placed last atop the pile. Gladius in it, her scabbard had been placed on the ground next to it and her pugio.

Naked and still covered in the blood of her enemy, the woman she'd grown to care deeply about, and that of her brothers in arms, she'd stood tall. Her shoulders were straight, arms at her sides and eyes facing forward.

The Prefect of the garrison looked her over, his gaze taking in every inch of her body. She could feel it like a lover's caress, even as she didn't watch him. In that moment, she didn't care what he did. In truth, she wished he'd grab her own sword and send her home, finally and blessedly home.

Instead, he'd wandered around her in a slow circle, never once touching her. He was eyeing her, much like she felt a wealthy sheep herder studied his flock. She didn't move a muscle, just waiting until he spoke and told her her fate so she could prepare herself.

"Why did you do it?" he finally asked, once again in front of her. "Why did you murder two of your brothers?"

"I did not murder them, sir," she said quietly.

"No?" he challenged, bushy eyebrows raised. "They are currently dead, one without a head."

She nodded. "They are, sir. They stood by while a village woman was hacked to death by one of the enemy," she said. "Our job here is to keep the peace and protect those who cannot protect themselves." She had to pause, as she felt emotion, as unwanted as it was, rising in her throat. She swallowed it down and continued. "They failed at their duty."

He studied her for a long moment. Though she continued to stare straight ahead, she could see in her periphery his intense gaze. "And," he finally said, beginning his stroll again. "You felt it was your duty to act as judge and executioner of that failure?"

"In that moment, yes, sir," she said honestly.

"In that moment," he repeated. "So, if it were another moment of failed duty, you would do the same?"

"In that moment sir, yes, I would do the same."

"And, should I do the same?" He paused in front of her again. "Play executioner? Or, perhaps allow their barracks mates to avenge them?"

"If that is what you see fit," she said easily. "I welcome it."

She'd been sent to clean up and given what amounted to a burlap sack with holes for head and arms to put on. She had what amounted to rags wrapped around her feet, and shackles had been placed around her wrists. She'd been tossed into a wagon and, after a long, bumpy ride, had ended up at a harbor.

It had only been once she'd been loaded into the cage she currently sat in that her shackles had been removed. She'd been loaded by crane into the hold of the ship she sailed in now.

She'd been told nothing, given nothing, and never allowed to return to her barracks to collect the few personal belongings she'd had. But then, she thought, what did she really have? Nothing belonged to her that hadn't been bought with money earned in the Roman army. Earned. Earned, doing what? Conquering? Taking? Killing?

She was exactly where she deserved to be.

Looking around, she could see the cargo that was stacked and secured all around her. It was amusing, in all honesty. She wasn't being treated like the common criminal, she was being treated like shipping materials. Her gaze was caught when the door at the top of the steep wooden stairs opened, the light from above shining down and making her squint.

Her eyes had adjusted to the small amount of light that came in through the porthole at the other end of the cargo area. Quick, booted steps were heard before a man appeared, one of the crew. He glanced at her before going to his destination, which was a stack of what looked to be bags of flour.

She tried to speak, but her words failed her, throat dry and rough. Clearing her throat, she tried again. "Are we almost there?"

He nodded, then hurried back up the stairs with his load.

❧ ❧ ❦ ❦

Kazia was awakened by voices and noise. She opened her eyes and pushed up from where she was curled up on the floor of the cage. It took a moment, but she realized they were no longer moving, and the sounds of hurried steps and instructions called out from the decks above could be heard.

Apparently, they'd docked. Sure enough, with the turning of a wheel, the deck above began to open. The heavier cargo—like herself—would be lifted out and moved over to the docks by crane. She said nothing, simply pushed herself up to a sitting position. She winced, her body sore and aching from being in such cramped confines for…she didn't even know how long.

The door was flung open, and many sets of feet pounded down the stairs into the hold. No one paid her any mind, nor did she care for them to. She was just glad this part of her journey was over and she could get on to her death. This in-between part was awful. She honestly wasn't sure why she hadn't just been killed at the garrison.

Finally, the focus was on her cage. One of the men climbed on top of it to anchor it securely to the chain attached to the crane arm, the thick chain having been lowered down into the hold. Hopping down, he called up to the men up top, who then called out to the men on the docks who operated the crane. Kazia felt her stomach bottom out as the cage was lifted, her hands gripping the bars as it swung from side to side.

Squeezing her eyes shut, she tried desperately to not focus on the feelings in her gut and certainly not the floor of the hold, which was getting farther and farther away. She could feel the cold ocean breeze as she was brought out into the light of day. She could hear the seabirds screeching not far away as they flew by, diving for anything edible.

She heard the men calling out to each other from the ship to the docks and, for a breathless moment, she felt her cage begin to swing violently, the men on the ship barking orders to the crane operators to slow down.

This time, Kazia's stomach did give way. She had very little in her, but what she had fell through the bars and to the dock below. She was just glad it hadn't landed on anyone. Slowly, and with more control, the cage was lowered, dock workers gripping it to direct it to yet another wagon. She took a long, deep breath when finally it was settled.

Almost immediately, two men jumped up into the wagon and covered the large structure with white fabric, her world going from blue skies above to feeling like a baby bird forced back into its shell. With little fanfare, the wagon was moving, pulled by a horse whose hooves clopped on the ground.

No idea how long she'd been on that ship, as Kazia hadn't bothered to count days or nights or even hours or minutes. She'd slept as much as she could, though her dreams had been haunted by Ione. Sometimes they were back in the baths, Ione straddling her lap. They'd kissed as they had that last morning. So soft, so utterly wonderful. Other times, she'd watched her die all over again, but this time *Kazia* was the one wielding the blade.

She'd not saved her. She'd not kept her safe, as she'd promised to. Kazia felt no guilt over the death of the two legionaries. What she'd told the Prefect, she meant. They'd failed in their duty. The Romans had conquered a land and conquered its people. At the very minimum, they owed those people safety.

She lay back against the bars, her behind and back screaming at her, as yet again her body was jostled. Unable to help it, she snorted in bitter amusement. Here she was again, in another cage heading to another unknown destination. It took her back to that horrible night when she'd been but fifteen. Now, nearly nineteen, she was full circle.

What seemed to take days but was likely an hour or less, the wagon began to slow down, the clopping of the hooves echoing and sounding as if they were clopping on stone. The wagon slowed then stopped. Several men's voices were heard surrounding the area, discussing amongst themselves the best way to get the cage out of the wagon and to the ground for "presentation."

Presentation? Kazia sat upright, still unable to see anything as the cage was still covered. She could hear grunting as the cage began to move, Kazia once again holding on to the bars to steady herself. It sounded and felt like it was being inched out of the wagon until finally she was free-floating, carried. A handful of moments later, the cage was slowly lowered until she was rocked a bit as it was placed on the ground.

She heard the wagon and horse trot away, which made her stomach lurch. Clearly she was where she'd be staying. But why all the fuss? Why wasn't the cover just taken off, shackles put on, and the door opened for her to walk to wherever? She heard more voices, these not that of the men who had moved her out of the wagon. These were big, boisterous voices. Male, and one in particular was making her skin crawl.

"I have bought the Beast of Britannia!" he boasted.

With that dramatic declaration, the covering of the cage was whipped off to a chorus of, *Ohh!* A group of a dozen or more old, fat men stood several feet from the cage, the quality of the material of their tunica and gold goblets they held befitting to the impressive courtyard Kazia found herself in. It was decorated with beautiful statues and well-maintained vegetation and gurgling water features.

Kazia's gaze moved from the scenery and large villa back to the men. They looked at her with wide, expectant eyes as if waiting for her to do something. She moved to her hands and knees now, eyeing every person there, trying to weigh their intentions with what she could do in response.

"Already on her knees," one of the men muttered, the other men laughing as the man who had spoken raised his goblet in salute to her as he gave her a lecherous smile.

The man who claimed to have bought her walked

closer to the cage. Curiosity burned in his dark eyes as he sipped from his goblet. He met her gaze before his own looked over every aspect of her as he wandered around the cage.

Kazia said nothing nor did she do anything. She had no idea where she was nor why she was there. But, from the look on the faces of her little audience, she had an awfully bad feeling that more blood would be spilled, and soon.

"Simply marvelous," the man said, as if to himself, as he made the full circuit, ending up back in front of her. The look in his eyes wasn't exactly lust as in sexual intent, but almost more expectant excitement in general. "You speak Latin?" he asked.

She stared at him, wondering why on earth he was asking such a question. She'd been in the Roman army for more than three years. What else would she speak?

"She *is* the Beast of Britannia," one of the men said. "Perhaps she speaks that foul Gaelic."

"Ah yes," the first man murmured. "Is that it?" he asked her, amusement in his eyes as he sipped his drink. "Do you speak that bastardized language?"

"Do you?" she asked in perfect Latin, an eyebrow quirked. Her gaze never left his, even as laughter arose amongst the other men.

"Perhaps a little civilized after all." The man chuckled. He let out a loud, sharp single whistle, eyes never leaving Kazia's. A small army of well-armed men seemed to come out of nowhere, surrounding the cage. Three by the door, one holding shackles. "Get her bathed," the man ordered. "And," he said to Kazia. "If you hurt any of my people, I will have them kill you where you stand."

❧ ❧ ❧ ❧

Understanding that these people were likely no less captives than she was, Kazia made no trouble for the armed men who led her through the halls of the fine villa shackled and surrounded. She was led down some stairs and into the largest, most fine bathroom she'd ever seen. The marble tub was massive, and it sported running water. There was even a private, indoor toilet.

As much as she didn't want to be, she was impressed and awed. The guards who had escorted her inside didn't leave until a veritable swarm of women showed up, taking over once the shackles were removed. From their clothing, she knew they were slaves. They said little to her but went about getting her bathed and, to her stunned shock, removing any and all body hair.

Again, there was no reason to hurt these women, even as Kazia desperately wanted to throw them aside and escape their suffocating and admittedly painful ministrations. After she'd been bathed, four of the women held her down while a fifth, armed with a razor, had shaved her underarms and legs.

Kazia had watched with morbid fascination, even as she was utterly baffled on why they were doing this. But it was when her legs were spread and the same woman moved in with the razor to shave a more… *delicate*…part of her body that Kazia nearly did throw them aside.

The woman with the razor, who was all but lying atop her legs to keep them still, looked up into Kazia's wide eyes.

"If you do not let us do this," she said, voice

quiet. "He will blame us."

Kazia met and held that angry gaze before, reluctantly, she nodded. She had nearly bitten through her bottom lip as the woman did what she must. It hadn't been painful but had left her incredibly confused. She'd never had anyone near her most private place before, and she could feel a warm little ball of sensations deep in her stomach, the same kind that she'd felt when in the baths with Ione.

She gasped when the woman's knuckle grazed a certain spot that made her eyes shoot open wide. Looking down the length of her body, she saw that the woman didn't react, very intent on her careful and meticulous shaving. When finally the torture was complete, the women scattered, almost as if little cockroaches that found the shadows as the sun rose.

Left alone in the large room, Kazia stood there, cleaner than she'd been in years, naked and shaved save for the hair atop her head, which hung partially over her forehead as the dark strands dried, and her eyebrows. Her skin felt tingly and more naked than naked. Bringing up a hand, she brushed her hair back and looked around, trying to see if there was any escape.

The main door opened within seconds, and the man who seemed to own the villa *and her* stepped inside, flanked by four of the armed guards. She made a mental calculation of what it would take to disarm one and kill the other four, including the old fat man, and get out.

"I wouldn't," the old man said, bushy gray eyebrows lifting in an expression of warning. "You may get past my guards here, but trust me, Beast, you will not get out of this villa alive."

"Do not call me Beast." She glared at him. "I am not the one who buys human beings. The *beast* of which you speak, would be you." She was stunned the words had fallen out of her mouth, as more often than not words were not her chosen path. But she was angry, confused, and felt violated.

He looked at her with amusement in his eyes. "No," he agreed. "You do not. You cut their heads off."

Oh, how she wanted to cut his off in that moment. Hatred sprang into her heart and burned there like a flame. "Why am I here?" she said, voice low and dangerous.

"You are here as my special guest," he said, smiling brightly. "You are also here as entertainment for my *very* special guests."

"The men outside?" she asked.

"Among others," he said with a nod.

She took a step closer to him, gaze never leaving his. She didn't stop when she felt the point of a blade at her throat. In fact, she took yet another step, refusing to react when she felt the metal dig into her flesh.

"Pull back," the old man said, his eyes never leaving hers.

Kazia was surprised when she felt the sword moved but not removed. "If any one of those men, or anyone else," she warned, voice deadly, "gets anywhere near me, I will rip them to shreds." With lightning-quick reflexes, she throat-punched the guard and grabbed his sword from him as he staggered backward, coughing and gasping. She held the blade's edge to the old man's throat. "Understand me?" she whispered.

With that, and a terrified look from him, she dropped the sword where she stood and took a step back from the old man.

Chapter Seven

Britannia: 852 CE

The lone figure stood outside the circle of huge stones, two long ones standing on end, another one across the top. They were set around in a huge, perfect circle, the stones' placement creating a circle of "archways," or as she knew better, doorways. Inside the inner circle were more stones standing upright and topped by a longer stone, five in all, and set in a semicircle. A row of much smaller stones were planted in the ground along the inside of the outer circle and trailing inside with the semicircle.

For eternity, many would wonder what all this was for, especially later in the future after the outer circle of "archways" had already been removed by those who no longer needed them to travel and couldn't chance someone stumbling into them. Science would call this a henge, a *stone* henge. Senara just called it cold as hell and was ready to get back to Duras, or as their destination was this morning, Bowhar.

As she waited outside, not able to enter, she pulled her heavy blue cloak with gold stitching tighter around her body, her hood pulled into place. The sun was rising, its golden rays stretching fingers out across the stones, changing the direction of the shadows to dump her into even colder temperatures.

Senara hugged herself tighter beneath the cloak as she began to bounce on the balls of her feet to stay warm. She'd known better than to dress in her usual, as she always froze her ass off in Britannia. It had been a long time since she'd dealt with this weather as a child living in Armorica. She had certainly become spoiled in Duras and Bowhar over the last many centuries.

As the sun popped over the tallest stones at the center of the circle, a cloaked figure emerged out of the archway of the center one. The cloak of dark gray was pulled tightly around the petite figure, the rising sun setting her dark auburn hair aglow. The morning flame around her head put what Senara knew was a beautiful face in silhouette as she hurried to the outer archway closest to the woman in the blue cloak.

"Good morrow," the woman called out, a smile in her voice.

Senara returned the smile that she knew was there, though she couldn't quite see it yet. "Good morrow, Brielle." When the smaller woman reached her, the two shared a hug from much shared history.

"I appreciate you coming," Brielle said.

Senara smirked. "I was literally in the neighborhood."

Though she appeared to be a young Druid, no more than twenty-five, Brielle was older than the stone structure they were walking away from. Brielle was one of the small number that were part of a sub-group of the most ancient of the Ancients: the super Ancients.

Born before the time of Christ, Senara was of the Ancients, but Brielle and her small group of peers had been born just about before time itself.

This group of a hundred or so were spread all across the globe and had been part of the earth's earliest civilizations and the birth of modern Man. They were the eyes and ears of the gods. And, if an Ankou or Druid were fortunate enough to have one befriend them, they were fortunate, indeed.

Each went into voluntary Shkee every five hundred years or so, Brielle's coming up in another hundred years, perhaps. It was a state of hibernation, an ageless soul in a human body at rest. With eons of years of existence between them, a sudden and destructive exhaustion hit swiftly. If this happened, it was like an implosion of a star, the power within exploding outward in devastating result.

The literal time and calendar keeper of years, in their chronological count, was in Bowhar, a place for Ankou, Druid, and those known as exceptional humans, or enlightened, to cohabitate.

In Duras and Ryarch, land of Ankou and Druid respectively, time held little meaning. That was a consideration on the earth plane, as regular humans had a lifespan, so time was sacred. This was also true for the super Ancients. There was a person whose sole job was to keep track of the super Ancients and their energy cycles for Shkee.

The two women walked in companionable silence for a bit, Brielle's long, auburn hair pulled back from her face and held in a single braid that joined the rest of her mane down her back. Her eyes were a green made of a thousand rolling hills and wild grasses. Her brand of beauty was that of sweet innocence, but her eyes could make a grown man tremble with their intensity when she chose.

Druids were seers, after all, and if one locked on to you, they would plunge your soul for all its secrets. And, Senara had come to notice in her many years that so many of the Druid blood carried the flame of their touch into their hair. If not red or a rich auburn, like Brielle's, it was golden blond. Exceptions existed, certainly, but it was a strange part of the blood.

"Have you seen her yet?" Brielle asked after a while, her gaze never leaving the path before them.

Senara brought up her hands to brush her hood back, revealing short, midnight tresses that just barely brushed her ears and curled at the nape of her neck. The strands lifted lightly in the morning breeze. "Who?"

"She is of The Lost." She glanced over at Senara. "I've been seeing her in my dreams lately."

"Druid?" Senara asked as they stepped up to the door, a naturally occurring one stretched out between a crag in a stone face surrounded by other huge boulders and trees, the telltale shimmer of the space only noticeable to the blood. This door would take them to Brittany, from which they could enter Bowhar together.

Brielle shook her head. "Ankou." She stopped just before entering the door. "And, you've seen her."

Senara's eyebrows drew as she followed, stepping through the door and…

…into a bustling seaport off the rocky shores of Brittany. Ships were docked at the harbor and being loaded and unloaded, dock crew scurrying around, not even noticing the two cloaked women who had just appeared from behind a small copse of trees. Set back from the docks was a marketplace, largely selling fish and some of the goods coming off the ships.

The air was filled with the pungent scent of fresh seafood, which made Senara's stomach roil a bit. Though she hadn't lived upon these shores since before the country had been unified into the current one, that smell still sat with her, and she still hated it.

Her gaze fell to her companion when she heard a

small laugh. "What?"

"You look like you're about to vomit," Brielle noted.

Senara blew out a breath and nodded. "Not far off."

Smiling, Brielle lightly squeezed Senara's hand in a brief affectionate hold before releasing her. "So, this woman—"

Her words were cut off when suddenly a little blur blew between the two women, nearly knocking Brielle to the ground. Senara immediately shrugged her cloak off one shoulder as she drew her back-mounted sword, which the cloak had been hiding. She looked back behind them to see three men running toward them, looking as though they'd been chasing whatever had pushed the two women apart.

"Stop them," Brielle said, running after something or someone.

Nodding, Senara turned and walked toward the men, blocking their path. Though she held her sword in her hand, she knew she wouldn't need it. These were merely humans, not much worth her effort. But, given a task she was, so performing the task she would. She twirled the blade casually in her hand as she sauntered their way.

She gave them a sexy little grin as, without warning, she sliced her blade sideways through the air as if she'd just sliced through a wall of hanging fabric. One fell to his knees, another flat on his ass, while the third staggered off and into a booth of wares being sold. She knew they'd be fine, just gave them a little something to deal with while Brielle was dealing with her own issue.

Turning away from them, she saw that her friend

was kneeling in front of a young girl up the way, where apparently she'd caught up with the little sea urchin. The girl had a head full of long, light blond hair that Brielle was currently carefully pushing out of an absolutely angelic face. She was the most lovely child Senara had ever seen.

As she walked up to the pair, the girl looked up at Senara, eyes the color of the most beautiful sky surrounded by the deep seas meeting her gaze.

Never good with children, Senara gave her a little smile then looked to Brielle. "Who is this?"

"Trying to find that out," the Druid said softly. "Why were those men chasing you, sweetheart?" Her voice was so gentle to this child, who looked no more than nine or ten. She was filthy, her clothing not more than rags on her tiny frame.

The girl's eyes met Brielle's, but only briefly, as she was looking around. She looked as though she'd bolt at the first given chance. "I know not," she finally murmured. Her voice was small, high-pitched in its youth.

Brielle glanced up at Senara, who met her gaze for a moment before she, too, was looking around. Yes, this child looked like she lived on the streets, as so many did. Had she stolen something? But, why on earth would three grown men chase her for such a thing? Would one not suffice?

"What is your name?" Brielle was asking, pulling Senara's attention back to the other two. "Don't want to tell me?" she asked sweetly when the girl said nothing. When she got a small shake of the girl's head, Brielle smiled at her. "All right, I will not push you. Have you somewhere to go?"

When the girl refused to answer yet again,

Senara felt herself becoming impatient and irritated. She shifted her weight to her other booted foot as she surveyed the area once again, though this time to keep her from shooting off her mouth than because she was concerned.

"Here," Brielle said, holding out some coins to the child who still stood before the kneeling woman. When she didn't take them, Brielle gently took one of the girl's small hands and peeled her little fingers back to reveal her palm. The coins were set there, and the fingers closed around them. "Get some food and a place to shelter," she said softly, her voice almost like a spoken lullaby.

Smirking, Senara could see the child was being affected by it. Lord knew *she'd* given in to it once…or a half-dozen times. Brielle had the fire touch, like all Druids, and was one of the ancient seers, but that damn voice of hers. When she wanted it to, which was the point, she could make anyone do just about anything.

The Druid raised her head and left a soft, almost loving kiss to the girl's forehead before she pushed to her feet. The young one looked up at her with far more trust than she had moments before. In fact, in those beautiful eyes it was almost a longing. A motherly touch, perhaps?

With a gentle smile, Brielle lightly cupped the girl's cheek before the young one turned and took off, disappearing in the throngs of people in the marketplace.

Senara watched her for a moment before she turned to see if the men had gotten themselves back together. Not only had they, but they were nowhere to be seen. This left her a bit uncomfortable as she took a step away from Brielle as she searched the faces of those nearby or even farther down to the docks.

Nothing.

Turning to the Druid, their gazes met.

⁂

Though her house and primary residence was in Duras, Senara kept a small cottage in Bowhar, where she was at the moment. Just returning from a long mission, she was tired but knew she had a debrief by Macha the following day, as her mission had involved a murdered Druid. As Ankou, her energy was not compatible to enter Ryarch and speak to the goddess, so Bowhar was where such cross-blood meetings took place.

Speaking of cross-blood meetings, Brielle planned to spend the night when she was finished with her own meetings, thus why she'd been heading to Bowhar. The two were very close friends and sometimes lovers, if the mood so struck. Mostly, however, Senara looked up to the smaller woman as a mentor. She was brilliant, patient, and had taught Senara as much about herself as she had the Druid blood.

She'd also been there that horrible night when Senara had been just barely a teenager, her parents killed by the conquering Romans in their peaceful little village. She'd been hurt badly, and a man had come along in a blue cloak with gold stitching with a woman who mesmerized a terrified young Senara with her kind smile and sweet Siren song of a voice in a dark gray cloak.

Literally unable to say no, the teenager had been swept away to Bowhar, and then finally to Duras to join her Ankou blood.

That had been more than nine hundred years ago, according to the clock of Bowhar. Now, Senara stood in her bathroom after stepping out of the shower. Nude, she looked at herself in the reflection of the mirror. She had the appearance of a woman in her midtwenties, as did most of them, considering they stopped aging the moment they reached their full power.

She'd been twenty-six, nearly twenty-seven in earth-plane years. Now, nearly a thousand years old, those she'd known in Armorica were dust in their graves. She looked into her eyes, which depending on the light and her mood could look a light grayish-blue or silver. The angrier she got, the less color they held.

Right now, they were the color of a light storm with a touch of blue skies hidden in their cloudy depths. She looked away from them and to her face, which she'd been told many times was beautiful. Her features were angular, with full lips and eyebrows as midnight black as the hair on her head.

Her gaze scanned over her body, strong yet very feminine. She knew Brielle, in particular, liked her breasts. Her skin was pale, a contrast she liked against the black leather pants she usually wore. They wrapped around her thighs and ass like a lover's caress. Her black leather boots, which stopped just below the knee, topped off her preferred dress from the waist down.

As tight as she liked her leathers was as loose as she loved the white billowing blouses she wore on top. A contrast in terms that was Senara to a T.

Looking away from her reflection, she finger-combed her damp hair as she padded to the one bedroom. She hadn't decided if seducing Brielle was on her agenda for the night or not. Truth was, that girl they'd dealt with in Brittany was on her mind, and she had no idea why. A waif of no consequence to them, she couldn't get her eyes out of her mind.

Growling in frustration, Senara went ahead and got dressed in something simple and comfortable in which she'd sleep, if nothing else happened.

There had been something about that girl that she just couldn't put her finger on. Something in her eyes, those absolutely lovely eyes. Someday that kid would be a knockout, she thought. In another ten, fifteen years. But that obviously wasn't it.

She grabbed the clothing she'd been wearing that day and gathered it all up where she'd dropped it on the way to the shower and stuffed it all into the laundry basket in the corner of the small, simple, and basic bedroom. Like the rest of the small cottage, no frills, just the necessities. She saved the specialness for her home in Duras.

Walking to the kitchen to make herself something to eat, she heard the front door open, and a glance showed her Brielle enter. The two shared a smile of greeting as the Druid closed the door behind her and reached up to untie her cloak as she stepped into the small living room.

"Long day," she muttered, sounding tired.

"Aye," Senara said. "I was about to make food. Hungry?"

In the simple dress she wore, almost like a peasant gown, Brielle made her way into the kitchen after laying her cloak over the back of the couch. Shaking her head, she plopped down into one of the two chairs at the table.

"Thank you, no." She rested her head back against the wall that the table was tucked up against for the sake of space, eyes closing. "You are troubled," she murmured.

Senara was amused, not surprised that her friend could feel it. "I am. I keep thinking about that girl today," she explained as she whipped herself up something simple to eat—a thick slice of homemade bread and a chunk off the block of cheddar. She poured them both a glass of cold, fresh water, which she knew Brielle would want, and carried her bounty to the table.

"I can see why," Brielle said, eyes opening to half mast as she watched Senara get settled. "I've been working with you on slowing down to feel the energy of those around you. Of recognizing your own kind for some time, Senara."

The Ankou got settled and looked across the table at her. "My own kind. That girl is Ankou?"

Brielle studied her for so long, she was making Senara feel a bit shifty in her chair. Finally, she spoke. "You felt it. Didn't you." A statement.

Senara smirked, setting the second glass of water in front of her companion. "Honestly, all I felt was irritation that she was so rude to you"

"She was not rude," Brielle insisted, wrapping her hand around the glass before taking a long drink. Her eyes once again closed, but this time in pleasure. As she set the glass down, the gorgeous green eyes peeked open again as she looked at the woman eating mere feet from her. "She is a survivor, Senara," she said softly. "And, someday, she will rule Bowhar."

Chapter Eight

*D*ark brown hair, short but shaggy strands *falling into hazel eyes, which looked straight ahead and were filled with a rage that could be felt. Defined cheekbones, a nose ever so slightly crooked, perhaps from being broken at some point. Full lips, no smile. A gorgeous face and the mask of hatred.*

The image zoomed out to show the entire body. A stunning example of female might, with a physique that looked as though it had been carved by the masters. No clothing was worn, only chains; a collar around the neck had a chain that disappeared out of the image, but no doubt was attached to something. Metal cuffs were clasped around both wrists and ankles, chains leading from each also vanishing out of sight.

Rome—80 CE

Kazia—age 20

Slave—Possibly of The Lost

Silvery-blue eyes opened, staring sightlessly for a moment until they blinked a few times, their owner falling back into reality. Senara closed her eyes again and brought her hands up to cover her face. She took a steadying breath before her hands fell back to the bed, and she allowed herself to fully wake up. She was naked in her bed and alone. Distantly she had the memory of a kiss to her cheek as Brielle left.

Pushing herself to a sitting position, she ran her hands through her sleep-mussed hair. Well, that and the fact that Brielle had a thing for holding her head by the hair when she orgasmed, which was usually an intense experience for them both.

Pushing the covers aside, she crawled out of bed and headed to the bathroom to shower so she could get out and get her meeting with Macha taken care of. With her new target sent, she'd need to start research as soon as possible.

As she went about her morning routine, Senara went over the information she was given, over and over again. When Frank, the Projectionist, sent it, the file was essentially burned into the brain, not like a normal dream that evaporates with wakefulness. As she showered, she studied that face in her mind's eye. Did she know her? Did she know the name?

The name, no. But there was something about her face that struck Senara. Well, her eyes, really. It wasn't the murderous glare, as that was representative of her current state. No, it was deeper, the soul behind them. Shower finished and drying before she dressed, Senara considered. Glancing at her reflection in the mirror above the bathroom sink, she looked into her own eyes.

Gasping, she remembered. Yes! Four years ago she'd been in Lacedaemon, Greece on a mission. Hiding in plain sight as an old man, she'd been there to take out a man who was there, ironically, abducting children to sell into slavery. But it had been a child, a girl in her teens, who had so shocked her that her mask had slipped right off.

Bracing her hands on either side of the pedestal sink, Senara looked past her own eyes and into those of the woman. She now suspected this was who Brielle had alluded to the previous day. The soul who had come into the seer's dreams as well. One of The Lost, she'd said. Her target information had backed up that suspected assessment.

What had it been that day? Back in the bedroom, she quickly stripped her bed as she considered, tossing the soiled sheets into the laundry basket, which would be taken back with her to Duras once she finished her meetings in Bowhar. What had shocked her so deeply that she'd lost her mask for a moment? She smirked, thinking Brielle would be so proud. She'd recognized the young woman's Ankou blood. She'd *felt* it.

Why was an Ankou in the Mediterranean, who was not a slave? They had their own gods, and Ankou, of the Celts, wasn't one of them. It was not the time of the far future where a body could hop an airplane and be on the other side of the globe in hours. This was the territory of the Ancients for a reason.

Though there was some exploring and continental conquering, most cultures were still widely isolated from each other. The technology didn't yet exist for mass mobility and melding. Those born of a so-called ancient time were familiar with the cultures and languages, and fared better in mimicking than.

Ankou born in, say, 1792 had more in common with the culture and technology of 1933 than the time of Julius Caesar. Ergo, the Ancients and the Moderns. All, regardless of era, were given their time in the Underground to get their fill of unending information for their missions to come.

So, this brought her back to her target. Why had she been in Greece? And, why hadn't she been accounted for, even if she was?

"Because," she muttered, using her hands to push down the bedding in the basket. "She is one of The Lost." Looking down at the bare mattress that was her bed, she sighed. "All right. I will find you, Kazia."

❧❧❧❧

Bowhar was a huge and beautiful place where a person could walk from one type of topography to another. Where she was headed was the beautiful representation of the gorgeous countryside that was ancient Ireland.

She could feel the cold of the waves heard pounding against the cliff face nearby, and in the distance see the massive arches, one leading to Ryarch, the other to Duras. But, where she was headed was the mark of the Druid, the stone "archway."

They were all over the landscape of antiquity, and all led to Ryarch or back to the earth plane. This one, however, was one that Senara would be allowed entrance to, as it went directly to Macha's chambers in Bowhar. Stepping inside the small, stone structure, instantly she found herself walking down a long, stone corridor, the walls the same tall, rectangular shape as the entrance. It was more like walking into an ancient pyramid than a tunnel or cave.

Her booted steps echoed off the stone, cool and smooth to the touch. The long shaft finally opened into a space of absolute beauty. It was a single room, the ceiling an intricate leaded glass dome, which allowed in the sunlight or light of the stars. The coffered walls were in rich, dark cherry wood.

The floor was of simple stone with a firepit at the center of the room, the flame ever burning. Huge throw pillows were tossed onto the floor for one to make themselves comfortable. When Senara entered the room, Macha was already there. The woman warrior, tall and in her armor, glanced over at her. Her raven was upon her shoulder, the goddess's hand raised up to it as the huge bird was pecking treats from her palm.

"Welcome, Senara," Macha greeted.

Her red hair was like a mane of fire around her head, framing a face with beautiful, feminine features, though a proud, strong jaw. She had piercing, light amber eyes. It almost looked like they were made of the very fire reflected in them from the firepit, despite the sunlight shining down through the dome.

The armor she wore over her torso was made of leather and metal, made to fit a woman's body. The leather trousers were fitted, showing muscular thighs that ended in leather boots to just below the knee. The hand that wasn't raised for her raven was resting upon the pommel of the sword belted at her hip.

"Thank you." Senara headed toward the firepit and chose a pillow covered in green silk to lower herself to relax upon.

"Good, my love," Macha murmured.

The magnificent bird squawked as it finished the food, then with a mighty flap of wings propelled itself up and out of the dome, the very center swung open for the bird to come and go. Both women watched until the bird was out of sight. Turning back to her guest, the Queen of the Druids lowered herself to the pillow next to Senara's.

"What news?" she asked.

"Marguerite is dead," Senara confirmed. "Though I do not believe the man they hold responsible is behind the murder, Macha."

She studied Senara, those unusual eyes unsettling as they seemed to penetrate her very being. "You do not believe it was his hands around her neck, then?"

she pressed, doubt in her voice.

"Oh, it was," Senara assured. "But I do not believe if was of his own volition. I believe he was being influenced." A woman very hard to intimidate, Senara had to force herself to stay put and hold the gaze that always reminded her of a lion, both in color and the ferocity it was capable of.

"Influenced," Macha said, voice deadly calm. It wasn't a question and wasn't necessarily a statement.

She looked away from Senara, finally breaking that penetrating, almost painful gaze. She looked into the flames of the firepit. The muscles in her jaw were pulsing, and Senara could feel the heat in the room rising, the flames not growing in size but somehow growing to an even more intense color of orange just by Macha's emotions alone.

"And," Senara added. "The fact that her soul has not yet been seen in Ryarch—"

"He took it," Macha interrupted.

Nodding, Senara said, "Aye."

"Bastard," the goddess murmured. Slapping her hands on her thighs, she pushed to her feet. She held out a bracer-covered forearm for Senara to grip and be helped to her own feet. "My gratitude, Senara."

"Of course." She gave the goddess a smile before she was released and allowed to leave.

❧ ❧ ❧ ❧

"Can I see that again, Frank?" Senara asked, gaze riveted to the huge screen before her.

The current scene froze then, with three rows of static bars, the image scrambled backward until it was stopped and moved forward at normal speed again.

Senara brought up a hand and absently stroked her chin as she watched the young woman being stabbed over and over again by a ruthless killer.

It was heartbreaking and awful. But, what hit her the most was to have to hear that absolutely inhuman cry of grief and pain as Kazia held her. Senara blinked rapidly as she felt the sting of emotion behind her eyes.

"Enough," she called out. Instantly, the screen went dark. Closing her eyes for a moment, she took a slow, deep breath to steady herself.

"Horrible tragedy, isn't it?"

Senara didn't have to look to see who had stepped up next to her. "Bring your popcorn, did you?"

He snorted, turning to face her. In his ever-present monochromatic outfit of brown baggy trousers with a rope belt and plain tunic shirt, Ankou demanded her gaze, which she gave. "I need you to fully pay attention to her state of being, Senara."

The two turned away from the screen and began to walk out of the huge, dark space. "Thanks, Frank!" she called out behind her.

"Anytime!" was called back.

"I know this is a surveillance mission," she said, the two exiting the building that held the Conference Room, and kept walking.

They meandered through the busy streets of Downtown, not much paying attention to those around them until they'd passed beyond. Big, fat snowflakes began to appear. Arching her neck, Senara opened her mouth and stuck out her tongue, grinning when one landed upon it. She allowed herself to enjoy the coolness as it melted in the warmth of her mouth.

"What exactly are you wanting me to find out?" she asked, continuing their conversation. The snowfall slowed, the little crystalized bits of water now colorful leaves falling from the trees above.

Ankou caught one of brilliant yellow and began to twist it in his fingers as they continued. "We need to find out if she is who we believe she is," he said. He shrugged, then added, "Clearly she'll have no memory of anything, no idea. But…" He glanced over at her. "That was why I asked Frank to show you the emotional highs from her life, Senara."

Senara had to look away, as she yet again saw that final moment on the screen that was shared with Senara. "Emotional lows, you mean," she muttered.

Ankou stopped her with a hand to Senara's arm. She turned to face him, feeling really angry in that moment and she wasn't entirely sure why. It wasn't Ankou's fault what that woman had been forced to endure in her life, but damn it all, *whose* fault, then?

"You know as well as anyone," he said, the soft, understanding tone she'd come to expect and crave from him lacing his words. "Those of the blood, Druid or Ankou, have an innate understanding and memory in their soul of something bigger." He indicated all that was around them, including her house just up the way. "You all have emotions, yes, and you all react with emotion, yes." Reaching up, he gently used the tip of a finger to wipe away the tear that was threatening to fall from one of her eyes. "But, it is a steeliness in the eyes that gives it away."

Ashamed at her own emotions beginning to get away from her, she looked away but nodded. "Yes."

"You will know, Senara," he said, waiting until she looked back at him. "You will know." He placed his hand on the side of her neck and raised his head to leave a kiss to her forehead. "Come see me when you return." With that, he turned and walked away, disappearing through a door.

Senara stood where she was for a long time, just staring at the spot where he'd been. She'd done countless missions before, by herself and as part of a team. Yes, each one was different. Yes, some had challenges, and some were even dangerous. But something about this one felt…different.

Letting out a long, slow breath, Senara turned and headed to her house. It was a white two-story, a house she'd fallen in love with the moment she'd set eyes on it. Something about its simplicity spoke to her. She knew so many of her peers who preferred to live as they'd known in their mortal lives. Nothing wrong with that, it just wasn't what she wanted for herself.

She walked across the expansive front yard, the front lawn autumn-crisp. Her boots thudded dully on the stairs to the large front porch and, finally, inside. Straight ahead were the stairs to the second floor, to the right the living room, and to the left of the stairs, a hallway that led back to the kitchen.

She went up the stairs, her laundry basket waiting for her just off to the side. She'd dropped it off before heading to see what Frank had cued up for her. Now, she stared down at it but wasn't seeing the tall, woven basket with its matching lid. Instead, she was hearing that horrible cry again in her head and seeing the lost look in those hazel eyes that had appeared so many times in the gathered memories she'd watched.

She knew that sound. It had been the same sound her heart had made the day those Roman bastards had murdered her parents and taken from her everything and everyone she knew and loved. It had been a sweet young Druid named Brielle and a mountain of a man, as gentle as he was huge, simply called Big Bear, who had shown her the way and taken her home.

Though if she were honest, she still missed her parents and what could have been every single day, but when she'd reached Duras, it had been more home than home.

"Damn it," she muttered, angry at herself as her hand came up to wipe at more damn tears. She *hated* to cry.

Grabbing the laundry basket, she carried it to the laundry room where she'd take care of it later. Right now, she wanted to get herself centered and ready for this. This mission was about this woman Kazia and finding out information—not her own sorry past, and certainly not tears.

Chapter Nine

Her friend and one of her Yewa counterparts had gone ahead of her to give her an idea of what she was walking into. The look on Willem's face had said it all. So, when Senara arrived at the Crystal Palace to catch the door, she'd kept her own form, but as she'd done that long ago day, using her chameleon abilities, she'd changed her hair from the short style she kept it in her daily life and changed it to the long styles of the women, braided atop her head.

She wore the type of tunica a woman would wear where she was going, and stepped through the dark archway and into the Crystal Palace. The red swirls of energy snaked their way around the otherwise pitch-dark space. She could feel the cool breeze as the scarlet caressed her skin. As she formed her intention of destination, the energy began to come together, bottlenecking until it formed the door she'd need.

Taking a deep breath, she stepped through the door...

...and into the back hallway of a Roman villa. Looking around, she saw the floors were marble, as were decorative columns denoting entry into every single room she could see. Little statues and busts were tucked into niches in the walls, and she could hear what she'd been hoping she would. Taking a deep, steadying breath and marking mentally where her door was located when it came time to retreat, she headed onward.

Her sandals made little clopping sounds on the polished marble floor of the opulent villa. She peeked into every room she passed, noting most seemed to be bedrooms. Her heart was racing as she got closer to the noise. It was excited chatter and laughter. As every chameleon was, she was a master of languages. She spoke fluent Latin, but it wasn't her favorite, by far.

She saw closed double doors up ahead and knew the other side was where the party was. She was about to take a step toward the doors when she heard harried steps farther down the hall, headed her way. Deciding to play dumb, she wandered away from the doors like she was looking for something.

A young slave girl, as evidenced by the collar she wore, was hurrying to the door carrying a tray filled with several silver goblets. She started, nearly dropping her tray when she saw Senara step out of the shadows.

Senara yelped in dramatic surprise, hand to heart. "Goodness!" she exclaimed with a little nervous laugh. "I got lost. Can you direct me?"

The slave girl bowed and indicated Senara should follow, which she did. She was led to the double doors, the young woman—no older than fourteen—pulling one side of the heavy doors open with her free hand while trying to keep the tray balanced upon the other. She gave Senara a deferential bow of her head again, allowing her to enter first.

It was so hard for Senara, who wanted to take that heavy tray from the girl's hands and use it to beat the living hell out of the man who owned her, then free her. But that was not possible for endless reasons. Most notably, she wasn't there for the young woman— not *that* one, anyway.

The one she was there for was the one that was

naked and chained in a cage at the center of the room up on a dais. Much like what had been sent to Senara in her target information, Kazia had a slave collar around her neck, though two long chains extended from it to the bars on either side of her.

The metal bracelets on her wrist and ankles were connected by four other long chains connected to a ring in the floor. The cage itself was ornate in its metal design, and large enough for a grown woman to recline, though not fully stretch out.

My god...

Throwing that out of her mind, Senara raised her chin slightly in indifference as she gazed upon the Beast of Britannia, so said some of those talking nearby. Giving the woman in the cage a side glance, which was not returned, Senara wandered deeper inside the room, trying to get a feel for what this was.

Soon enough, that was made very clear. As more drinks were consumed, more clothing began to come off. The room was filled with at least fifty people, perhaps pushing one hundred. It was a mixture of men and women, though most of the men were older and obviously wealthy. The women were younger, many beautiful, and, she suspected, a good number of them slaves.

The air was getting thicker and thicker, the Bacchanalia in full swing and amping up. Music was being played at the far end of the large chamber, and it was definitely setting a mood. Huge pillows were all over the floor, as all furniture had been moved out or had never been part of the room to begin with.

The pillows seemed to be in place of that. Some of the revelers were sitting on them, others leaning back against them. One woman was currently being urged to bend over one, the man behind her with clear intent coming into view as his tunica was pulled up to his waist.

The last thing she needed was to be mistaken for one of the party favors, so Senara focused on her own energy. She took several deep breaths and used some of the lessons Brielle had taught her over the many years—how to affect her own reality by changing the perception of others.

In short? She all but made herself disappear, except to Kazia, whose energy she forged a link to. Glancing over to the cage, she saw that the woman of the hour was looking at her, studying her.

The eyes reminded her of Macha's, which were those of a lion, both in color and in ferocity. Even so, there was very much a soul behind them, emotions and feelings. But as Senara looked into the hazel eyes looking back at her, they were the eyes of a person without a soul, without a care, without anything to lose. She'd already lost, and so was she.

The material of Senara's white tunica flowed around her as she walked slowly over to the cage, no fast or quick movements or actions. She was treating this woman as if she were a caged animal, because at the moment, she was. She kept a safe distance.

Though she could take care of herself, the last thing they needed was for her to have to kill her surveillance target in the middle of an orgy because she tried to strangle her with her ankle chain.

Senara said nothing, just allowed Kazia to look at her, hoping against hope that she'd recognize her. She'd been able to recognize that day on the street that, for whatever reason, young Kazia had been struck when she'd seen Senara appear out of the alleyway. And now, with the party in full swing all around them, yet not a soul pulling Senara into the fun, maybe she'd feel she was something special, something to pay attention to and trust. Someone there to help.

Kazia, who was lounging back in her cage like a sated tiger, was indeed watching her. Her eyes were impossible to read, as there was nothing there but primitive awareness. There was no curiosity, no lust, no hate, nothing. It was truly scarier than if she'd been glaring, hissing, *anything*.

Taking a step closer but never taking her eyes off those staring back at her, Senara decided to try her luck, see if she could get her to react. Nothing. Honestly, she wasn't sure if Kazia would start to purr or growl. Her focus was definitely locked on Senara, that much was clear.

Raising her chin a bit in challenge, Senara cocked her head to the side slightly, her eyes boring into Kazia's. Something not to be done with a wild animal, but she knew the woman was still in there somewhere. She was concerned, as she felt they were losing time before this lost one was lost for good.

Before another thought could enter her head, Senara was grabbed by the throat, Kazia's face mere inches away from hers on the other side of the bars. The rage that burned in Kazia's eyes now was truly terrifying.

"Enjoying the show?" Kazia growled, fingers of iron tightening around Senara's throat.

Knowing she had to think quickly, Senara switched to Gaelic, knowing that Kazia spoke the language and that not a single pompous ass around them would dare lower themselves to speak it or understand it. She didn't try to move away from the grip that was making it difficult to breathe, nor did she show any fear. Instead, she met that gaze that nearly burned her alive where she stood.

"I can get you out," she said.

If Kazia was surprised by the language, she didn't show it. "You lie," she hissed.

"I do not," Senara gasped, her throat nearly closed to the point of the inability to get words out, or air in.

No choice, Senara used her chameleon ability to morph her energy into another random person just long enough to slip right out of Kazia's viselike grip. In the split second a new mask was put on or taken off, the entire energy makeup of the chameleon became like smoke.

Gasping for air as she solidified back into herself beyond Kazia's grasp, Senara met a stunned gaze.

"We will talk again," Senara said as she rubbed her neck, knowing now was not the time.

She'd done what she'd been sent to do, and now it was time to go. She needed to speak to Ankou. As she was about to turn away, she stopped, surprised to hear Kazia's voice again.

"You're like him. Aren't you?"

Senara looked back at her. "'Him' who?"

Kazia said nothing, simply eased back deeper into her cage, taking the same, almost lazy posture she'd been in when Senara had first seen her. Her gaze never left Senara's, however. The daring in their hazel depths made it quite clear she was in an alert mentality, regardless of what her body language seemed to convey.

Forcing herself to look away, Senara took in the space around her and was frankly disgusted at the gluttony of every caliber. It was definitely time to go.

One more glance to Kazia, and Senara turned and left.

⚜ ⚜ ⚜ ⚜

Senara was admittedly shaken when she got back to the Crystal Palace. She stood there for a moment, blowing out a breath as she considered what had just happened. Why? Why was she so moved by this situation? Blowing out a breath, she left the energy hub and headed directly to Ankou's.

It always amused Senara that the God of Death, God of the Underworld, so feared and dreaded, was not much more than a fatherly pussycat who lived in a simple two-story, Tudor-style house, and apparently had an affinity for the color brown. Well, his human, Duras façade, anyway.

Entering, as expected she found herself in the entryway where she could either go up the stairs or into the room straight ahead. That room, which she entered, was the main space of the home that was utilized by Ankou and those who came to speak to him. The room was soothing and beautiful, with wood paneling on the walls that weren't taken up by built-in bookshelves, filled with leather-bound tomes, and the massive fireplace, which was currently popping with dancing flames.

And of course, a fan favorite, the massive window in one wall with a stained glass white rose at the center in the little nook that housed a large, padded window seat. Ankou stood before the fireplace in between the two twin wingback chairs, hands clasped behind his back. He looked as though he were waiting for her. Saying nothing, he glanced over at her, quiet expectation in the air.

"I believe it is her," Senara said, walking across to the window seat and lowering herself to the padded comfort. "She certainly is of the blood, regardless."

Ankou turned to face her, bringing his hands out from behind his back as he rested one atop the chair nearest him. "Tell me about her," he said. "How is she?"

"Other than the fact that she is nude and chained in a cage like an animal and is the entertainment and inspiration in an orgy?" Senara drawled. "I would say she is fine." He glanced over at her, a bushy eyebrow quirked at her sarcasm. "You asked."

"Indeed," he muttered, looking back to the flames. "Did she say anything? Do anything?"

Senara was confused.

"Why are you so deeply concerned about this woman, Ankou? I know you love all your children, as it were," she added, meaning all of the blood. "But I have never seen you like this."

He smiled and nodded. "I do, and I will answer your questions after you answer mine."

Allowing her sandals to slip from her feet, Senara drew them up beneath the flowy material of her tunica. "She didn't say much, no. But," she added, a hand coming up and absently touching the skin of her neck. She honestly expected it to be warm to the touch, Kazia's fingerprints scorched into the skin. "She has a speed I have never seen before. Literally," she said, snapping her fingers. "I did not even blink, and she was on me."

Ankou looked over at her, concern on his grizzled features. "On you? Did she hurt you?"

Senara shook her head. "I do not take personally how she acts right now, Ankou. She is cornered. And, I do believe she is afraid."

"Tell me about this speed," he said. "Tell me about *her*."

"Well," Senara said with a tired sigh. "I told you of her inhuman speed to move. But also, she is beautiful in a way I have never seen before, Ankou. She is sculpted perfection in body, the power…" She shook her head. "I was not prepared for that," she admitted softly. "And, it wasn't just physical. You can *feel* it."

He was quiet for a moment, as if turning over in his mind what she'd said. Finally, he looked at her again. "Do you feel a pull to her?"

Senara blinked a few times, surprised by the question, but she decided to give it its fair due of consideration. Finally, she admitted, "I do."

Nodding, he turned fully away from the fire and walked over to her, looking down at her. "There is a reason." He held his hand out to her.

Taking it, she was pulled to her feet, and he led the way to the side door in the library, one which she knew could lead anywhere. She was not disappointed, as stepping through, they were stepping onto the soft, warm sand of a beach. The gentle lapping of waves flirted with the sand before easing back out shyly to the ocean.

Releasing her hand, he again tucked his hands behind his back as they began to stroll. The warm softness felt wonderful beneath her bare feet and between her toes. She knew he had something significant to tell her, as she knew Ankou tended to pace when troubled. A walk along the beach was the ultimate in pacing.

"If Kazia is who I believe she is," he began. "And," he added, glancing over at her. "From what you said and the pull you feel, I do believe she is—she was born in Bowhar, not Greece, and her parents were not Greek. Her mother, Eulah, was born in Duras. Like you, she was a chameleon. Her father, a man I did not know well, was Druid."

Stunned, Senara looked over at him, drinking in all he had to say. She said nothing, anxiously waiting to hear more.

"I did not want Eulah to leave Duras, or even Bowhar, but she did, pregnant with who I think was Kazia."

"They went to the earth plane?" Senara asked. At Ankou's nod, she considered for a long time. "So," she finally said. "Kazia is both? Druid and Ankou?"

Ankou nodded. "This does happen, though not often. But much like if a child has a parent of different ethnicities, the child tends to favor one side or the other." He glanced over at her, Senara meeting his gaze. "Same is true with the blood. There are some who have no idea they carry both, as the other blood has shown very little in their abilities."

"Wow," Senara whispered.

"What you describe," Ankou said. "The speed, as well as her success in the Roman military as a woman. Her strength, her physique..."

"Druid?" she asked.

Ankou didn't speak for a moment, but when he did, Senara was stunned by what he had to say.

"As you know, Senara, the Druids can manipulate reality." He waved a hand over the beach upon which they walked. "Hide an entire settlement before our eyes here in the sand."

Senara smiled, thinking back over the astonishing things Brielle had shown her. "Aye."

"I believe Kazia's blood has been melded together.

As you also know, the chameleon changes its physical appearance." He reached out and lightly touched Senara's hair, still long and braided in her mask.

"Oh, right," she said with a chuckle, the hair morphing into her normal, short style.

"I believe the ability to do this, her mother's ability—which is why I believe you feel the pull to her, your shared abilities—and her father's ability to manipulate reality, have combined into her *internal* structure. The power you witnessed and felt, Senara," he continued. "It is almost like a deformity of a most advantageous nature."

"Wait." Senara stopped Ankou with a hand to his arm. He looked down at her. "Are you saying the muscles, the power, all of it, a façade? Manipulation of those who look upon her?"

Ankou brought a hand up and with incredibly gentle fingers stroked her neck where the iron grip had been. "Did that feel like a façade?" he asked softly.

Tears came to Senara's eyes—again. She turned away, needing a moment. Looking out over the ocean before them that seemed to go on forever, she took a deep, steadying breath. Clearing her throat, she calmed herself.

"How did she end up in Greece, then? Why is she not here? Or in Bowhar, or Ryarch?"

"That, my dear," he said, draping an arm over her shoulders as they began to walk again. "Is the rub. Eulah has not been seen nor heard from since she left, and we cannot find her energy anywhere, nor Macha, her father's."

"Clearly," Senara said, "Kazia was separated from her parents."

Ankou nodded. "Yes. Either sold or given to the

Greek couple who raised her." He shrugged, looking very troubled. "We must get her home, Senara. With no understanding or knowledge of who she truly is, yet having this great ability, she is extremely susceptible."

"To what?"

"Not to *what*," he said, meeting her gaze. "To *whom*."

Chapter Ten

I t's all clear down this hall, Senara," Willem said, his voice in the woman's ear who was making her way barefoot down the darkened passageway.

With the stealth of a cat, Senara used Willem's eyes to guide her. Though very much solid in Duras and Yewa, he was "dead" on the earth plane, so was not seen. In other words, a ghost, though he could communicate with Senara in her mind. She stopped when it was hissed in her head to do so.

Pressing herself up against a wall, Senara waited. Moments later, she saw what the issue was. Two guards, who seemed to be patrolling the property overnight, walked down a nearby hallway. She waited until they were gone, then, with Willem's blessing, continued.

Her bare feet not making a sound on the polished marble, Senara was all eyes, her head constantly on the move to make sure she wouldn't run into anything in the darkness, as this guy had statues and small decorative pillars everywhere.

"Turn left at the fork in this hallway," he instructed. "She's in the third room down."

Nodding but not daring to respond verbally, Senara continued. She gasped and nearly cried out when she saw someone coming right at her. Hand to heart, she rolled her eyes when she realized it was a damn mirror. *Son of a...* Irritated at herself as she tried to calm her heart, she knew she'd reached said fork in the hall, so turned left and continued on.

Slowing her pace, Senara looked behind her

often as she began to get nervous. She had her blade with her this time in case she needed it but was hoping with everything in her that it wouldn't be necessary. She came to the third door, which was made of wood and ribbed with iron. There was no door handle nor door pull, simply an iron ring at the center of the door and a large lock for a key, which she did not have.

Not a problem. Bringing up her hand, she focused on the locking mechanism inside and then, with a small build of energy, sent her intention, which sent the tumblers rolling until the lock clicked quietly. Looking around one more time, she pushed the door open just enough to slide inside, then reached inside her cloak for the small dagger she'd brought. Quickly pulling it from its sheath, she left the leather between the door's locking mechanism and the doorframe so it wouldn't lock, then turned to the room.

It was a small square with stone walls. The narrow window at the back was the only source of light, which sent a rectangular spotlight to the figure curled up asleep on the cot. She lay on her side, a threadbare blanket covering her. Senara thought she looked like a little girl, her hands tucked up under her chin.

Stepping up to the woman, Senara surprised herself when she reached a hand out, the very backs of her fingers barely brushing the side of her face.

"Hurry, Senara," Willem said. "We have little time before the guards make their rounds again."

Nodding, she pulled herself out of her reverie and brought the dagger up. As carefully as she could, and so as not to awaken her, Senara did what she'd been sent there to do—get a piece of Kazia's hair. Using the deadly sharp dagger, she quickly sliced through several strands, though not enough to make it obvious, and wrapped them in the cloth Brielle had given her. All that tucked away safely to an inside pocket, she was about to turn and leave when hazel eyes blinked open.

The eyes that looked up at her were not those from the cage several nights ago. These were of a young woman who looked so very lost. Senara looked down into them, again unable to stop her hand as it once again reached out. She rested her fingers against the softness of Kazia's cheek. The other woman didn't flinch, didn't move to attack, just looked up at her. Senara could feel a deep, profound need within this young woman—a need to…what? Belong? She caressed the softness of her skin for a moment before she smiled and leaned down.

"Soon," she whispered against a cool forehead before leaving a kiss there.

"Go now!" Willem exclaimed inside her head.

A final caress of her fingers and Senara quickly moved away from her. Pulling the door open, she looked back to the chained woman on the cot who was watching her before she grabbed the dagger sheath and eased the door closed until it clicked into place. Her heart in her throat, Senara was knocked out of her confused reverie when she heard the footfalls of the coming guards.

Keeping the dagger handy, she sprinted down the hall, knowing the one she was in was their next turn. Heart racing, she reached the end, which was a dead end, but there was blessedly another of those statues in a nook. She all but held her breath as she tucked herself behind it. She shifted the energy away from herself but was still cognizant of their every move, breath, and word.

The two men walked up to Kazia's door, one

tugging on the iron ring. When it held, they turned to walk away but then stopped. Senara could feel the grip of the dagger in her hand, the space she was tucked into way too confined to bring out her sword. One looked her way but didn't focus on her, just seeming to have sensed something.

Damnit, go away! She watched them, almost screaming in her mind for them to move on. The second one said something to the first, their words too quiet and far away to hear.

"Willem," she whispered as quietly as possible. "Get their attention. I cannot get to the door."

"Will do."

As any good ghost can do, in an adjacent hallway, something went crash in the night. The guards stopped mid-conversation and bolted off in that direction. Able to breathe for a moment, Senara eased herself out of her hiding place without knocking the statue over in the process.

"Go now!" Willem yelled.

Again, at a dead sprint, Senara booked it down the hallway, not even looking to see if anyone was nearby as she rounded the corner and kept going. She could see the large fountain at the center of the courtyard where the door was. Putting more speed behind her pumping legs and arms, she heard shouting far behind her but didn't even stop to look. A moment later, running steps could be heard.

The open doorway at the end of the hallway that led to the outdoor though walled-in courtyard was suddenly obstructed as a man stepped out in front to block her exit. She kept running, sending her hand waving across her path, which sent a bolt of energy his way. He was thrown against the wall to his right, clearing the doorway.

She saw that the man was trying to get up, and as she blew past him, he reached for her cloak, which fanned out behind her like a cape. Though he didn't get hold of the material, he did send her careening through the door…

…and into the Crystal Palace, landing on her shoulder. She lay there for a moment, stunned. Two hands reached down and gripped her under her arms to help her to her feet. Still dazed, she looked into Willem's concerned brown eyes.

"You all right?" he asked.

Nodding, she did a mental inventory to make sure everything had come back with her.

"Oh no," she said. looking down at her hands. She only saw them as the floating bits of red energy passed over them. "I dropped the dagger." She checked everything on her to make sure it hadn't fallen into a pocket or even gotten tangled up in the material of her cloak, as well as bent down to feel around on the floor. Nothing. "Damn it," she muttered.

"Do you have her hair, though?" he asked.

Panicked for a moment, she reached inside her pocket and, with a breath of relief, felt the wrapped bundle, which had been the entire reason for going in the first place. "Aye."

"We'll have to send a cleanup crew in to get the dagger."

Nodding and furious with herself, she ran a hand through her hair. "Damn it," she said again.

"It happens, Senara," he said, the two heading out of the Crystal Palace.

"I know, but I am better than that."

"Look," he said, stopping her with a hand to her arm. "I know you're angry and upset with yourself, but we got the job done." He gave her a sweet smile before dropping his hand from her arm. "I need to go. Let me know if you need me."

"Thanks, Willem," she said, watching the man with the buzz-cut light brown hair whistle his way down one of the many paths that led away from the beautiful structure she stood just outside of.

Reaching into her pocket, she retrieved the wrapped hair and looked down at the little bundle. Next stop, Britannia.

❧ ❧ ❧ ❧

The two women hurried from where Senara had met Brielle just outside the circle of stone archways to a cave system half a mile away. As it always seemed to be, the weather was punishing with frigid rains and winds, both women clutching their cloaks to keep them from flying up around them.

"My goodness," Brielle murmured once they entered the smallest of the caves, which was just large enough for the two to enter and be out of the direct temper of the weather. She pushed her hood back before continuing on. "Come."

Senara followed along, also pushing her own hood back. She followed the Druid through a series of stone corridors until they ended up in a cave deep in the mountain. It was about the size of Senara's bedroom back home, carved out of the rock from time and water. The most amazing thing about spending time with Brielle was that no matter where they were, they were never in need of light.

The moment they'd stepped into the first cave, the Druid had begun to glow softly, just enough to open up a room to a comfortable level of vision. To look at her directly, the human eye didn't pick up on the source of the light or that it was even there. It was out of the periphery or simply the effect in the space that made it visible.

Once they reached the larger cave, Brielle tossed her hand out as though she'd tossed a handful of dice. A fire erupted in the center of the cave upon the stone floor, then with a little coaxing of her hand, eased down into a campfire-sized flame.

"All right," she said, reaching up to undo her cloak, which she let drift down to the floor at her feet, hidden beneath the material of her ever-present peasant dress. Somehow, though, despite the rather drab green color of it, she made it look beautiful just by her very presence. Looking to Senara, who stood nearby, she held out her hand.

Saying nothing, Senara reached into her own cloak and retrieved the precious package, resting it in Brielle's palm.

"Thank you," the Druid said softly. She reached into hidden pockets in the skirts of her dress, bringing out various items in pouches. Lowering herself to the stone floor, her lower body was covered by her skirt as she organized things in the little apron created by it that she spread taught over her lap. She glanced up at Senara. "Sit," she said, patting the stone floor beside her.

Doing as asked, Senara used her cloak as a cushion to sit on as she watched her friend do whatever it was she did. She'd tried once to teach Senara the arts of powders and potions, but Senara just didn't have the patience and was terrible at it. It took someone with a very steady hand, a keen eye, and innate understanding. None of these things she possessed.

Brielle had told her it took what she called a "still soul" to do such work, whereas Senara was pretty much full of piss and vinegar at any given time. Nonetheless, she fully enjoyed watching her friend and mentor do her work. If Senara hadn't understood what she'd meant by a "still soul," all she had to do was watch the very woman who'd said it.

It mattered not what Brielle was doing—walking, running, standing still, lying down, talking, or fucking in the throes of passion—there was a deep stillness to her that was so calming to be around. So often, Senara wished she had some of that, wondered what it would be like to have her own inner peace. She'd always felt like something was missing within herself or her life, and she had no idea where to look for what it could be.

Brielle brought out a mortar and pestle, setting it on the stone floor before her. Senara's eyebrows drew. "Where on earth were you keeping that?"

Brielle simply smiled as she began to open the little pouches she'd set aside. Crushed crystal, grasses, what looked to be pine needles and shreds from a feather were placed into the mortar. She took hold of the material the dark strands of hair were wrapped in, carefully spreading the material out on the ground.

"You did well," she said softly. She picked up a single strand and held it up. "Roots."

"Completely by accident, I am sure." She grinned at Brielle's chuckle.

The Druid placed the hair into the mixture, raising the small stone mortar to just below Senara's chin. "Spit."

"What?" Senara gasped. "Why?" When Brielle said nothing, simply continued to look at her with those intense, grass-green eyes, Senara began to gather moisture in her mouth before she did as asked, the wad landing atop the unmixed ingredients.

"Thank you."

Wiping her lips with the back of her hand, Senara watched with rapt fascination as Brielle used the pestle to slowly and carefully grind it all together. Something caught her eye. Glancing to the fire before them, Senara noticed that within the flames and all that was expected in such, she began to see what almost looked to be figures, though only partial ones, before they vanished into the flames, only for something else to appear briefly before it, too, was gone.

Looking back to the stone mortar, Senara's breath caught. The contents no longer looked like a bunch of vegetation, tiny bits of crystal, hair, and spit. It was now all a powder of an electric blue. Her gaze went to Brielle to see her lips were moving as she continued to mix the contents, though no sound came from them.

Setting the pestle down atop one of the pouches, Brielle continued with her silent chanting as she got to her feet, the mortar held in both of her palms. Feeling she should stand, too, Senara did, moving just a bit behind the other woman, as she had no clue what was about to happen. Within a moment, the chanting was heard, Brielle's beautiful voice soft at first but growing louder,

As if responding to her melodic voice, the flames began to grow, shadows dancing across the ceiling of the cave. Looking up at them, Senara realized they were shadows, silhouettes of people. Her eyes opened wide as she took it in, though they quickly flicked back down to the flames as Brielle scooped her hand inside the mortar, the bright blue powder filling her palm.

Her chanting continued in a language Senara did not know, the sacred language of Ryarch. Without looking at her, she held the mortar out for Senara to take, which she did. Now both hands free, Brielle held them together, the blue powder mixture in her palms. The words came out of her as her eyes closed.

With a *whoosh*, the powder caught fire, the flame burning in Brielle's braced hands. She stopped chanting, her eyes slowly opening.

"Show us," she said softly.

The column of fire that had grown from the original smaller fire on the stone spread out into a veritable wall of it. The flame burning in Brielle's hands turned the same color blue as the powder it had ignited from. The flame began to morph into a strange smokelike material that flowed over to the wall of fire, mixing in with the orange and gold of the flames.

However, as though ink were spilled into a glass of water, the blue began to trickle through the flames, initially seeming to be in random patterns. After a few moments, all of it had left Brielle's hands, which fell back to her sides, and a picture began to form— much like a stack of cards with a figure or thing drawn on each that, when shuffled, the illusion of a moving picture is created.

This was similar, the blue   "ink" on the page of fire. Two adult-sized figures in a wagon, one male and one female. A moment later, a baby was in her arms. A moment later what looked to be a huge net swooped down over the trio, the next showing an empty wagon continuing on its merry way.

The images cleared only to be replaced by two

sets of hands, one holding a tiny baby, the other, coins. When that faded away, the blue silhouettes of the man and woman from the wagon were chained to a wall, and the very ink that created their visage seemed to melt away, the figures getting smaller and smaller until nothing was left, the ink flowing into a standing silhouette, which got bigger and bigger as more and more of that ink flowed into him.

All went dark, the wall of fire vanishing. Senara could hardly breathe. In the pure darkness, she cradled the mortar against her chest and brought up her hands in front of her mouth for a second, shaken.

A moment later, another fire was started, much like the initial one upon the stone floor. Brielle stood looking down at it, deep in thought.

"He had no use for a baby," she said at length, her voice so soft Senara almost missed it. Finally, Brielle glanced over at Senara, who couldn't speak, her throat so full of unshed emotion. "She was no use to him yet, so rather than wait, keep her alive until she was nine or ten years old when a child—especially a girl—comes to her power, he sold her."

Senara tried to speak, but nothing came out. Swallowing, she tried again. "What did he do to her parents?"

"Drained them of all their energy," Brielle said simply, looking back to the fire. "He can survive without it, but he would be just an evil man with a deadly ability to influence. In order to maintain his ability to change his likeness, he must take the energy, as he cannot produce his own as Macha and Ankou do." She paused. "As *we* do." She looked back into the flames. "What he takes in, he can bastardize into his own version of the same ability."

Senara swallowed again, stunned by what she'd just seen. "Who?"

Brielle looked deeply into her eyes. "Bahutha."

Chapter Eleven

Pillows pushed aside, Ankou, Macha, Brielle, Senara, Willem, and an Ankou called Big Bear stood in Macha's Bowhar quarters. All eyes had been on Brielle as she'd explained what had been revealed to her and Senara.

"So," Ankou said. "Kazia *is* one of The Lost, then?"

Brielle nodded. "She is. And," she added. "Bahutha may very well be going after her now that she's grown and is reaching her power."

"My fear as well," Macha added.

"A daughter of an Ancient," Big Bear said, huge arms crossed over a barrel chest. The Native American man looked to each person, his long, thick braid trailing down his back. "An awfully tempting catch."

"She's extremely powerful," Willem said. "Physically, mentally." He shrugged, looking at his cohorts. "Not a bad idea for a personal bodyguard, huh?"

"Or," Brielle added flatly. "Someone to carry out his agenda."

They were all quiet for a moment as they absorbed that thought. "And," Ankou finally said, breaking the silence as he looked to Senara. "You say you believe she's ready to go?"

"Without question." Senara remembered the look in those tortured eyes that last night she and Willem were there. "I do not think she cares where she is going at this point. Just ready to go." She indicated

Big Bear and Willem. "Though it is good to bring in a team, I do not believe she will fight us."

"So," Macha said, hands on hips as she looked to those gathered. "You are our extraction team. Go get her."

❧❧❧❧

"We are going the long way from Macha's yet again," Senara said, glancing over at her friend. "You know this, right?"

Brielle grinned. "I do."

The two were walking through the marketplace near the harbor. Green eyes were scanning the area as they went, Senara beginning to look around as well, curious what exactly Brielle was looking for.

They'd left Bowhar through the borderlands, which was the main area exceptional humans lived—those who were human but had abilities of their own not tied to Druid or Ankou. It was a vibrant area filled with both residential and commercial structures. Much of the fish hauled into the harbors of Brittany were brought there to sell to the Bowharians.

The borderlands was where the huge archway was to traverse from Brittany into Bowhar and back. It was an archway that was identical to those to enter Ryarch or Duras on the other side of Bowhar, where the population was much more Ankou and Druid.

The women had stopped at the market in the borderlands, Brielle buying a bag filled with apples, cherries, strawberries, and grapes. Much of the fruit wasn't available in Brittany, mainly because of the season. Her purchases in hand, the Druid walked with Senara along the Breton harbor, her gaze everywhere.

Senara tried to figure out what her friend was looking for but was at a loss.

"Why are we here?" she finally asked.

Brielle said nothing for a moment, instead turning to head toward a part of the docks that was away from the ships and markets. A lone figure sat on a half wall that looked over the water.

"Her," Brielle finally said, heading in that direction.

Senara followed, noting the long, light blond hair that blew in the breeze around narrow shoulders, slumped as she sat by herself. Yes, it was sad that this child was alone, but Senara was still perplexed by Brielle's interest in her. Of course she'd heard what had been predicted, this child someday being an important figure, but certainly Brielle could be wrong.

"Good morrow," Brielle said, using her voice to immediately put the girl at ease.

The young one looked back at them from where she sat, legs dangling over the half wall. As her heels thumped lightly against the wall, Senara was reminded that this *was* a child, regardless of how it seemed she was a two-thousand-year-old soul in a tiny body.

The girl said nothing but remained where she was as Brielle sat next to her, her back to the water.

"I brought you something." Brielle held out the burlap bag to the girl, who studied it for a moment before her cerulean gaze moved back up to meet Brielle's patient one.

Senara watched, intrigued by what this girl would do. She saw a pink tongue sneak out, the girl's bodily needs betraying her aura of control. Brielle said nothing more, simply held out the bag for the child to take, which she did. Again, a small spark of her true age bled into her eyes as they brightened when she peeked inside the bag.

Unable to help herself, Senara smiled when an apple was brought out, a little hand wrapped around the large piece of fruit. Immediately, the girl began to eat it, nearly humming in delight as she couldn't seem to eat it fast enough.

"As you're eating," Brielle said, a hand coming up and, with motherly care, brushing the long hair out of the beautiful young face. "I want you to hear me and remember what I say. Okay?"

The girl eyed her, nodding as she made quick work of the apple before moving on to the cherries.

"I want you to remember my name," Brielle said, her fingers continuing to comb through the fair hair. "I am Brielle," she continued softly. "If you are *ever* in trouble, you say my name. But," she added, lightly tapping a fingertip against the girl's forehead. "In your mind, pretend like you are calling for me, like I'm across the room. Understand?"

The girl nodded again, her intense gaze boring into Brielle's, almost as though looking into her very soul. Senara felt affected by it, and she was standing a couple feet away.

"Good girl." Brielle cupped the side of her head before leaning over and leaving a kiss on her forehead, as she had done the last time. "When you are ready," she said softly, so softly that Senara almost missed it. "You call me or Senara." She indicated the woman named, never taking her eyes from the girl's. "We will get you home." She smiled and used that same finger to playfully tap the tip of the girl's nose. "Only when you are ready."

The girl nodded for a third time, sparing a glance

up to Senara, their gazes meeting and holding for a moment before she looked back to Brielle and then her bag of fruit. Senara was moved by that simple look, a look she felt to her soul. In that moment, she felt it too. This child would play a role in her life and certainly the bigger picture, but she had no idea what.

"Brielle," the girl said, her voice so small and beautiful.

"Yes, my sweet?" the Druid said, looking down at her as she'd pushed to her feet.

"I am Enori."

Brielle lowered herself to sit next to her again. She gathered the girl into a warm embrace, which the little one seemed to absolutely sink into.

"An honor to meet you, Enori," she murmured into the hug.

⁕⁕⁕⁕

Dressed in her leathers with sword mounted to her back, Senara took one last look at herself in the mirror mounted to her dresser. She adjusted her shoulders a bit so the flowing material of her blouse settled a bit better. Running a hand through her hair, she was ready to go. Looking into her eyes, she could see they were intense already, nearly silver.

Hearing a knock on her front door downstairs, she took a deep, steadying breath, then headed out. Big Bear and Willem waited for her to respond on the front porch.

"Boys," she greeted.

"Mind if we come in for a sec?" Willem asked.

Saying nothing, Senara stood aside, allowing the two men to enter before she eased the screen door closed so it wouldn't slam. She followed the two into the living room where Willem plopped down on the couch, but Big Bear remained standing. He crossed his arms over his chest, feet wide. It amused her. To the average person, he looked so menacing when she thought his name *should* have been Big Baby Bear. A sweet, cuddly guy.

"What is on your mind?" she asked, hands on hips as she looked from one to the other.

"Well," Willem began. "I was just thinking earlier today about what this gal has been put through."

Senara nodded. "Yes. She has been very traumatized."

He nodded. "Exactly. I just wonder," he said with a little shrug and glance to Big Bear. "Where do we put her when we get her back here?" He indicated the house and Duras around them.

She eyed him. "What do you mean? She'll go where she wants to go, just like anyone else brought home. If she—"

"She's feral, Senara," he said.

Arms slowly crossing over her chest, she shifted her weight to one hip as she cocked her head to the side. She pinned him to the spot with her gaze. "Are you suggesting we leave her in a cage?" she drawled, daring in her voice.

"No, of course not," he protested, hands raised in supplication.

"She may need detox," Big Bear said, his deep voice making Senara's head whip in his direction.

"You would not *dare* suggest that," she hissed. He said nothing, just held her gaze with his deep brown eyes. She turned away from him. "You both can go to hell," she murmured. "Let us go."

She was so angry she could nearly see red. She shoved the screen door open, not caring as it slammed into the house. She could hear the two following her, and it took everything in her to not draw her sword and gut them both. How *could* they?

"Senara," Willem said, his touch on her shoulder timid.

Whirling on him, she glared. "Do not touch me, Willem. Of anyone, how could you agree to such a thing?"

"Senara," he tried again, tone soft and conciliatory. "You know damn well neither of us," he said, indicating himself and Big Bear, "would ever do or suggest anything to hurt anyone. Definitely not you." He looked into her eyes, his pleading. "But you know as well as we do that coming here won't get rid of her pain."

She looked away from him, knowing damn well he was right. But she also knew she damn well wasn't going to let him know that.

≈≈≈≈

Their differences pushed aside for the mission, Senara waited for the door to gather in the Crystal Palace then stepped through…

…and into the small square room in the Roman villa. Big Bear stepped through after her, Willem already inside. Immediately, her gaze went to the cot, and immediately she was confused then concerned.

It was empty.

Looking around, she saw that the iron rings were still attached to the stone of the walls, which Kazia's chains had been connected to. No chains, no shackles, just the iron rings. For just a moment that had her hopeful that they'd just moved her to another locale, until she saw the heavy chains in a coil on the floor, along with the neck, wrist, and ankle bracelets.

"We have to find her," she said quietly. She started to head toward the closed door to the prison-like room when Willem's voice in her head stopped her.

"No. You and Big Bear stay put. Let me see if I can find her, then I can direct you guys. Probably best if you went back to the Crystal Palace. You can make a new door wherever she is."

Nodding, Senara turned back to Big Bear, who still stood next to the door they'd just used. "Good plan," she said to Willem. "Let us go back and wait."

The two went back to the Crystal Palace. She was worried. Very, very worried. Hands on hips, she began to pace. It was beyond possible that they'd moved her or even had her as part of some stupid event in that moment. But something in her gut told her they'd been too late and she was no longer there, for whatever reason.

It seemed to be hours but likely was less than thirty minutes when Willem appeared. He met her gaze and shook his head. "She's not on the property."

Senara turned away, running her hand through her hair as she fought two powerful drives: tears and gutting someone.

"We were too late," she blew out.

"Let's meet with Ankou and regroup," Big Bear said.

Nodding, Senara led the way out of the Crystal Palace, knowing there was nothing more they could do right now. The three stood outside of the beautiful structure, which looked like a domed building made of diamonds or a billion shards of glass, the red threads of energy that shot straight down from the swirling sky veining through it.

"We need to see if we can pick up on when her energy was last in that building," Big Bear said. "Do you feel her?" he asked her.

Concentrating, Senara placed her hands on her hips and looked down at her booted feet, though she wasn't seeing them. She reached out with her senses, desperately trying to feel something, *anything*.

Finally, she shook her head and met his gaze again. "I do not."

He brought up a hand and stroked his chin. "All right. We'll see what Ankou wants to do." He gave her one of his huge bear hugs, squeezing with a playful growl before offering the same to Willem. "Talk soon," he offered as he began to walk away. "The wife is making lasagna for dinner."

"Where's my invite?" Willem called out as the big man walked away. He laughed when Big Bear turned and walked backward as he gave a dramatic shrug. Willem laughed. "Creep." Turning to Senara, he placed his arm around her shoulders. "Come on," he said. "Let's you and me go have a beer."

"I hate beer," she muttered.

"Great! Then I'll have yours."

Unable to help herself, she laughed, smacking him in the stomach. They headed to her house, making a stop Downtown for him to get his beer. Funny thing about Willem was, he'd been born just a handful of decades after she had been, but he was the most well-adjusted of any of them when it came to futuristic things. She was pretty sure he'd been born—and died—during the wrong time.

Reaching her house, they went to the kitchen, where she tossed him a church key to open a bottle for himself as she poured herself some water. A little food for them to nibble on as they chatted, and she got settled at the table across from him. She studied him for a moment as she sipped from her cool and refreshing water.

"Do you regret doing it?" she asked at length.

He didn't respond for a long moment as he tossed a cube of cheddar into his mouth and chewed.

"I felt I had no other options." He met her gaze, so much pain in his normally bright and friendly brown eyes. "My father was such a zealot," he said. "Everything was religion to him, to the point of forcing his one and only son into the monastery." He brought the brown bottle up to his lips and took in the liquid.

"What was it like?" she asked softly. "Living there."

Setting the bottle down after his drink, he sat back in his chair. "Empty. It was so goddamn empty for me, Senara. All day, all you did was pray, ask for forgiveness—"

"For what?"

He snorted. "For speaking. For having a bad thought. For farting, who knows." He waved off the question. "And, all for a god I felt in my bones was not for me." He grinned. "Good guess, huh?"

Grinning, she nibbled on a cracker. "How long were you there? Did you see your family?"

Shaking his head, he wrapped his hand around the bottle. "I was there for eight very, very long years." He met her gaze. "Never saw my parents once during that entire time." He rolled his eyes. "Let's not forget about the stunning tonsure we had to sport." He raised a hand and made a circle in the air with his finger above the crown of his head. "Ridiculous."

She ate some cheese, questions rolling around in her mind. She had a lot, but her stomach roiled, so she limited herself to Willem's situation and their current discussion. "How did you do it?" she asked softly.

So many emotions passed across his face as he seemed to consider her question. Finally, he let out a beer-scented sigh. "I used my rope belt from my robes," he said quietly.

Surprising herself—and, from his expression, him—as she wasn't exactly a touchy-feely kinda gal, she reached across the table and covered his hand with her own. "I am sorry, Willem. I cannot imagine that was an easy decision to make."

He smiled at her, turning his hand over and gently cradling her smaller hand in his own. "Funny thing was," he said softly. "The hard part wasn't making up my mind, it was knowing what it would do to my mother." He gave her a rueful smile, so much sadness in his eyes. "Even though I hadn't seen her in almost ten years, my last thoughts were still of her."

"I am so sorry," Senara said again. "Have you made your peace with her?"

He shook his head. "Ironically, *he* was the one of Ankou blood, not her. He threw all that aside for his zealotry." He gave her hand a squeeze before releasing it to grab his bottle of beer again. "So," he concluded before taking a drink. "I never got to see her again."

"And, your father?"

"He asked Ankou long ago to be released to go to his Heaven, wherever that is."

"Well," she said, grabbing her own glass. "You may piss me off, but I am glad to have you here."

He grinned and raised his beer bottle, which she tapped with her glass in salute.

Chapter Twelve

Four months ago:

Yet again, Kazia found herself in a cage in the back of a wagon. She was jostled as she sat there with her head leaning against the perpendicular set of bars. She'd awoken after her very strange dream of the beautiful woman coming to see her—an angel?— to loud voices and footfalls. Next thing she'd known, the door to her cell had been slammed open and the little fat man who owned her had barged in, demanding answers.

Apparently, there had been a break-in of some sort, and a dagger had been left behind. He'd shoved that dagger in her face, asking who had come to try to take her. She'd never seen the dagger in her life, and all she could do was stare up at him blankly. Truth was, she wished he would have just used that dagger to end her misery.

Alas, he had not. Getting no answers from her, answers she didn't have, he'd stormed out. An hour later, his guards had come in and clothing had been thrown at her to put on, not much more than a short tunica. Once dressed, she'd been shackled at the wrists and, surrounded by well-armed guards, she'd been led out to the cage already loaded into the back of the wagon.

"Are you happy?"

Starting, Kazia lifted her head to see a cloaked man sitting on the opposite side of the cage from her.

His cloak was dark brown, hood pushed down to reveal a man who looked to be in his thirties, perhaps. A somewhat plain-looking man, the type that was easily overlooked in a crowd, with features that didn't much stand out, including his dirty blond hair and dull blue eyes.

She studied him for a long moment. She knew she'd never seen this man, but she knew his voice, his energy. She knew it was *him*.

"Who are you?" she asked, voice rough from lack of use.

His smile lit up his otherwise insignificant face. She knew that smile, knew that cloak. Where had she seen them before?

"I'm the only friend you've got at the moment." He shrugged a shoulder in the casual posture he held, sitting cross-legged in the confines. "She *said* she'd be back for you but then what?" He quirked an eyebrow. "She left you there to rot." Tsking his tongue, he shook his head. "*I* got you out, Kazia."

As she looked into his eyes, she felt her defenses easing, which was a change considering she'd been on guard now nonstop for what felt like years, though she honestly had no idea how long it had been since that horrible day in Britannia. But somehow this man made her feel like it was okay to relax despite the craziness that he'd just shown up in her cage.

"Where am I going?" she asked.

His smile grew. "Where you always should have been. You're off to the Ludus Magnus," he said, reverence behind his words.

She stared at him, stunned. "The gladiator school?"

He nodded. "You are a fighter, Kazia. Not a party

favor for a pervert and his insatiable wife and their friends."

She was so sleep and food-deprived, it took a moment for her brain to catch up on what was happening, all the new information she'd been given. If this was true, she was relieved. "And," she finally said. "You did this?"

"Of course I did," he said. "I did it for you."

She studied him. "Why?"

"Because," he said simply. "I do my best to look out for those who cannot look out for themselves." His gaze bored into hers. "Those who are abandoned, mistreated." He gave her a pointed look. "Those who are not loved by those who should love them most and protect them."

She forced herself to look away, a strange weight lifted from her shoulders when she did, as though a spell had been broken. She had nothing more to say. In that moment, she just felt empty, alone, and cold, though the coldness had nothing to do with the outside temperature. She felt like her heart was made of ice.

Yes, she thought as she rested her head back against the bars. Fighting was good. All she was, right? All she'd ever been good for. And maybe it would finally be the way she could just go home.

Kazia closed her eyes, that thought leaving her with a smile.

❧ ❧ ❧ ❧

"Wake up!"

Bam, bam, bam.

Nearly jumping out of her skin, Kazia shot up from the narrow bed in the very small room she had in the training facility, which was similar to the ones they all were given. Shaking the sleepies away, she hopped up and grabbed the clothing she wore every single day.

The subligaculum that covered her midsection—sort of—was a piece of cloth shaped in somewhat of a long triangle with the longer side having a more rounded end. The two pointed ends were brought around to tie in a knot at her lower belly. The long part of the cloth was brought up between her legs to cover her behind and privates. The excess was pulled up under the knot at her lower belly and flipped over it to hang in a bit of a loincloth-type look.

Like their male counterparts, she and the other two women were bare chested. Her garment tied into place, she sat on her bed to put on her sandals, footwear with an almost boot-like structure of leather that covered the shins up to the knee, the leather straps wrapped around her calves to buckle into the front.

No weapons were allowed to be kept in their rooms, so she quickly made her bed to the perfection they'd been taught—which she luckily already knew from the military—and headed out. To their credit, the school fed those in training well. Truth was, she hadn't been fed so well since before her mother died.

Friendships among those in the training school were discouraged. They were there to learn how to become killers, which, from the skill she'd already seen from many, no doubt all of them already were. And, very often, their fellow trainees were their combatants, and not just in the gladiator school. They learned and fought each other in the arena the facility was structured around.

Spectators could pay for one of the thirty-four hundred seats to watch them train with their lanistas, most retired gladiators of a specific expertise in weaponry or fighting style. They'd be pitted against each other in interesting combinations to bring out their best skills. Kazia yearned to be challenged. Her female counterparts were wonderful fighters but not much of a match. She literally had to restrain herself in order to not kill them in the middle of training.

The most she'd gotten out of it was when she and one of the women were paired against one of the men. Even then, there wasn't much challenge for her. She tried to keep the boredom off her face but knew she wasn't so successful when later that afternoon, her lanista stopped her as she was headed back out after the midday meal. At her name, she stopped at the mouth of the tunnel that would take her back into the facility's arena and waited.

"I have a question for you," he said, the man short in stature but massive in body size.

He had broad shoulders and chest, and his arms were three times the size of her own, which were incredibly impressive, even if they had been on a man.. She said nothing, simply waited for what he had to ask.

"I've been watching you, Kazia," he said, voice deceptively soft for his size and ferocity in the arena. "I sense you're capable of far more than you've shown us."

She nodded. "I am."

"Do you feel you're being challenged adequately?" he pushed.

"I don't know that that's for me to answer," she said, shrugging. "After all, you're the one who did this for six years and lived to fight another day."

He nodded. "I did. Your first match is coming up in the Colosseum," he said. "I've spoken with your owner, given some suggestions. Agreeing with me, he wants us to mix things up with you. He has great hopes for you."

Kazia felt a little twinge in her gut, knowing that disgusting little man whose villa she'd been a chained slave in still owned her, still directed her life. "All right," she said, hands on hips. "What is the plan?"

His grin said it all even as his words were only, "You'll see. Either you'll succeed to great fame, or you'll die." He slapped her on the shoulder before walking away.

⁂

It was two nights before her inaugural fight. She'd had a long day in the school's arena and, after a good dinner and bath, she was ready to settle in for the night. She was turning down her bed when there was a knock at the door. Surprised, she turned in the narrow walkway between the bed and the opposite wall and walked to the door. Pulling it open, she saw a young slave who worked for the school doing various things. Kazia had often seen her helping serve meals.

The young woman, who looked to be no older than Kazia's own age of nearly twenty, had long, light brown hair and pretty blue eyes. She looked up at Kazia, who said nothing, waiting for her to explain her presence.

"I was sent here to train you," she said.

Kazia was confused. "Train me?"

The young woman nodded toward Kazia's room, silently asking for permission to enter. Granted, the young woman, whose name Kazia didn't even know, stepped passed her and to the bed. Closing the door,

Kazia watched, baffled when the pretty young woman set down a wrapped package she'd brought with her on the bed, then reached down and, in one fluid movement, brought her tunica up and over her head.

Stunned, Kazia just stood there, mouth open. The young woman was naked beneath her garment, which was tossed to the floor. Seeming unfazed by her state of dress, or lack thereof, the woman unwrapped the package she'd brought with her.

Once the fabric was peeled back, Kazia saw it looked like a severed penis, though it was clearly not made of flesh and blood, connected to leather straps in a very strange contraption. Finally, the woman looked to Kazia.

"Do you know what this is?" she asked. The smallest hint of amusement flashed across her face when she looked at Kazia, who no doubt looked as stunned as she felt.

"No," Kazia managed.

"Have you been with a man before, Kazia?" the woman asked, walking over to her, all business as she eased the shift Kazia wore to sleep in up and over her head. When Kazia shook her head, the woman pressed further. "A woman?"

Instantly, a lance of pain slashed through Kazia as she saw Ione's face, one that often haunted her dreams. Shaking her head again, she murmured, "No, not really."

Nodding, the woman reached to the bed and grabbed the strange thing she'd brought. "This is leather," she explained, looking up into Kazia's eyes as she took hold of the penis, which now Kazia realized was indeed fake. Though relieved, she was confused. "This attaches to you," the woman explained, using gentle but firm touches and movements to get the straps buckled around Kazia's hips and between her legs until finally the phallus jutted out from her crotch.

Swallowing, as she was filled with so many feelings and sensations all combating each other, Kazia managed to speak. "Why are you putting that on me?"

Taken by the hand, Kazia was led to the bed. The woman pushed down the covers before climbing atop the narrow structure,

"Your owner has instructed you be taught," she explained. "He and his wife have plans for you after your match."

Pulled down on top of the woman, Kazia barely caught herself on her hands before she crushed her. She saw the small look of apology on her lovely face before the woman opened her legs, carefully easing them out from Kazia's raised body until Kazia's hips were nestled between them, the phallus strapped to her awkwardly trapped between them.

Absolutely no idea what to do, Kazia froze. The woman beneath her smiled sweetly at her, her hands on Kazia's back rubbing as if to sooth a jittery colt. "It's okay," she said softly. "Do you know how to kiss?"

"Um," Kazia murmured, swallowing again. "I did that once." Again, she thought of Ione, and despite the fact that she'd been dead for more than six months, Kazia still felt guilty. And now, as the back of her head was cupped and she was pulled down to this stranger's lips, that guilt returned.

The kiss was soft, the woman so gentle with her. Kazia knew neither of them had a choice in what they were doing, so she allowed herself to relax. In some ways, that very much surprised her—she was enjoying it. The woman who was kissing her, lips and tongue quite talented and clearly experienced, was just as much of a slave as Kazia was. Just because Kazia had a different title, there was no difference.

Neither of them could just up and leave without being hunted down and killed for desertion. Neither of them could say no nor question what they were being told to do. Would this woman be here kissing Kazia and teaching her how to have sex if she had a choice? If the woman beneath her were to answer honestly, no doubt her response would be no.

For that matter, Kazia's answer would also be no. But, here they were. She lowered her upper body, amazed at the feeling of her breasts pressed against small ones. They were so soft. She felt a hand trail up from her back and into her hair as the kiss deepened. From the small sigh she heard from the other woman, she guessed she must be doing something right.

The woman's other hand moved down between their bodies, Kazia's hips jerking at the unexpected feeling of the backs of her fingers against her pubic area.

"Relax," she said softly, looking up into Kazia's eyes as the kiss broke. She took hold of the phallus. "Lift a bit more." When Kazia did as instructed, the woman directed the tip to her own opening. "Slow," she murmured.

Nodding, Kazia looked down the length of their bodies and watched in wonder as the length of the phallus disappeared inside the woman's body. When her hips were flush against hers, the young woman raised her knees a bit closer to her chest, her hands returning to Kazia's back.

"When you're inside of someone," she said softly. "Pay attention to their breathing, their face. This will help you know where their pleasure is, and make sure you don't hurt them."

Nodding again, and still a bit stunned at the very unexpected situation she found herself in, Kazia began to move her hips. It felt very strange and wasn't a natural movement to her, but she had to throw that aside. She followed the advice given and paid careful attention to the lovely young woman's face, her body language, and the little noises she made as the phallus moved gently inside of her.

It was an amazing feeling once Kazia got more used to the concept, and her brain stopped flipping over the idea that a woman could do such a thing to another woman. Her entire body was suffused with heat, her lower regions pulsing with each gentle push inside of the woman's body.

"You're doing so good," the woman murmured, her words breathy and eyes hooded. She trailed her fingernails down along Kazia's back and over her ass, which moved between her spread thighs, before trailing back up. It sent delicious little thrills through Kazia's body.

Looking down into the woman's face, Kazia could see the pleasure, could hear it in her increased breathing. In that moment, it became her sole goal to give that to her. She knew that, like herself, choice and pleasure were small and rare events in their life. This woman may not have had a choice but to have sex with Kazia, so she was determined to make it a good experience for her.

Raising herself to brace on her hands, she followed her own instincts, and though she quickened her thrusts somewhat, she kept them steady and long, nearly pulling fully out before pushing back in. Her gaze fell to the woman's breasts as her back arched, her pleasure seeming to increase. Kazia felt the woman's fingers wrap around the backs of her shoulders, nails lightly pressing into the tanned skin there.

"Faster," the woman gasped.

Shortening her strokes, Kazia used the power in her body to thrust hard and fast, her hips slapping against the skin of the woman beneath her. The woman began to groan deep in her throat, head arched back as her lips fell open, Kazia's own lips opening in sympathy. She felt her own pleasure building and threatening to explode out of her. It did just that when the woman cried out, her nails now digging into Kazia's flesh.

With a surprised gasp and small cry, which she tried to keep in, Kazia's world became pure pleasure that began between her legs and flowered throughout her entire body, nearly making her fall atop the smaller woman. It took her breath away, the movement of her hips stopping for a moment as she ground herself against the smaller woman, who whimpered in response.

Panting, Kazia lifted her head from where it had fallen to the pillow. "Did I hurt you?" she managed.

Smiling, her unexpected teacher shook her head. "No," she gasped, wrapping her legs around Kazia's hips to still her movements, as Kazia had no idea when to stop or what she was supposed to do. The woman hugged her to her, Kazia relaxing into her body. Admittedly, it felt amazing to feel their bodies so intimately pressed together. "Wonderful," the woman whispered into her ear, giving her a tight squeeze before releasing her.

Kazia lifted her head again and saw the smile she was given. It wasn't that of seduction or even of a lover.

It was a smile given to the person you were given a task to complete with, and it was completed well. The woman lifted her head and left a soft kiss on Kazia's lips before gently urging her off her.

Her body released from the woman's legs, Kazia eased out then climbed off the bed. She stood there, looking down at the phallus, which glistened with the woman's spent passion. She looked up to her companion, who had also climbed off the bed and walked over to her. With the same gentle touches as when she'd put it on her, she unbuckled the harness and removed it.

"Tomorrow," she explained softly as she did her task. "I will be here with you again after the breakfast service." She met Kazia's eyes. "They don't want to chance you getting hurt in training before your big day, and there are specific things I was instructed to show you how to do."

Nodding, Kazia watched as the phallus was rewrapped in the cloth and the woman grabbed her garment off the floor. "What is your name?"

Tunica back in place, she picked up Kazia's discarded shift and walked over to her, holding the garment out to her. "Flora," she said.

When Kazia tugged hers back on, she met the young woman's gaze. She felt a bit of a kinship to her, no doubt because of their situations and certainly what they'd just done. Surprising herself, she took the smaller woman in a hug, an embrace that initially Flora seemed surprised by and was stiff, but then returned it. For a long moment the two women just held each other before, with a kiss to Kazia's cheek, Flora left.

Chapter Thirteen

Beneath the Colosseum were small cells, either for the fighters or for animals or props. One man was assigned to handle the weapons used while another helped the gladiators with what little armor they were given. Kazia was in her own cell, already in her dark brown subligaculum and gladiator sandals. She'd been told by her handler that she'd been given that color of breeches so it wouldn't show when she shit her pants in fear.

As she paced in her cell, feeling once again like a caged beast, the man came in with her supplies for the fight. In his hands, among other things, he held a small round shield called a parmula, and a short sword with the blade slightly curved. She'd trained with it and learned it was called a sica. Of the three gladiator types, she'd been cast as the Thraex, armed in the Thracian style of warrior. How appropriate, she thought, considering Thracians were part of the Greek world.

She stood still as the man bent down to attach the armored greaves that protected her lower legs, watching him do his task with deft efficiency. She wondered what went through his head as he did this, knowing that it was entirely possible that one of the fighters he was arming would not return alive.

Finished with that, he grabbed a heavy leather and metal belt that was wrapped around her belly just above the waistline of her subligaculum. This was for support and protection, and perhaps to not be so easily gutted.

While doing that, his hand accidentally grazed the underside of her exposed right breast. He flicked up an apologetic look to her, but she cared not. Her tan lines from her military days were long ago baked away as she'd spent the last four months topless, just like her male counterparts.

She'd long ago stopped seeing herself as any sort of sexual being, though her experience with Flora the day before had confused that apathetic view. In that moment, however, she pushed that aside. It didn't matter, as she didn't care if she survived this match or not. At least she got to experience sex, she supposed, forced or not. And, it wasn't with a man.

He finished his task by helping her slide her sword-using arm into the manica, essentially an armored leather sleeve and shoulder covering, which he strapped into place across her chest.

"Here you are," he said, handing her the helmet she'd be using.

She looked down at it, a strange looking helmet, for sure. It was metal with a brim all the way around, a high crest, and a wide visor that covered the entire face with two large holes to see through, though they were covered by metal mesh. They reminded her of bug eyes. It was difficult to see well through them, but luckily she'd had a lot of practice at the school.

His job completed, the man headed out of her cell, closing the door behind him, though it wasn't locked. Cradling the helmet to her side, she lightly tapped the flat side of the sword against her bared thigh as she paced, blowing out a breath as she tried to focus.

"You have no need to be so worried, Kazia."

Whirling around, she was surprised—and not—

to see the cloaked man leaning back against the closed door. His ever-present dark brown cloak was clasped around his shoulders, much of his body hidden beneath the heavy garment. Pushing away from the door, he made his way over to her.

She stared at him, his pale blue gaze finding hers. Immediately, she felt a calm come over her, a protection surrounding her like a cloak of her own. He nodded down at the sword she held as if for permission. She handed it to him, watching as he took it, turning it this way and that before he glided a finger down along the curved edge of the blade.

His gaze flicked up to meet hers, a downright devilish grin upon his face. "You'll do some damage with this today," he said, voice nearly a purr. "Won't you?"

"I will do whatever I have to do to stay alive," she heard herself saying, though the words surprised her, as she didn't much care.

"No," he said, handing her the sword back. "You will do all that you must to give them a good show." He took the helmet from her, holding it up. He ran his fingers over the visor, which fully hid her identity. "Behind this, Kazia," he said. "You are no longer the girl from Greece. No longer the blacksmith's daughter, and no longer the lost girl thrown away."

Instantly, Kazia felt herself tense up. She felt almost overwhelming fury pass through her at his words. They were words that reminded her all too well of who and what she was. Hand tightening on the grip of the sword, her jaw muscles tightened as well, and she glared at him. In return, he gave her a knowing smile.

"Save it for the arena," he said softly. He looked

her over, looking like a doting father, the one she'd never had, before his blue eyes settled back on her own. "Make me proud," he said, handing her the helmet back. With those words, he turned and walked to the cell door. A final look at her over his shoulder, he left.

⁂

Lifting her helmet into place, Kazia stepped onto the platform that would be cranked by slaves to lift her to the arena floor. She sent a thumbs-up when she was ready. Heart pounding, she widened her stance for balance as the platform began to lift on its pulley system. Her fingers loosened then tightened their grip on her sword as she headed closer and closer to the final destination.

She could hear the uproarious crowd, which was nearly deafening. She was used to an audience and the cheers, but less than four thousand was a far cry from eighty thousand eager souls, all there to watch someone bleed. It was daunting as she reached the arena. She stepped off the platform and out of the shadows and into the sun on the sand-covered arena floor.

Her gaze took it all in, the massive structure that was the Colosseum, filled to capacity with those who had paid their hard-earned denarius to see a good show. As she walked in, the cheers turned to surprised shouts and boos. No doubt because she was a woman. Those displeased cries turned back to cheers as her opponent entered—a man. She was very surprised, but deeply pleased.

Her opponent was, not surprisingly, cast as Murmillo, which was essentially dressed and armored as a Roman legionary, the crème de la crème for those in the stands. Kazia was already cast as the villain, both as the so-called Thracian but also a woman. It was *her* blood they were cheering to see spilled.

"Not today," she muttered, looking up into the stands that encircled the entire arena.

She and her combatant were the main attraction, the main event. Other fights and shows had already been executed for the entertainment of the masses, and the bloody spots in the sand stood testament to that.

Something caught her eye to the left. A quick glance showed her the cloaked man standing near the box for Emperor Titus.

The crazy thing was, none of the guards protecting Rome's leader nearby seemed to even notice him. He nodded at her, that same smile upon his face as had been there earlier in the cell beneath the Colosseum.

She gave him a quick nod of acknowledgment, then turned her focus back to her opponent, and none too soon.

She didn't see it but *felt* a swing coming her way. The crowd cheered as her opponent used his gladius to try to slice her left arm, which was exposed and would have been a devastating wound, nearly ending the fight before it began.

With the speed she'd used on the battlefield, she ducked, her foot lashing out and catching him in the left thigh with the power of her most powerful body part—her legs. He grunted and staggered backward but remained on his feet. She knew it would cause a terrible charley horse, and the surprised look in brown eyes told her he certainly hadn't been expecting that.

As the cheers began to turn to boos again, Kazia knew the crowd hadn't expected that, either. With the entire Colosseum against her, she knew she had some serious work to do to win them over, or to be victorious *despite* them.

Again, the man in the cloak caught her eye, his smile beaming at her. She sent a smirk his way before focusing solely on her opponent. She could see he was angry; no doubt simply by being in the arena with her his ego was wounded, just because as a gods-given right as a male, he was supposed to be superior to her.

She intended to keep the wounds coming. She'd had to prove herself her entire goddamn life, and this man's entitled fury was just fuel on her very large fire.

With gritted teeth, she went after him. As he swung at her again, she used the round shield as an extension of herself, her left arm slipped through the leather strap on the back. She knew she couldn't out-weapon him, as that was the point of the battle of "Greek versus Roman"—to highlight the perceived weakness of the lesser culture. So, she had to use her speed, surprise him into making stupid mistakes.

She yelled out a battle cry as she whirled, shield to his head, her own sword leaving a nasty gash across his unarmored shoulder while using another kick on the back of his knee. He nearly went down, turning his body to use his much larger shield to smack her side, sending her staggering away from him.

He barely got back to his feet before she was on him again. He grunted as he took a slash to his left pectoral with the sword in her right hand as she backhanded him with her shield, sending his helmet askew, a second backhand knocking it off altogether. The crowd was on its feet as he staggered away from her, trying to fix his helmet. She sent him flying backward with a kick to the gut.

Splayed out flat on his back, he looked up at

her with wide, stunned eyes. She walked over to him, circling him like a vulture, hands out as if to say, *Gonna get up?* The crowd was laughing now at her antics. She played to it, bringing a hand to where her mouth was, unseen behind the helmet visor, as if stifling a yawn.

She could see he was extremely angry now, and out for vengeance. With gritted teeth, he popped to his feet, slamming his helmet into place as he did. The crowd was once again cheering, though Kazia wasn't entirely sure for whom. All she knew was, the fight was on. This was what she'd been craving for so many months.

He was going at her like a true warrior now, and she was meeting him blow for blow. He got in a good slice to her left forearm, and though it stung and was bleeding, she didn't care. She relished the pain, for at least it reminded her she was alive. She was relishing the fight, too, the two taking up a huge footprint at the center of the arena.

The clang of metal knocked against the leather-covered wood of the shield, then the clang of blades meeting. It was constant as they danced, first in his direction, then back in hers. They were both bleeding, and the sweat easing inside the wounds made them sting like mad, but she couldn't focus on that. She knew he, too, had to be in pain, but like a good warrior, he ignored it.

She could see the determination in his eyes, and it reflected what was in her heart. The crowd was cheering, and at this point it felt like they were just excited for a good fight. Even so, in the training school they'd been taught that it was a balance between a good fight and a long fight. The crowd got bored with a long fight, and that would never bode well for either of the two combatants.

Both breathing heavily, they were staring each other down, taking a moment to catch their breath, but she could see that he, too, was trying to find a way to break the stalemate and bring the fight to a close. This was her debut in the Colosseum, so there was no way in Hades she was letting him win, nor would she settle for a draw.

Without warning, she let out a growl of attack and, with all she had, she sent him wheeling, helmet flying off and bouncing along the ground as he landed on his back once again. His legs flew up as he landed, and he tried to use that to propel him back to his feet, but she used her blade to slash his hamstring, a loud cry of pain leaving his lips.

Rolling to his stomach, he crawled away from her, his wounded leg useless as the slice had cut into the meat, leaving the back of his thigh flailed open to the bone. He was trying to get to his sword, which had also flown when he'd been sent to the ground. The crowd was roaring in appreciation now, and it filled Kazia with a sense of purpose and mission.

She stalked after him, and as he reached for the gladius, she used her own blade to slash him down between his shoulder blades. He cried out in agony again. She didn't go deep enough to kill or cripple him, but enough to make a very bloody splash with the crowd's reaction. It was also very clear that he wasn't going to be able to continue the fight.

Knowing she was safe from him, she looked to the Emperor's box to see what he wanted her to do. The man looked to the crowd, where some were emphatically gesturing for her to kill him, others to let him live.

Again, playing to them, Kazia took a step toward him with sword raised, then took a step back and lowered it, a step in, a step out. She held her arms out like, *What do you want me to do?* Laughter rippled through the crowd once more. Finally and dramatically, Emperor Titus gave her the gesture to let him live.

Bowing in her deference to him, she took a large step back from the prone man, offering him space and safety from her blade. The Colosseum erupted in cheers of approval. Not sure if it was what she was supposed to do, it felt like the right thing to do. She made her way over to her wounded combatant and, tossing her sword to the ground and kicking his away from him, grabbed him beneath the arms.

"Up," she said. "Let us get you to your feet."

It took some doing, and a lot of grunts of pain from him, but finally, working together, they got him to his feet. The crowd was on theirs once more at the generosity of spirit. She stayed with him, supporting his not insignificant bulk as he hobbled toward the door he'd appeared in at the start of their fight.

Reaching it, he turned to her, pain evident in his face. She reached up and whipped off her helmet, hair standing up in crazy ways from sweat.

"You should not have done this," he said through gritted teeth, pain lacing his every word.

"And we should not be trying to kill each other for entertainment," she responded. "Yet, here we are."

The platform appeared, two slaves upon it to help the injured man. Kazia watched them take over, getting him onto the platform before it was lowered out of sight.

Chapter Fourteen

To her shock, after the match Kazia had been whisked off to the massive domus of her owner, Felix, and his wife, Mona. Apparently, where she'd been chained like a dog for two months had been their country villa. This home was in the heart of Rome. Once she'd reached there, she was taken to a bathing chamber, even more opulent than the one in the villa, and bathed and her wounds tended to.

It was a different batch of female slaves this time, but they were doing much of what the first ones had done so many months ago. Kazia didn't fight it, knowing better. And besides, she was tired, she was hurting, and she was grateful for their help. She did as they asked her to do, moved this, turned over, lifted that, and was finally dried and dressed in a fresh tunica and sandals.

Afterward, she was sat down on a stool, and a particularly lovely young slave stood before her with a comb, working on the strands of her damp, dark hair. Kazia's gaze was at about the eye level of the young woman's breasts and, admittedly, they kept catching her eye.

"Do you like her?"

Trying not to move her head, as she didn't want her hair pulled out of her scalp, Kazia glanced to her left with her eyes.

Mona stood in the doorway of the large bathing chamber. She was lovely, curvy, and with her dark hair piled atop her head in a becoming style. The look on her face was knowing amusement.

Feeling very ashamed, as the poor woman doing her hair had no choice but to be there and she certainly had no choice but to wear the clothing she was. The material was meant to drape and caress every curve it touched.

Clearing her throat, Kazia looked back to the wife, no more than ten years older than she, though her husband was at least thirty years her senior.

The wealthy woman looked to the slave. "Kiss her."

About to protest, Kazia saw the woman's dark eyes turn even darker as she stared her down. It seemed she was daring her to do just that. *Remember your place.* Despite her apparent victory that day in the Colosseum, Kazia was no better than this girl. A hand to her jaw turned Kazia to look at the slave girl again. With apology in her eyes, Kazia accepted the kiss.

The young woman's lips were soft, and her tongue was even softer. The slave buried her fingers in the very hair she'd just been combing into a semblance of order as the kiss deepened. Kazia had no idea how far this was supposed to go, because she had the very distinct feeling that this wasn't meant as some sort of reward for a fight well won, but for the wife's own voyeuristic pleasure.

Suddenly, the slave was gone, her mouth replaced by that of the wife. Knowing full well this woman had a proverbial hand around her throat, Kazia continued the kiss. Her partner was clearly very excited, her kiss breathy and wet.

"Such a missed opportunity," she finally whispered against Kazia's lips once the kiss broke. "Naked and in chains, all that time." Her dark gaze bore into Kazia's. "You will join us," she said with finality, glancing over at the slave girl as she stood erect from where she'd been leaning over to reach Kazia's seated form.

Looking down at Kazia, the woman caressed the side of her face with her fingers, painted lips quirked in a little smile. Without another word, she dropped her hand and left the room. Even without her presence, the air was heavy, as though she were still there. Kazia had no idea what to say, her guilt stabbing at her gut as she felt her wandering eyes had set the poor girl up for gods only knew what.

With a quiet, "May I finish?" the young slave stepped back into Kazia's personal space.

Kazia nodded. "I'm sorry," she whispered.

The young slave said nothing, though gave her the smallest of smiles in acknowledgment of her words as she continued with Kazia's hair.

❦❦❦❦

Kazia had been paraded about, a giant feast held in her honor. She'd never seen so much food in one place in her entire life, and the irony was, she'd only been able to eat here and there as she'd been pushed from one group to another. Never in her wildest dreams did she think she'd be hobnobbing with the wealthiest of Rome, and frankly, she wasn't impressed.

Yes, they were dressed in the finest of materials, and impressive gold and baubles had been upon fingers, earlobes, and necks, but she found them all to be shallow and uninteresting. She would have much preferred to be standing back with the slaves, or chatting with them in the kitchens.

She allowed none of this to go to heart or head. One thing she'd learned over the years of working for her father and his blacksmith's shop was that the poor were deemed only as good as their usefulness to the wealthy. Right now she was exciting, an anomaly in the patriarchy that was Rome and the brotherhood of the gladiators. The second her sword failed them, she'd be nothing more than a footnote of a footnote in history.

Finally, a scantily clad slave, a young man, found her and took her with him deeper into the large house. They went upstairs to a second-floor bedroom that was massive. Inside was a large bed and furnishings to allow a large get-together to take place there. He led her to the bed and a wrapped object left upon it.

"You are to undress and put this on," he instructed, then with a small bow, left her alone.

Recognizing it as the same package the phallus had been wrapped in that she'd used with Flora, Kazia groaned inside. She was tired and she just wanted to go back to her room at the school and sleep. Not to be, clearly. She unwrapped it, and sure enough, it was the phallus and leather harness.

Closing her eyes, she took a long, deep breath before removing her tunica. She tossed the garment to the bed and took hold of the contraption as the door to the room opened. Glancing over at it, she saw the young slave girl from earlier, the one who had been working on Kazia's hair after her bath.

She wore a robe and nothing more. Her chestnut hair was down and brushed around her shoulders and down her back. She was truly lovely. Her hazel eyes never left Kazia's as she walked over to her, clear intent in their depths. She dropped her robe once she reached the bed, revealing a beautiful body, though Kazia had to do her level best to not react to the scars upon her back, clearly remnants of more difficult days for the young slave, who looked to be around eighteen or nineteen.

Even still, Kazia couldn't take her eyes off a very shapely behind as she crawled onto the bed. Once she reached the pillows, she turned and lay on her back. Looking down her own body at Kazia, who still stood at the foot, she slightly cocked her head to the side as she straightened one leg, the other bending at the knee with a foot flat.

Her gaze scanning over the beautiful body, Kazia continued what she was doing. Her day spent with Flora had been a lot of putting on and taking off the harness, so she pretty much had it down. Though she knew neither of them had a choice, she hated the fact that her body was very much reacting to what it was seeing. She was beginning to pulse, and as she got the flat end of the phallus pressed against her growing need, she gasped slightly.

"Beautiful, isn't she?" was murmured into Kazia's ear from behind her.

Proud of herself for not whipping around and slamming whoever it was to the floor by their neck, Kazia stiffened instead. She nodded, recognizing the wife's voice. "She is."

Kazia felt naked breasts brush against her back, wincing slightly as one of her many bruises from the match earlier was touched.

"Sorry," Mona whispered, the softness of her hair breezing across the expanse of Kazia's back as soft kisses were trailed over the injuries.

Kazia forced herself to not react in any way, as they were extremely painful, and though the woman was being very gentle, it still hurt. Again, a quick fantasy of just going to bed flashed through her mind, but it was very obviously not to be for some time.

The kisses moved up along her spine to her upper back and across her right shoulder until the woman was facing her. Mona's kiss was already heated when it reached Kazia's mouth, already very ready for whatever she had planned for Kazia.

The kiss ended, and Mona's dark eyes looked up into Kazia's. "Watch," she whispered before turning away from her and crawling onto the bed and toward the slave woman.

Doing as asked, Kazia stood where she was, phallus securely in place and ready for whenever—and for *whoever*—it was needed. Mona crawled over to the slave woman on all fours, looking much like a big cat ready to pounce.

The beautiful young woman's legs parted for her as Mona settled herself atop her. The two women began to kiss, and the way the young woman seemed to know exactly what her mistress would do, Kazia figured this was not the first time she'd been brought to this bed.

As Kazia watched, she had to admit, it was the most sensuous thing she'd ever seen, and all her years of complete ambivalence to men made complete sense. She knew in that moment that there was truly nothing more beautiful in creation than a woman.

And, as Mona's mouth explored gorgeous breasts, the slave woman's eyes opened and met Kazia's. Her lips were slightly open as she seemed to be enjoying what was being done, but she was looking at Kazia as though it were the gladiatrix's own mouth that was lavishing her right nipple with a tongue.

Kazia's body was beginning to burn, and as

Mona's mouth moved down the beautiful body of her slave, she moved her own body farther down the bed. When her mouth was about to explore the young woman's most private place, Mona glanced over her shoulder at Kazia as she moved herself to her knees, her ass lifted and inviting.

It was easy to see how ready she was, even from Kazia's position a few feet behind her. Her sex was swollen and wet. The look in her dark eyes held no question of what she wanted. She turned her attention back to the feast before her. The slave's eyes fell closed and her breasts thrust forward as her back arched.

The woman before Kazia was beautiful for sure, but something about her was dark, and Kazia did not like her. So, she focused instead on the slave woman as she climbed onto the bed on her knees up behind her owner's wife. She took hold of the phallus in her hand, guiding it to a very slick opening before easing it inside. The kneeling woman groaned in concert with the entry.

Fully inside, Kazia placed her hands on womanly hips as she began a slow, even thrust inside of her. She watched the slave, watched as her body undulated with the ministrations of the mouth between her spread thighs. She took in her face and her lips, so full and slightly parted. One hand reached down to tangle in the dark hair of her mistress, the fingers of the other pinching the nipple of her own right breast.

It was easy to imagine that was Kazia's fingers, or her mouth, even. And, when those eyes opened once more, hooded in sensuous delight, they again found Kazia's and wouldn't let them go. It was far too easy to imagine that Kazia was gently thrusting inside of *her*, that those wonderful little noises she was making were because of the phallus deep inside.

Kazia felt herself becoming lost in what was happening. It wasn't just the sex and attraction to the young woman she felt, but all of it. She felt addicted to the day, to the *power* of the day. As much as she knew this wasn't her, she wanted to be nowhere else. It wouldn't have much surprised her if she'd seen the man in the cloak standing in the corner watching, encouraging her to take what she'd earned.

Was this what he'd meant? With that thought, a surge of power washed through her, a feeling of aggression that made her grab hold of Mona's hips tightly and slam into her, skin slapping ruthlessly against her ass as she buried the phallus into her over and over again.

The woman lifted her head from between the servant's legs and braced herself on hands and knees with the onslaught. Her cries were nonstop, as were Kazia's thrusts. Finally, Mona's loud, guttural cry erupted from her with her orgasm, which nearly sent her collapsing against the slave woman's spread thighs.

Kazia's chest was heaving from her exertion, and with the look of desire in the slave's eyes, she knew she wasn't done. She pulled out of Mona, who rolled over onto her back on the bed. Her eyes were closed, and a forearm rested across her eyes as she seemed to be desperately trying to catch her breath.

Phallus still glistening with Mona's release, Kazia crawled the couple feet forward, the slave's legs opening wider to accept her as she lowered her hips and easily entered her. They were breast to breast as Kazia was pulled down against her. Their kiss was hot and filled with her moans as Kazia began to move her hips once again.

Unlike the almost animalistic rutting thrusts into Mona, these were slow and deep, the kiss all-consuming. Kazia felt like she couldn't get enough of this woman's mouth, even as she was deep inside her body.

She felt like her very soul was connected to this woman in that moment, felt so pulled into her that she had to break away. Lifting her head, she saw the woman looking back up at her, and for just a moment saw near-black eyes, the vibrant hazel of the slave woman missing.

Blinking several times, Kazia shook her head. She was exhausted, and she'd consumed entirely too much wine at the feast in her honor. Looking back at the beautiful young woman who was caressing her back as she continued to thrust inside her, she saw those hazel eyes meeting her own, though they fell closed in pleasure as Kazia increased her thrusts.

From her increased breathing and constant moans—as well as her own—Kazia could tell the woman beneath her was close. She felt Mona's hands caressing her back and ass as she raised herself to her arms and slammed into the young woman. At nearly the same time, they both cried out, the woman's hands gripping Kazia's biceps, squeezing with her release. Kazia hissed from pain, as that was where one of her cuts were from the fight. It was superficial, yet painful.

Her orgasm rocking her hard, Kazia slammed into her one final time, grinding her hips until finally her body was done. She had no energy left, everything gone, like an extinguished torch. Her arms failed her, and she collapsed atop the smaller woman, who immediately wrapped her in a hug.

Kazia tried to catch her breath, gentle fingers

running through her hair by the slave and over her back by Mona. It was partial tactile bliss and partial tactile overload. After a moment, she knew she had to be crushing the other woman, so she raised herself. She looked down into her face, giving her a sheepish smile.

"Sorry," she murmured, giving her a soft kiss before pulling out of her, then off.

Mona moved aside so Kazia could roll to her back. She was so tired and was grateful when she felt kisses to her face and murmured words in her ear.

"Sleep, now," Mona said, fingers trailing down between Kazia's breasts. "More later."

≈≈≈≈

After Kazia had unbuckled herself from the phallus, the covers had been pulled up and she'd been shocked to find herself in the middle of a Mona and slave girl sandwich. All three women had nearly passed out, but Kazia awoke to a roaming hand and kisses on her neck.

The room was pitch-dark, so she had no idea which one of them it was, though she could feel a still body to her right. That had been where Mona had been, last she knew. The lips made their way up her neck and along her jaw until they reached her ear.

"Sorry" was whispered so softly Kazia almost didn't hear it. "I just needed you one more time."

It was the slave woman, and truthfully, Kazia wanted it, too. In response, Kazia reached over and urged the smaller woman to move atop her. She did, her softness pressed against Kazia, which made her sigh into the mouth that found her own. The kisses were slow, sensual, and lazy.

She had no idea if she'd ever be able to touch this woman again, so decided to get one last bit of time with her. She sensed the other woman was feeling the same thing. It wasn't anything more than pure attraction and lust, but in a dark world of oppression and servitude, it was a moment in time of brightness. Of choice.

The woman's thigh fell between Kazia's, pressing against growing need, Kazia's own strong thigh doing the same for the woman who sighed into their kiss at the contact. She was already so wet, which made Kazia herself wetter.

Their movements were very slow so as not to move the bed or make too much noise, their kissing similar. It was wonderful, and once again, Kazia felt like her soul was opening up to the exquisite creature atop her, rocking against her.

Kazia's hands slid down the smooth plane of her back until she cupped a beautiful ass, using her short, blunt fingernails to trail back up until her hands spread out again across the softness of her skin just below her shoulder blades. Their kissing became deeper, more breathy as the pleasure was building.

The woman brought up a hand and wormed it between Kazia's head and the pillow, holding Kazia's mouth firmly to hers as the kiss grew more passionate. Kazia almost couldn't breathe, but she didn't break away, couldn't make herself break away. The thrusting against her body became quicker, shorter.

Finally, the woman lifted her mouth from Kazia's, the gladiator taking in much-needed air as, with a small whimper muffled in Kazia's neck, the slave came. Kazia's eyes squeezed shut and she bit her lip until she tasted blood to keep in her own cries of release. As they had earlier, they held each other as they both tried to come down from their shared experience.

Finally, the woman lifted her head just enough to murmur into Kazia's ear. "You're beautiful when you come."

She initiated a slow, soft kiss, tongue gently stroking against Kazia's. Responding, Kazia felt like she was being lulled into a state of calm and peace. Her body felt light, and she drifted away.

Chapter Fifteen

Senara stepped from the Crystal Palace into an absolute nightmare. The sky had already been thrust into inky blackness, turning the afternoon to midnight. She immediately began coughing, the smoke so acrid, making her eyes water.

She hadn't worn a mask on this mission, as she felt if she came looking unlike anyone else there, perhaps her target would see her as the savior she was in that moment and cling to her to get out of a city that was destined to be destroyed.

The chaos was already underway, the violent eruption spewing volcanic pumice, ash, and deadly gasses high into the air. What goes up must come down, and screams filled the air as fire rained down upon a people unknowingly warned for more than a decade that this day would come.

The door was placed in an alleyway, and she quickly looked around for a landmark. She noted some graffiti on the side of the building and then headed out to search. The clock was ticking, and Senara had only precious minutes to find one tiny needle in a pile of terrified, screaming, and running ones before she, too, was forever immortalized as a cavity in stone of what once was, instantly incinerated.

She could feel the heat swell over the land and cried out as panic began to swell along with it. She felt like the lone fish swimming upstream as people ran from the nightmare that was nearly on top of them. Eyes wide, Senara looked everywhere, as *this* was supposed to be where he was in that moment, damn it!

A cloud of thick, acrid smoke eased over the city like a smothering blanket, anyone running out of it suddenly appearing as if by magic. *There he is!* Nearly in tears of relief, Senara scooped the child into her arms, the boy not fighting her as everything was happening at once, and she grabbed his mother's hand.

Nearly pulling the woman out of her sandals, Senara took off at a sprint, pushing her energy forward to knock people out of her way as they went until they made it to the alleyway. She was so grateful when she saw Big Bear step out of the door. She literally used the inertia of her hold on the woman's hand to propel her into Big Bear, who caught her and vanished inside the door.

About to step through, Senara stopped for a brief second. The graffiti caught her eye again. It was for a gladiator, heralded by his fans. Something inside her head clicked, but before she could even ponder, she was yanked by the back of her shirt and sent flying backward through the door, the screams of those left behind ringing in her head as she landed on her back in the Crystal Palace, a crying and coughing three-year-old in her arms.

Immediately she began to cough violently, just like the little boy and his mother. The child was taken from her arms in time for Senara to roll to her side and then slowly to her hands and knees. Her head hung as her body retched the thick smoke from her lungs.

Before she knew what was happening, a medical team was swarming in, the woman surrounded and lifted onto a rolling gurney and whisked away as she, too, was coughing. The little boy was next, and then Senara. She couldn't breathe, and her eyes were watering so badly that she could barely keep them open.

The medical team was running with the three gurneys, the dark tunnel pushing out before them even as it closed up behind them, until suddenly they were out and in a large, cavernous space. Huge doors pushed open, and the trio and their respective medical teams were thrust into almost blinding light, after what the three had just gone through and then the darkness of the tunnel.

Senara had been in this area before, but never as a patient. She wanted to yell at them to let go of her and that she'd walk it off, but she couldn't even get in a word edgewise as her lungs were seizing. It felt like she had a fire burning deep in her throat. She'd only been there for a scant few minutes, so how on earth were mother and son?

Once she was settled in a little curtained-off area, she was sat up, her body limp as she felt so weak. Her shirt was cut off her by a gentle set of hands while another held something to her lips.

"Drink this," they murmured.

Doing as asked, she grimaced at the taste but nearly swooned as whatever it was she'd been given instantly coated her from the inside, from her mouth down into her lungs and belly, like a loving mother's caress. The fire was turned down to a small simmer, which she figured would likely just take time to heal.

"My god," she whispered, head hanging as she sat there.

"Are you all right?" one of those attending her asked gently.

Nodding, she closed her eyes, which burned so badly. "My eyes hurt," she said. "My skin hurts."

"Let's get you into a shower."

She was eased off the gurney and the rest of her clothing was removed, along with her boots. The curtain was pushed aside to reveal a small door in the stone wall beyond sliding open. A small cave-like room was revealed. Helped off the gurney, she padded naked into the room. Inside was a waterfall about two feet wide and used for showering purposes. A small nook was carved into the stone for shelving, which held hygienic incidentals.

Left alone, the door slid closed behind her as Senara walked to the warm water that spilled over the lip of the stone from an unseen source. She stood beneath its spray, powerful enough for a nice washing but not powerful enough to make a person feel like they were being skinned. Raising her face to the spray, she used her hands to push her hair away from her face, which felt tight and no doubt was covered in soot.

"Turn around."

Senara did as she was told, not entirely surprised to hear Brielle's soothing voice. No doubt Big Bear had them call for her, as the medical facility was housed in a section of the Underground, which was mutual territory for the Druids and Ankou.

Brielle, fully dressed but standing out of the spray, was just setting one of her pouches aside, a purple powder in her palm. Using a bit of the water, the Druid began to create a froth in her hands. With extremely gentle touches, she smoothed the froth over Senara's face and her closed eyes.

"Keep your eyes closed," Brielle murmured. "But this will sooth them."

Senara nodded, nearly moaning in relief as the skin of her face stopped burning and her eyes began to feel as if they'd been rinsed by clean, cool water. "So much better," she murmured.

"Good."

"How is the mother and the boy?" Senara asked, turning her face back to the water when she was instructed to, the gentle spray washing away what Brielle had smoothed over the heat-damaged skin, which felt refreshed and brand new.

"You care?" Brielle asked, her hands gently smoothing more froth over the expanse of Senara's back and shoulders.

"What kind of question is that?" Senara snapped.

"A fair one," the Druid said evenly. "Turn."

Senara did as asked, glaring at her friend as those hands and the magic salve upon them was spread across the front of her shoulders, upper chest, stomach, and breasts. The touches were meant to soothe and heal, not seduce. Senara looked away, annoyed.

"You make me sound so cold," she said, a bit hurt.

"No," Brielle said softly, using a touch to Senara's shoulder to urge her to turn to face the spray to rinse. "You have always been very committed and dedicated to Ankou and the mission." She created more froth before bending down and working it over singed legs. "Your priority completion in perfection."

"Is that a bad thing?" Senara challenged, running her hands down over her chest to help the water rinse away what had been slathered all over her.

"Not at all," Brielle assured. She ran her hands over a shapely behind before pushing to her feet. "Rinse."

Senara turned to once again face the Druid as she allowed the water to rain down over the backside of her body. "But," Senara pushed. "You are saying I have been more about the mission than those who are the target." A statement.

Brielle looked into her eyes, a dark auburn eyebrow raised in question. "You dispute that?" She fell to her knees once more, smoothing her creation over Senara's thighs, knees, and calves.

Senara looked down, noting Brielle's face was nearly level with a very sensitive part of her body. She grinned when she received a questioning glare from the woman kneeling before her. A bark of laughter escaped Senara's lips at the tsking of a tongue. Clearing her mind, she continued their conversation.

"What we do," she said, voice not harsh even though it was firm, "is not easy on the heart, Brielle." She looked away, feeling…shy? Vulnerable, perhaps? Neither a favorite emotion for her.

"I know that," Brielle murmured softly, pushing to her feet. She reached around Senara to rinse her fingers before she placed her hand on the side of Senara's face. Looking deeply into her eyes, she smiled. "Caring is nothing to be ashamed of, Senara." She caressed the other woman's cheek before her fingers fell to cup the side of her neck. "Something in you has changed." Her intense green eyes were looking into Senara's very soul.

As much as Senara wanted to look away, she couldn't. "I cannot begin to bring my heart through the door, Brielle."

Brielle's eyebrows rose. "You don't bring it through your *own* door, milseán," she said softly. "Turn and rinse."

Senara did as instructed, relieved to be able to look away from Brielle's eyes, which saw far too much.

Clearing her throat, she said, "I think I know where she is." She waited for a snort or a laugh or chiding that Senara had just proven Brielle's point. None of those things came, just a soft question.

"Where?"

"I think she is still in Rome, and I think she is alive." She turned her head to glance over her shoulder. Brielle stood back out of the spray and waited for her to continue. "I think she has been forced to fight."

❧❧❧❧

The sun was hot as it beat down upon the balding head of the mask she wore. She led her *wife* to their seats in the maenianum secundum imum with the rest of the wealthier citizens, come for a day's worth of entertainment. The structure was massive, the climb to their seats taxing on the older man she was portraying.

Getting seated, she glanced over at her companion, a none-too-thrilled Big Bear. She reached over and patted the knee of the sixty-something woman who sat next to her. "You look so pretty, honey," she said sweetly.

Cackling quietly at the glare she got, neither of them thrilled when they lost the coin toss on characters to play, she looked away and over the arena below. Currently, things were quiet, though soon enough it would be the lavish parade to open the games. From what she understood, it would be music and dance with costumed entertainment. The fighters and the Roman elite would be honored as well.

As they waited, her focus was with those seated around them. When Brielle had triumphantly told her she'd found the Beast of Britannia, Senara had been overjoyed and relieved that she'd been right. No, she hadn't expected the "forced to fight" to be in the arena of the Colosseum, but rather in an army somewhere. But they'd found her, and she was alive.

The fact that Senara had no longer been able to feel her, and even Frank hadn't been able to focus in on her energy to tap into her memories, was deeply troubling. This meant her own, personal energy was being usurped by something or someone.

So now, she and Big Bear were on a surveillance mission. Step one: find her. Step two: watch her. Step three: extract her.

This time, she thought, still angry with herself for waiting too long the first time, she wasn't leaving until Kazia was leaving with her. She wanted to get sight of her, read her personally, then begin to formulate a plan. They had to figure out why and how her own energy was being suppressed. Where was it going? Worst-case scenario, which they all feared, had she been taken over?

She focused her attention on what those around her were saying, and she could tell Big Bear was also. The woman he wore at the moment looked frumpy and bored, but she could see the man beneath the mask. He was all ears, just like she was.

"It's an absolute disgrace having that woman fight with the men," one of their fellow audience members was saying.

"She sure as Hades doesn't fight like any man!" another responded.

"She's not worthy to fight here," the first man insisted.

"You going to be the man to put her in her place, Marcus?" another goaded with a chuckle.

"*Beast of Britannia*," the man said bitterly. "Send her back where she belongs."

"I heard she's Greek," Senara's mask said, voice deep and as grumpy as the permanent expression on his face.

The men, who were seated in the row below her, glanced back and up at her. "I heard that, too," one of the men said.

"See?" the angry one added. "All the more reason to get her out of Rome!"

"My wife," Senara said, reaching over and taking Big Bear's hand, which squeezed her fingers a bit tighter than was necessary, "heard about her and wanted to see it for herself." Her mask chuckled. "Reminded me of my military days, so we came to see for ourselves."

"You're in for a treat," the younger of the two said. The other one just grumbled, turning back around with his arms crossed over his chest.

Senara glanced over at Big Bear, who met her gaze before they were distracted by the sound of the parade beginning. The procession had already made its way all through the streets of Rome but now had finally reached the Gate of Life, which all eyes were now looking at on the eastern side of the Colosseum.

It was a procession of floats pulled by exotic animals, including elephants and zebras. Young, beautiful women and handsome men stood atop it dressed as mythological characters, frozen in a tableau of splendor and wonder and Roman glory.

It was gold chariots and the hyperbolic supremacy and pomp that Rome was best known for. Though supposed to be entertained and impressed, Senara was disgusted but had to hide it. That arena was filled with slaves, both of the two- and four-legged variety. The worst part, however, was when the Colosseum went up in deafening roars of excitement.

The gladiators had arrived. Bringing up the end of the procession   was the reason Senara and eighty thousand of her closest friends were seated on the hard stone benches. The two combatants were already dressed in their armor, though both wore cloaks of outrageous finery, which neither could possibly dream of affording outside of the arena.

The moment Senara saw her, she was unable to take her eyes off her. Strong, assured, and filled with a confidence that hadn't been there the last time Senara had seen her. In fact, of all the images she'd been shown, the only time she'd ever seen such self-assuredness had been while in battle, while doing what she'd literally been born and her body sculpted to do.

She was stunned to see that, like her male counterpart, Kazia was bare chested, her breasts and torso as deeply tanned as her incredibly powerful arms and legs as they carried her around the arena as the two gladiators followed the procession. Hearing something, Senara focused on the crowd around her, as a chant had begun.

Beast! Beast! Beast!

Looking back to the gladiatrix, Senara saw that Kazia and her companion, soon to be combatant, were stepping up to the Imperial Box, the festooned Emperor Titus looking down at them. In unison, the gladiators yelled out in loud, strong voices:

"Ave Imperator, morituri te salutant!"

"Good god," Big Bear's mask whispered, her voice just barely heard.

Senara nodded. *Hail, Emperor, those who are about to die salute you!*

Chapter Sixteen

The images on the screen reflected in her eyes as she took in every detail created for this woman she'd be portraying. She took in her name, her age, her background and family history, all of which had to come off her tongue as though it were part of the fabric of her own quilt of life. Lashyn, aged twenty-one and her Egyptian owner's favorite Circassian woman.

As a teenager, she'd been taken from Circassia and sent to Egypt, where she was now the personal body slave of Anise, wife of merchant Jabari, and part of his harem. Of course, Anise *was* the wife of Jabari in real life, neither changing their names. No need, as neither would fall upon any record and meeting any Roman had ever had.

It was a rarity that Druids accompanied on Ankou missions, but Senara knew Jabari and Anise very well, and the couple would be perfect for what was needed. They had the look that was required, with the rich, dark skin and features of that part of the world. Plus, as a former slave hailing from the very region of commerce, Jabari could talk the talk and help Senara understand her role.

The images came to an end, Senara left in the stony silence and darkness. She felt him walk up beside her, though he said nothing. Turning, she looked at the silhouette she knew all too well.

"Can you do this?" he asked finally.

Nodding, she ran a hand through her hair. "I can, Ankou. I must."

"All right, then. We leave for Bowhar in the morning," he said. "I'll create a door so you, Jabari, and Anise will leave together from there."

"All right. I'll head to the Warehouse to get outfitted for myself and the correct clothing to bring to them." The pair turned and headed out together. "This will be a long-term mask, Ankou," she reminded. "Sadly, I do not think this will happen overnight."

His nod was able to be seen as they stepped out into the beautiful sunny day that was that part of Duras. "Did you and Big Bear see any sign of Bahutha while you were there?"

"No. That is one thing I want Anise to focus on. Good thing about this time," she added with a smirk. "Women were seen and not heard. So, Anise is there to be the beautiful wife while keeping those lips shut."

He chuckled. "Seen and not heard means a whole lot of watching."

"Exactly," she agreed with a grin. "And," she added as they headed in the direction of the Warehouse, where they'd part ways. "You are okay with Big Bear coming in when he is needed?" She spared him a glance. "The second part of the plan we told you about." She added softly. "Should we need it."

He met her gaze, his chocolate-brown eyes looking as troubled as she felt. "Yes."

⁂

It was a risky strategy, but the team had decided Senara not use a mask for this one. Nobody on the ground had seen her but Kazia. If she was recognized by the gladiatrix, regardless of her reaction, that was good news. If she did not, they knew it was likely she was not in control of her own faculties and had either been, or was in the process of, being taken over.

The domus utilized near that of Kazia's owner had been carefully selected and set up. The door from Bowhar had been placed in the bedroom of Jabari and Anise. Few would be going in there, so it was out of the way. The home wasn't as large as the one effectively next door, but it would still pass for the look of the assumed wealth of those within. And, it was a temporary situation, as the wealthy merchant was in town for business, not to set up a residence.

This being a known fact gave the whole thing a lot more wiggle room to just blow into town for a short time before blowing back out—with Kazia in hand, if everything went as planned. Senara's Lashyn would be taken along to essentially serve as the plaything for the couple, the toy they just couldn't leave at home.

This was another reason Senara wanted to bring the couple. The three were close, and this sort of situation would be awkward as it was, let alone with someone she didn't know or trust as much. They had to be able to pull this off without a single crack in the chemistry. Though nothing would happen between the three physically, the intimacy of caring—or at least knowing each other well—had to be believable.

She was in her own quarters getting ready for the dinner. There was a knock on the door. "Come," she called out, knowing at this point they didn't need to worry about eyes and ears. The entire house was filled with "slaves" from Duras to bolster Jabari's claims of wealth.

The garment she wore looked something like an elegant, modern-day sports bra of white, though was edged at the deep neckline and around her middle with a thick decorative band of gold stitching. The white skirt-like garment began low on her hips, a thick band of gold at the waistband as well. It wrapped around her hips and flowed down to just above her ankles. Sandals finished the look, as well as gold armlets cuffing her biceps.

The outfit was quite comfortable, actually, and she wouldn't mind wearing something similar at home. The door opened, and she smiled when she spotted her friend and colleague walking over to her, looking every bit as elegant and beautiful as the wife of a very wealthy Egyptian man should. She gave the older woman a bright smile before turning back to the mirror.

Knowing there may be physical contact, she kept her own hair, which also would make her stand out. This was part of the point. Anise stepped up beside her, watching as Senara ran her fingers through her hair, making sure it was perfect. Anise was a lovely Black woman who looked to be in her forties or early fifties, her complexion flawless and beautiful smile stark white against her skin tone.

"You look stunning, my darling," Anise said, crossing her arms over her chest. "Good thing Jabari knows I would start his testicles on fire should he even look your way."

A bark of laughter escaped Senara's lips as she looked over at the other woman, who was grinning. "No threat, Anise. No. Threat."

The older woman stepped over behind Senara, the two women studying the younger one's reflection in the mirror. "Now," she said softly, one hand on Senara's hip, the other resting upon the bare midriff. Her dark skin was a beautiful contrast to the creamy paleness of a muscular stomach. "You feel her here," she said softly, dark brown eyes boring into Senara's. "Yes?"

"Not anymore," Senara admitted.

"Tonight," Anise said softly, removing her hand. "If she is there, connect with her, Senara." She shook her head. "Whatever that takes."

⁂

Music drifted through the air out in the courtyard that the domus was built around. A gurgling fountain sat at the center. The dining guests milled about with goblets of wine and chatted. Lashyn followed Anise around dutifully, holding her goblet and her plate of food to reach over and nibble from and for the other guests to marvel at. Though many Romans had dark hair, lighter eyes—especially those as unique as Senara's—were rare, so she was becoming quite the party favor.

She kept glancing to Jabari as her "owner," who had to remember to keep giving permission for others to speak to his property.

"I have heard of the beauty of the Circassian women," one man said, his gaze taking in her eyes, yes, but also every inch of her body. It was making Senara's skin crawl, and she wished she had her sword. "What is the name of such a beauty?" he asked her.

Again, a glance to her owner for permission, which was granted. "Lashyn," she said demurely.

"Beautiful," he said. "Just like you."

She gave him a shy smile, even as she entertained visions of gutting him. Instead, she gave him a bow of gratitude. "Thank you for your kindness," she murmured.

Jabari called for her, so she bowed again to the man before skittering off to her master. He wrapped his arm around her waist, pulling her against his side possessively. She played along, hand resting upon his chest. The irony was, Jabari was one of the kindest, most giving men she'd ever known. He adored his wife and their sons, so no doubt it wasn't easy for him to portray a greedy monster who peddled in flesh.

To make it easier on him but keep it authentic, she nuzzled into him, an obvious display of the fact that she *knew* who owned her and who kept her fed and happy. Also, it showed her devotion to him.

"I would like you to meet Mona," he said. "She is the mistress of this house, and she would like you to accompany her upstairs for a gift for Anise." He gave her a pat on the behind. "Go."

Mona was a woman who looked to be in her thirties. Eyes as midnight as her hair, she was voluptuous and lovely. Even so, Senara thought as she followed the woman inside the house and to the second floor, there was something very dark about her. She could sense a cruelty in her that could be unleashed unbidden.

They finally reached a massive bedroom with a massive bed as the centerpiece. Immediately, Senara felt drawn to it. Her stomach began to roil. Her solar plexus, just below the breastbone and the energy source for humans, was pulsing. She nearly cried in relief. She *felt* her! Kazia had been here, and recently.

Her attention was garnered when Mona stopped their progress into the room with a hand to Senara's arm. She turned her to face her. Senara kept her expression clear: no confusion, no curiosity, no interest.

Mona's dark gaze took in all that there was to see, resting on Senara's breasts. Senara could feel the heat coming off her in waves, and it was the heat of arousal.

"I've not seen anything like you before," Mona finally said, coal-black eyes finally raising to meet Senara's. "Beautiful isn't the word for you, my dear. Lovely, sexy, none of those are adequate." She brought up a hand, using a fingernail to trace down the length of one of Senara's arms. "How free is your owner with you, hmm?"

In that moment, Senara knew this woman had taken Kazia to her bed. She had no idea if it was a onetime thing or if they were lovers. But, as much as she didn't want to, if she had to play ball with this woman in order to get information or closer to her target, she would.

Jabari, Anise, and herself had discussed beforehand what Jabari's "rules" were, for just a situation like this. She was so grateful they had, so no matter what she said, they were on the same page.

"My master allows me to make my own choices," she said, a spark of interest entering her eyes. "He believes pleasure is to be shared, explored, and," she added, voice dropping a bit. "Given."

A slow, sexy little smile crossed Mona's lips. "Does he, now?" That fingernail moved back up Senara's arm and to her shoulder, then across her upper chest. "What is your name?"

"Lashyn."

"Have you been with a woman before, Lashyn?" Mona asked, dark eyes boring into Senara's, even as her fingernail trailed over her left breast.

"I have," Senara murmured, keeping her hands to herself. She had to play the game with this woman, and in her position, that meant do as you're told until you're told to do as you please. That had not happened yet.

"And," Mona pressed. "Have you been taken by a woman, like a man has taken you?" She stepped closer, their breasts nearly touching as her hands roamed down to cup a very shapely ass. "Inside you," she murmured into Senara's ear. "Thrusting, taking." She flicked Senara's earlobe with her tongue. "Fucking."

Senara's eyes closed, forcing herself to respond and react to what was clearly an act of seduction. She had no idea if Mona intended to follow through in that moment or, as Senara had seen before, merely was marking her perceived territory for a later date.

"No," she breathed, moving her head to the side as Mona left little kisses along the column of her neck.

"Then," Mona said, taking Senara's hips in her hands and holding her still as she pressed her own curvaceous hips into them. "You will be in for something you've never experienced before."

"By you?" Senara asked with a soft moan when she felt a tongue find her skin.

This was part of her job she struggled with. It didn't happen very often, but she was a very honest, direct person, so missions like this—taking on a literal hands-on role—was tough for her. But, she understood the importance of this, felt it in her very soul, so she pushed all of that aside and allowed herself to fully be Lashyn.

"I will be there, yes," Mona said, nipping at the muscle that connected Senara's neck to her shoulders. "But no, I will not be who is fucking you as such." She grinned against her flesh, a hand moving around between their bodies to cup Senara between the legs. "Though I will certainly participate in my own way."

Mona's mouth found Senara's as her fingers

stroked her lightly through the material of her skirt-like garment. It seemed the touches were more about showing domination or control of the concubine's body than about an attempt to make her prey come. Senara returned the kiss, loath to admit that the woman certainly knew what she was doing.

But, as the kiss continued, Mona's hand moved to cup the back of Senara's head, holding their mouths together. She felt a coldness enter her mouth, something that was trying to fill it and force itself down her throat, and it wasn't the woman's tongue. Panic filled her, and she used a small energy burst to push the other woman away from her, severing the kiss.

Staggering back a couple steps, Senara looked at Mona, and the woman whose dark eyes had twinkled with sensuous intent now looked at her with pure hatred—but for just a moment. A flash, then it was gone. Replacing it was a look of startled confusion, and Senara knew she had to continue to play along.

Hand to her chest, she let out a long breath. "Goodness," she whispered, giving the other woman a little side-eye. "As I said…choice," she said in a sensual tone.

❧❧❧

Senara burst through the door of Jabari and Anise's bedroom in the rented domus, running her hand through her hair as she entered the room. The two occupants followed, Anise closing the door behind them. The couple said nothing to her, as it was obvious she was agitated. Instead, they waited her out, Jabari taking a seat on the bed and his wife standing next to him, arm resting on his shoulder.

Taking a deep, centering breath, Senara looked to the expectant pair. "I felt her there," she began, giving Anise a little smile as she placed her hand briefly upon her own midriff. "Kazia has been there, and I believe Mona is controlling her."

"Mona?" Jabari asked, surprise in his voice. He looked up to his wife, who met his gaze before both returned to Senara.

"I need to know everything about this bastard," she said, voice dropping. She couldn't keep the feeling at bay that they were being watched. "No." She shook her head and headed to the door, waving the two to follow.

They stepped through the door…

…and into the passageway in the Underground where they'd entered to begin with, the part of the massive tunnel system that was in Bowhar. She turned to the couple, who looked concerned.

"I am sorry," she said. "I felt like we were being… watched, somehow. Listened to." Her focus went to Jabari, who she knew had extensive information. "Tell me about him, Jabari. How does he get to people?"

He quirked an eyebrow. "You believe Bahutha was inside Mona?" he asked.

"I do not know," she said, frustrated that she didn't understand the situation better. She felt out of control, and she *hated* that feeling. "But she kissed me, and I am telling you…" She looked to them both. "Something was trying to enter my body through my mouth."

Anise's hand went to her own mouth as she turned away, walking a few steps before turning back to look at them. She looked shaken. Senara glanced over at her before looking at Jabari when he began to speak.

"Bahutha's way is to manipulate into influence," he began. He used two fingers to point to his own eyes. "Through the eyes. It is like a hypnotic stare that gets inside you and influences what you do. But," he added, holding up one of those long fingers. "It is temporary, so he must do this over and over again to truly change a person's constitution."

Hugging herself, Senara nodded. "Understood. Can he enter a person's body?"

Jabari nodded. "He can. He has a physical form, currently that of a man, always in a dark brown cloak."

"Sometimes," Anise added. "He is seen riding a black horse with glowing white eyes."

"But," Jabari continued the tale. "He can send a piece of himself, his own darkness, into a person."

"Possession?" Senara asked, again feeling that awful coldness that had tried to fill her mouth.

"Not exactly," he said. "If he gets in, he will find the darkest part of a person and use it to his advantage." He brought up a hand and began to tick his words off on his fingers. "If they have issues with anger, violence, intense sexuality, which," he said, sparing a glance to his wife. "Sounds like our girl Mona." His gaze settled back to Senara. "He will use it to achieve his means."

"Is he using that to control Kazia?" Anise asked, the question taken from Senara's very own mind.

Jabari met her gaze and held it for a long moment before it swung back to Senara. "Entirely possible. Question is, habibi," he said softly, using the term of endearment for such a close friend as Senara. "Can you turn the tables and use the same power against him?"

Chapter Seventeen

The Gladiator School, which was connected to the Colosseum via underground tunnels, was a huge structure. Clearly not as big as the one whose shadow it literally sat in, but impressive nonetheless. Mona and her husband, Felix, had invited Jabari, Anise, and Lashyn over with them to watch their little pet train.

The day Senara and Big Bear had stepped into the Colosseum to watch the fight, it had been such a mixture of feelings for Senara. She'd felt nauseated, impressed at Kazia's brilliance and power, yet profoundly sad to see her there, humiliated by an entire empire, just to be entertained. Today was the beginning of the end for Kazia, the end of this nightmare that Senara wasn't even sure Kazia was fully aware she was living.

Today was also the day they were coming face-to-face in a very different situation than Kazia had been in the first two times. All this was in her head while she kept her expression free of any of her thoughts or feelings or observations. She was so grateful that Jabari was filling the quiet with his endless babble about anything and everything.

It helped both she and Anise keep their eye on everything, essentially disappearing   as the men and Mona took center stage.

The arena of the school was large, though not as big as the Colosseum. There was a goodly amount of seating for spectators, which was where they were at the moment. Down below, several of the gladiators and their trainers were working out issues on fighting styles, learning new weapons, or were just sparring. The space was large enough for several things to happen at once.

Despite a half-dozen men with gorgeous bodies moving, flexing, and doing incredibly impressive work with weaponry, Senara's gaze was focused on only one fighter. She was dressed like the men were, only the subligaculum and gladiator sandals in place. No helmets on, and most only had the manica in place on their sword arm for armor. It looked more like this was an exercise period of movement and creating muscle memory than any sort of real scrimmage happening.

Kazia was a standout simply because of her movement. She was taut like a spring, only to bounce away from her opponent then back at him on a side he wasn't expecting her to be. She was quick, she was deadly, she was beautiful. It was like a dance, and Senara was mesmerized.

Grinning, Kazia and her opponent stopped when he stumbled backward, seemingly over his own feet. Walking over to him, she extended her arm. He grabbed her at the forearm, the powerful gladiatrix pulling the large man to his feet.

She stopped, as if frozen in place. Her gaze moved to the stands. Senara met that gaze, and it held. Even from the distance, Senara could tell that Kazia was affected by her, and as much as she hated to admit it, Senara felt it, too.

She nearly felt herself push to her feet from the stone bench she sat on, about to heed the call, when the spell was broken as Kazia looked away. The man she'd been fighting again got her attention as their sparring began anew. Senara watched, her gaze falling over every bit of Kazia's body.

She was stunning, and Senara watched the muscles in her back work beneath the tanned skin as she blocked a blow, and then the incredible power of her thighs as she braced herself back on one leg before sending him flying into the dirt with a kick that honestly didn't even look like it had been a full attempt. If it had, no doubt he'd be halfway across the arena.

Kazia was utterly spectacular.

When Senara had seen her in that cage, she'd seen how gorgeous her body was at rest, but to see it in motion…she'd never seen anything like it.

"Magnificent, isn't she?" Mona murmured into her ear.

Senara said nothing, simply nodded.

"Tonight," Mona said, trailing her fingers down Senara's back. "Perhaps you two can be properly introduced."

Again, Senara simply nodded.

One of the trainers clapped his hands, bringing everything to a stop. He called out something to his gladiators, which apparently was their cue that the training day had ended. Mona and her husband pushed to their feet, their three guests doing the same.

Senara's heart was racing as they headed down the closest aisle and down toward the arena. It had a wall around it, like the Colosseum, though unlike the larger arena, it had a gate to access the arena proper from the stands.

Kazia was talking to one of the trainers as the group of five reached the arena. It was strange being on that level, Senara thought. Though it was a wide, open space, she swore she could smell the blood and sweat permeating the air. It was brutal, the training the gladiators went through, and all for what? Even more brutal fighting in the arena next door?

Gladiators were expensive to keep fed, housed, and trained, so owners preferred that they didn't kill each other, but it did happen. Maiming and horrible injuries certainly did.

Senara focused on the present, lagging behind as was her station as they stepped onto the sand that covered the arena floor. The man Mona was married to, Felix, called Kazia over to them with a whistle. Like a good dog, Kazia finished her conversation with the man she'd been talking to and headed to the group.

Stomach flipping, Senara steeled her expression and her spine. Kazia was even more gorgeous up close. She was tall, as tall as the men in their group and, amusingly, taller than the man who owned her. It was astounding to Senara that a woman so powerfully built and on display with every step she took was so incredibly beautiful. It was a dizzying contradiction in terms.

She was a gladiator. She was an amazon. She was a goddess.

Introductions were made and compliments given, and despite polite responses of gratitude to them, intense hazel eyes always found their way back to Senara's, who was always there to meet them. The two women stood not more than ten feet apart, as Senara stood back in her proper place behind Anise, who stood back in her proper place behind her husband.

Strands of dark brown hair, sweaty from the intense workout, draped over Kazia's forehead and nearly into her left eye. For reasons she wasn't comfortable with, Senara wanted to reach over and brush them away. She wanted to know what her skin felt like. Was it as warm as it looked, deeply tanned and heated by the warm day?

Were her full lips as soft as they looked, currently quirked in a small smile before they began to move as she spoke to a question someone asked, the words sounding distant and foreign to Senara's ears? They were so beautiful in contrast to the straight white teeth, stark against the deep tan of her face. Her gaze fell upon that bottom lip, fuller than the top.

Her gaze wanted to dip lower, but she forced herself to look away from the woman totally. She was losing focus, even as she focused completely on her target. One thing she did realize, however, was that there was no recognition in Kazia's eyes. There was only curiosity and a good deal of lust.

Senara looked down at her fingers, which fidgeted with a gold cuff bracelet she wore as part of the uniform of the concubine. She felt literal heat suddenly warm against her face. Looking up, she found herself once again looking into Kazia's eyes, though now the woman was only a couple feet away.

Mona stood with her, an almost possessive hand wrapped around a very defined bicep. Senara looked from Kazia to Mona, her black eyes pinning Senara to the spot.

"Lashyn," the woman said. "This is Kazia." She stroked the skin of Kazia's arm with her fingertips. "Kazia," she said, looking up at the woman she stood next to. "I've brought you a treat." Her gaze went back to Senara. "Lashyn. She is here for a brief time." She moved in a bit closer to Kazia, her breast pressed against her arm. "I wanted you two to meet."

"Nice to meet you, Kazia," Lashyn said softly, her accent in place. "You were impressive in the arena," she added, indicating where they stood.

Kazia's eyes never moved off her, her eyes, her lips, a quick drop to her breasts, then back to her eyes. There was fire behind her eyes, but no life. "Thank you," she said, voice surprisingly soft.

"She will be to our house for dinner tonight," Mona said, reaching her other hand out and using the backs of her fingers to brush along Senara's jawline. "You both will. Perhaps a little dessert, hmm?"

Kazia said nothing, simply nodded, her gaze never leaving Senara's.

⚬⚬⚬⚬

Senara was not unused to being looked at like prey or dinner, especially by an unwitting man who had no idea she'd just as soon cut off all his fingers than let them touch her, but she'd never experienced it in the manner she did later that night at dinner. Kazia was never far away, whether with a gathered group that was seated around the huge table, loaded with platters of food to be passed around and shared, or out in the courtyard visiting.

Kazia, of course, was passed around much like the food had been. She was a star now, a gladiatrix by her gender but a gladiator by preference of those who touted her a hero and the best fighter Rome had ever seen, Colosseum or not. But, regardless of what group or person she was in front of, her eyes always found Senara.

Wanting to get her alone, Lashyn excused herself from her handlers and headed back into the house and up the stairs. She didn't hurry, rather took her time. Her head tilted a bit when she heard a step on the bottom stair as she nearly reached the top. Her fingers trailed casually along the railing as she turned fully forward again.

She knew it was her, could *feel* that it was. Raising her chin a bit and adding a little extra sway to her hips, subtle but potent, Senara made her way down the hall. She passed the hallway she knew would lead to the private bathing room. She saw the doorway at the end of the hall for the large bedroom that Mona had taken her to the last time she'd been in the house, but she had no intention of going there.

Noting another short hallway, she turned down it, not sure where it led. There was a cluster of smaller bedrooms—guestrooms, it looked like. She turned into one of them, noting the bed, smaller than that in the large bedroom but still opulent in style, like everything else in the domus. She walked over to the window, overlooking the courtyard below.

The many lamps filled with vegetable oil lit all over the space below was the only light in the bedroom. Many shadows filled the room. She braced her hands on the wall on either side of the window, looking down when she heard footfalls head down the short hallway. Like her own, they weren't harried or frantic. Senara's heart pounded with each one.

They paused at the open doorway of the bedroom, but only for a moment. They entered the room, and she could again feel that heat, and it nearly burned her alive. Moving away from the window, she turned to see Kazia was not three feet away, and the look in her eyes was absolutely indicative of what she intended to do.

Senara was frightened for just a moment, but she knew she had to see this through. Her gaze moved to the door, trying to see if she could—

Gasping, Senara found herself pinned to the

wall, hands held in one ironlike grip above her head as Kazia's other hand was working to tug her skirt-like garment up. Senara looked up into her eyes, and there was nothing there. It was determination and lust, nothing more.

"Let me go," she said quietly, more to see what would happen than because she expected her request to be honored.

In response, the sound of material ripping and the cool night air touching the incredibly heated skin between Senara's legs. Both made her gasp softly. She tried to struggle against Kazia's grip, but there was no getting her hands free. Kazia's other hand reached down between Senara's legs, her fingers instantly covered with the growing wetness there.

A small, knowing smile graced full lips as Kazia met her gaze. Still, she said nothing as she brought those fingers up to that mouth that Senara was so entranced with and, without a word, tucked them inside. Senara's breathing hitched, but still, not like this. While the other woman was somewhat distracted, Senara used a burst of energy and pushed the larger woman away from her.

Kazia staggered backward, rage crossing her beautiful face. Her lower garment in tatters, Senara pushed away from the wall and bolted for the door, only to be caught up when an arm grabbed her around the waist. Her inertia swung her and Kazia both around until she was facing the bed, her body held hard back against that of the gladiatrix.

Like she weighed nothing, she was carried to the bed and tossed down onto it. She tried to scramble away but again was caught, this time by Kazia's body pressing her face down into the mattress. She was able to move her head to the side to breathe and could feel the hardness of what had been strapped to Kazia's hips all night press against her ass.

"Don't fight me," Kazia murmured into her ear.

"Why are you doing this?" Senara asked, her words breathy as her chest heaved with the exertion of their fight as well as, admittedly, a little fear and a lot of arousal.

She gasped when she was suddenly turned to her back, one of Kazia's knees forcing her thighs apart before she lowered her hips between them. Senara gasped again as she was entered.

Kazia began a slow, easy thrust inside her. "Because," she panted, looking down at Senara as the gladiatrix rose to her hands. "You want me to."

They were both breathing heavily as Kazia continued to thrust deep inside of her. Unable to help herself, Senara reached down as far as she could, pulling up the tunica the woman on top of her wore, needing to feel her skin. She pulled it up to her waist and pushed her hands up underneath. She could feel the strong back that she'd been admiring just hours before, the skin covering the muscles soft and warm.

Senara raised her knees closer to her chest, eyes growing hooded as Kazia's penetration was deeper. She looked up into her face, Kazia's eyes looking into hers. They didn't kiss, just stared at each other as Kazia moved between her spread thighs, the bed creaking beneath them. In those eyes, she swore she saw recognition there.

After several moments, Kazia's own eyes were growing heavy, her beautiful lips falling open as it seemed her own pleasure was building. She never increased her thrusts, just kept them long and slow.

Senara felt like she was in another world, just the two of them and the pleasure building inside them both.

Her hands moved up to cup the backs of strong shoulders, back arching as she was about to come. Her eyes squeezed shut and mouth opened into a silent scream as her orgasm exploded throughout her entire body, taking her voice and her very breath with it.

Kazia's hips became jerky as her body released with a strangled groan. Her head fell for a moment, and when Senara went to wrap her arms around her, Kazia pushed up and off her.

Climbing off the bed, Kazia stood there for a moment, chest still heaving as the phallus jutted out from her body obscenely. She stared down at Senara, who lay there still a bit stunned by what had just happened. Finally, Kazia ran a hand through her hair before she backed away from the bed, adjusting her clothing and tucking the phallus away.

"My second job complete," she said breathily, her breathing still uneven. Looking down at Senara with disgust, she said, "Dessert has been served."

With those quiet words, she turned and left the room.

✿ ✿ ✿ ✿

The moonlight shone in through the giant, stained glass window. The white rose at its center seemed to glow with the kiss of night. Senara was curled up in the window seat, looking out through one of the more clear panes of glass in the beautiful tableau. She wished she could curl herself up even more.

"Why are you here?" Ankou asked gently, entering the room. He did not light a fire, and she was glad. She needed the shadows.

"I do not think I can do this," she said, voice flat.

"Why?" He walked over to the window seat and sat down, her curled up body leaving plenty of room for his larger bulk.

She said nothing for a long moment before meeting his gaze. "Because I have gotten too close to the target," she whispered, ashamed.

"What happened?" he asked.

"Please do not make me say it."

He reached across the small amount of space between them and used gentle touches with a fingertip to wipe away the tear that was easing its way down her cheek. Hand dropping away, he looked at the wet spot upon his fingertip before rubbing the moisture into his skin with his thumb. He looked back over at her, fatherly concern in his eyes.

"Did she hurt you?" he asked.

Shaking her head, she looked back out into the night. "No."

"Then not all is lost."

Her head whipped around as she glared at him. "How can you say that?"

Never losing the understanding tone, he explained. "If Kazia were lost to us, Senara, she would have hurt you." His brown eyes held hers, even as she wanted to look away. "She has been whittled down to animal instincts in order to survive the life she is being forced to live, which is not much more than a glorified tiger. But also to survive the attack from Bahutha."

He reached over again and took her hand in his warm one. "Her moments with you, my dear," he whispered. "That was her desperately trying to be human."

Chapter Eighteen

Tink! Tink! Tink!

Oh, what a satisfying sound. The smile upon her lips was unstoppable as she watched her creation begin to take shape. How was it that, out of a crude bar of steel, with some heat and powerful blows from a blacksmith's hammer, an incredible tool or weapon could be formed? She was in awe, and more than that, she was happy.

Feeling that she wasn't alone, she stopped her pounding and glanced over her shoulder. There she was, leaning back against the building. She was far enough away to not get hurt, but close enough to watch. She said she loved to watch, and if Kazia were honest, she loved it when she did. She saw the love in the most beautiful blue-silver eyes she'd ever seen.

"What do you think?" she asked, holding up the beginnings of her creation.

"I think it looks like a blob of metal," she teased.

Kazia grinned. "Ye of little vision." She chuckled at the laugh she got.

With a jerk, hazel eyes opened. They blinked a few times before the surroundings came into focus. She was in the large bedroom, though it was still dark, early morning. She knew that as she could hear the birds singing outside. She lay there for a moment, allowing reality to snap back into place, but oh how she wanted to go back to… To what?

Her brain was fuzzy. She felt the good feelings

of whatever, and suddenly felt incredibly lonely, but wasn't sure why. Had no memory of why. Glancing to her right, she saw the figure lying on her side, the deep, even breathing of sleep emanating from her. To the left, it was the same thing.

She needed to go, had to get back to the training school, so as quickly as possible, Kazia crawled out of bed, trying not to disturb either woman. She pulled on her clothing and, as always, wrapped up her removable cock—as Mona liked to call it—and placed it in the drawer where it would stay until she returned.

She ran a hand through her hair as she headed quietly down the stairs, one of the guards that patrolled the palatial domus giving her a nod of acknowledgment as she passed him to head out into the start of a new day, a new day that would look like her every day. She glanced to the right when something caught her eye.

Looking up, she was surprised to see someone standing on the second-floor balcony of the smaller house next door to that of Mona and Felix's. She slowed her steps when she realized the person was a woman and she was looking down at her. As her eyes adjusted, she realized it was the concubine. What was her name?

The fog that was so often in her brain made her forget little things or even lose track of time. Maybe she'd taken too many hits to the head, she thought. But it seemed worse after what could only be described as an intoxicating night with Mona and whoever she brought to their play.

One night, to her horror, it was a man, but he'd had only one interest in Kazia, and it wasn't for any of her orifices. Turned out he had use for her "removable cock," too. Hadn't been her favorite encounter, but she'd made it happen without complaint or question, as was her job.

As she looked on, the woman left the balcony and headed back inside. For reasons she didn't understand and couldn't even quite hold on to before another random thought had taken their place, she was disappointed. They'd… She'd… Kazia turned away as she continued walking. Yes, she had been one of her given duties. But why did she have a strange feeling about it?

"Hello."

Kazia stopped at the soft voice. She saw that the woman had left the balcony because she had come down to the front door and was now outside. She was dressed in a flowing robe, very obviously naked beneath as the silhouette of her beautiful body could be seen from the lamp light burning outside the front door a few feet behind her. She was stunning, and the moonlight shining down into her face turned her eyes silver.

Kazia suddenly felt very shy. Clearing her throat, she spared her a glance. "Hello," she managed.

The woman hugged herself, head slightly cocked to the side as she studied her from where she stood, ten feet away. "You are up early," she noted.

Nodding, Kazia looked around, the street quiet and still. "I need to get back."

"To the training arena?"

Kazia turned more to face her, but the woman took a small step back. This, of course, made the gladiatrix freeze. Was she afraid of her? Then the fog evaporated just long enough to know exactly why.

For the first time in a very long time, Kazia felt a foreign emotion—shame. She looked down at her feet, not daring to take a step closer. She started when she felt a gentle touch to her chin, urging her to raise her head. When she did, she saw that she was looking into the beautiful face of the woman she'd been with a few days before.

This time, there was no fear in the woman's eyes, just compassion. How long had it been since Kazia had seen that, certainly aimed at her? She didn't know what to do with it, and she wanted to do what she'd been taught to do—get angry.

But there was something about this woman that made her feel at peace somehow. Certainly calm, anyway. The fog in her brain began to clear, and for a moment, just one beautiful, perfect moment, she felt like herself. She felt familiarity, she felt home, even though she had no idea what that word even meant anymore.

She wanted to say she was sorry, she wanted to beg for forgiveness and beg to be taken home, but she had no idea what that meant or why she'd even think that.

Her gaze took in the stunning face of the woman who looked back at her. Dark hair short, but long enough to run her fingers through. Her skin, pale in the moonlight as the sun had yet to take its place in the sky. It looked so creamy, and Kazia knew how soft it was.

"I know you," Kazia whispered, though she didn't know why she'd said it, the words just kind of falling out of her mouth. And the strangest part was, her instincts told her it had nothing to do with their time together in that random bedroom in Mona's house.

The woman—what was her name again?—nodded. "You do," she said softly, her hand moving to cup Kazia's cheek. Her thumb caressed the side of the gladiatrix's face.

Needing to touch that creaminess, Kazia's own hand rose. Her fingertips trailed along her jaw and to her throat. She felt the movement as the woman she touched swallowed, and she hoped it wasn't because she thought she'd hurt her. She was amazed at what she was feeling, the skin so soft, so warm and pliant.

She felt the hand on her face move around to the back of her head as it was urged down. The kiss was soft, not demanding nor invasive nor one of ownership. It was giving, it was comforting, and it made her want to cry. There was no tongue, as it wasn't that kind of kiss. Her hand once again moving around to cup the side of Kazia's face, the woman spoke against her lips.

"I told you I would come back for you." One final soft kiss, she turned away and hurried back to the house, her robe fluttering behind her hurried steps.

Kazia watched her go, so badly wanting to follow. She craved how she'd felt in that moment, as she felt the fog begin to ease back into her brain again. Her eyes closed and her hand came up as she covered her eyes. The blackness in her mind rolled in, making her feel a bit dizzy and unsteady on her feet.

Standing there for a moment, she waited for the worst of it to pass, leaving her feeling…flat. Colors weren't as bright, sound was more dull, and she felt nothing. Looking back to the house she stood before, she was confused on why she was standing there. Shaking her head, she continued on her way. Fight. She had to fight. That was who she was, what she did.

❧❧❧❧

"Again! Again! Kazia, hit again!"

With bared teeth, Kazia gave all she had. The sun was hot, they'd been at this for more than an hour, and she was desperately trying to not let the fog take over. She shook her head and blinked, fiercely holding it at bay. Her body was buzzing, even as it was sore and her arm stung like mad from the accidental slash earlier in the day from one of her sparring companions.

"Again!" the lanista cried.

Kazia was losing ground, her opponent pushing back with his shield. Finally, she lost her footing, and down she went. Her chest was heaving, sweat dripping into her eyes along with her dark bangs.

"Prohibere!" the trainer called when the other gladiator continued to go after her. Her opponent immediately stopped, and the lanista walked over to the fallen fighter and looked down at her, displeased.

She tried to catch her breath but just couldn't. She shook her head again, feeling like she was about to get sucked into the darkness that filled her head. Dropping her sword, she tried to stand but fell back to her behind. Trying again, she only managed to get to her knees before the darkness totally consumed her.

It was dark and very cold, like the grave. She stood where she was, feeling a presence next to her. That feeling was validated when a torch was lit and sparked to life. She was in a tunnel, the man in the dark brown cloak next to her holding the torch. He smiled over at her, the torchlight sending garish shadows to his features.

"Come with me," he said.

She followed, the torchlight creating a halo of guiding light for them on the narrow stone walls of the tunnel and rounded ceiling. Looking behind her, she saw that it was blacker than black, and she couldn't help feeling that something was about to jump out of that darkness and grab her. She had to force herself not to move up closer behind him.

The tunnel seemed to go on forever before finally, he took a right. Now, they were in a small space like a cave, but she noticed there were little nooks in the wall, like little carve-outs. With a gasp, she saw they were the perfect size for a human body to lay within. And, as the torchlight passed over those in this cave, that was exactly what inhabited the little nooks.

The carved-out areas were stacked upon each other in the wall, about two feet of solid stone between them. Gasping, she took a few steps back, gasping again when her back came into contact with the hard, cold stone wall. She couldn't take her eyes off those nooks, a body lying in each. This cave had eight of those.

All eight bodies were in various stages of decomposition, from all-out skeletal to the wound of death still visible. The still in the room was so incredibly eerie, even as she expected one or more of those bodies to sit up and look over at them.

Swallowing, she pushed away from the wall slowly but didn't walk any closer to the stone coffins. "Why are they here?" she asked.

Her torch-bearing companion turned and looked at her, the same ever-present smile upon his lips. "Because you put them here."

She met his eyes, which in the flame of his torch looked coal black as opposed to the dull light blue they usually were. Shaking her head, she looked back to the bodies. "No."

He walked over to her, a hand upon her shoulder. "What do you think you've been doing all these last years, Kazia?" he asked gently in the same almost fatherly tone he so often used with her.

He squeezed before his hand fell away and he walked out of the room. She had little choice but to follow or stay behind in the all-consuming darkness. As they went, the light shone over doorway after doorway after doorway of those little caves with the death nooks. She felt nauseous.

"You see," he continued, seeming unfazed by her reaction or what she was reacting to. "I saw you in Britannia, Kazia." He took a left into a long, straight tunnel, none of those haunting rooms adjacent. "The power and the mastery," he said, pride in his voice. "So well done!"

"I did what I had to do," she argued.

"Oh, indeed," he agreed, glancing back at her. "I'm not for a second implying that you enjoyed that, Kazia. You see, that's why I became so interested in you. You're loyal and dedicated and a true soldier." He paused, grinning. "Not a psychopath."

She followed as he once again continued, everything she'd seen and he'd said rolling around in her brain. "You have been around me here," she said, "but I remember you back in Britannia. On your horse that day. Watching."

"Yes," he validated. "I was watching a true master." He paused again, though she could see just up ahead, barely out of reach of the ring of torchlight, was a very wide entrance to something. He met her gaze. "You." He studied her. "For a long time, Kazia, I've been looking for the right one, the right warrior to lead the way."

She stared at him, confused. "Lead the way to what?"

"To the freeing of Bowhar," he said sagely. "A

realm that has been under the control of tyrants since time immemorial."

He reached for her hand, which reluctantly she gave him. He walked the few steps to that opening and pulled her along with him. Standing at the entrance, she saw that it opened up to a massive cavernous chamber. A strange, dim, silvery light with no source billowed up like fog from the ground.

With it was revealed an endless sea of silhouettes standing in perfect rows and lines, the two looking down at them as if those silhouettes were standing on ground a few feet lower than Kazia and her cloaked benefactor.

There were no faces, no features, no distinction between male or female, old or young. They seemed to be standing at attention, even as their heads hung, as if looking down at the ground.

"Like you," he continued. "They were all in chains." He indicated the silent masses before them. "Chained to an idea and bloodline that keeps them enslaved." He released her hand to reach up and cup the back of her neck in a gentle hold as he leaned in to murmur into her. "Now, because of you, they are free. And they are here to help you free the rest."

She swallowed again. "Who are you?" she whispered, sparing a glance to him.

He smiled. "I am father, mother, brother, sister, and best friend. All you need. Well," he added, a little sheepishly. "Brother, sister, and best friend, anyway."

He sent an arm out, the glowing fog moving to two figures at the front. They were still largely in silhouette, but they raised their heads to look up at Kazia.

It was a man and a woman, both with long, disheveled hair, the man's the same color as Kazia's dark brown, the woman's eyes Kazia's own hazel. They were *not the parents she'd known in Greece, but she felt a tie to them and certainly saw the physical resemblance, especially with the woman.*

"Your true Mamaí and Daidí," the cloaked man whispered in her ear, his fingers lightly combing through the shaggy hair at the back of her head. "One big, happy family."

Tears in her eyes, Kazia couldn't take her gaze off the two people, shaking her head as she felt the truth of his claim seeping into her very soul. Trapped. She felt utterly and totally trapped.

"No," she whispered, shaking her head more vigorously. "No!" Turning, she sprinted off into the darkness...

...the light of day blinding her as she blinked against the harsh sun's rays. Something caught her eye, and she saw a man standing over her with a sword in his hand, the sun winking off the blade. With the roar of a caged lion, she lunged up from where she'd been cowering on the ground, her own blade thrust so deep into his body that the tip emerged through his back.

She was close enough to his face to kiss him. His eyes were wide in stunned pain. With gritted teeth, she used incredible strength to rip the blade upward, tearing his innards as it went.

"What are you doing?" someone exclaimed.

Her blood-covered hand slipping off the grip of the sword, left it in the man's gullet as she turned to see another man charging her, face screwed up into vengeful rage as he raised his blade to strike.

She tightened every muscle in her body, ready to defend herself, when a mountain of a man with a thick braid down his back appeared seemingly out of thin air, tackling the man that Kazia vaguely realized was her trainer to the ground.

She was touched on the shoulder and whirled around, ready to sever the head off whoever with her bare hands when she was knocked backward by an unseen force.

Staggering back a few steps and finally to her butt, she looked up in wonder as the concubine lowered herself to kneel next to her. So struck and stunned, Kazia said nothing as she looked into that face, into those eyes, blue-tinted ice.

Everything inside of her calmed as soft fingers touched her face, pushed sweat-soaked hair back from her forehead. She couldn't look away, the fogginess in her mind, the animalistic fear clearing as she looked into her eyes.

The woman caressed her face again before, closing those magnificent eyes, she leaned in and touched Kazia's lips with her own. They were so soft, even softer than her caresses had been. Responding, Kazia sighed as she felt the rage subside, felt like she was coming back into her own body.

The first touch of a soft tongue made her sigh again. She wanted to cry, so relieved to not feel the fear that had been her constant companion for so long. Her own hand came up and buried itself in the softness of the short, midnight tresses. She was losing herself, losing herself…

Kazia grunted, her lips stilling as the woman slowly pulled back from her. Dumbly, she looked down and saw the grip of the blade sticking out from her chest, the woman's pale fingers still wrapped around it. Ribbons of crimson began to tickle her flesh as they trailed down over her stomach like tears.

Her gaze moved up to the woman, who was no more than six inches from her. She saw tears in those silvery-blue eyes. A wet cough left Kazia's lips, warm, coppery-tasting blood dribbling over her bottom lip.

She felt so weak and fell backward, grunting as her back made contact with the sand of the arena floor. The woman released the grip of the dagger and knelt over her, looking into her eyes.

Why? Kazia wanted to ask, but she couldn't gain a breath to speak, instead coughing up more blood. The woman caressed her face, a lone, lazy tear making its way down her cheek. The woman's eyes, she focused on them. So lovely, she thought, even as they began to dim, fade. The sun above was growing into evening, and finally into the full moon of night.

Lying there, she looked at that full moon, huge, silver, and magnificent. She felt so drawn to it. A beacon. Looking to her left, she felt the presence before she saw it. A hooded figure, in a black cloak. Slowly, the figure knelt down next to her as Kazia eased herself up to her elbows. She was transfixed by this faceless being, identity lost in the depths of the hood.

"Come," he said, voice deep but not menacing. Comforting. "It's time you came home, Kazia," he said. One of the arms lifted, a hand extended to her. It was the hand of what would be a child's nightmare, but in that moment she knew it was the bony hand of salvation.

The softest of smiles brushed her lips and she nodded. "Yes," she whispered, taking it. "Home."

Chapter Nineteen

Everything!" Senara called out, hurrying up the stairs. "Not a goddamn thing can be left behind. Not a bit of trash, not a goddamn hair from your head!" She clapped her hands to punctuate her words as she nearly ran into the room she'd been using to pack up her own belongings. "Let's go!"

Heart racing, she was doing her level best to keep her heart inside her chest. She could feel the sweat between her breasts and under her arms. She was on autopilot. She shoved everything into a burlap sack, not caring what it was. If it had been brought with her, it was going out with her, even if just to be burned.

"Calm."

Her head whipped around from her task to see Brielle enter the bedroom. That was nearly her undoing. Looking away, she growled, "What are you doing here?" She grabbed a pair of sandals from the floor and shoved them roughly into the bag.

"You know why I'm here, Senara," the redhead said softly.

Senara said nothing, just continued to shove items, including the bedding, into her bag. She whirled around when she felt a touch to her arm. "Do not touch me," she growled, nearly baring her teeth.

Brielle, as always, barely batted an eyelash. Without a word, she reached up and cupped Senara's face. She held firm when the other woman tried to push her away from her. "Stop," she said softly.

Whether she wanted to or not, Senara had no

choice but to. She felt the emotions rise and she was angry, because this was not the place and she did not want a goddamn audience.

"Stop," Brielle said again, fingertips caressing Senara's cheek like Senara were a skittish colt. She leaned up and left a kiss on her forehead. "We finish and go," she murmured against the skin. "All right?"

Eyes closed, Senara swallowed and nodded. "Yes."

One last kiss to her forehead and Brielle moved away from her, though kept her gaze on her as if making sure she was all right. "Soon," she said. "All this…" She indicated the room around them and the time beyond. "A memory." She gave her a soft yet beautiful smile then was gone, just the bit of her dark gray cloak fanning out behind her as the Druid hurried from the room.

Senara stood there for a moment, even after Brielle had left to do her duty of creating a reality of the domus as if it had been uninhabited for months, if not years. She didn't move but could still feel the soothing, warm energy that Brielle had essentially bathed her in moments before. Her entire body tingled with it.

She closed her eyes and took a deep breath before getting back to work.

Less than thirty minutes later, the entire place was empty, everything carried back through the door and burning in the bonfire that Senara stood before in a field in Bowhar. She was wrapped only in her blue cloak, all the bloodied clothing she'd been wearing tossed into the fire. Though she could feel the heat on her face, she felt ice cold inside.

The smoke was burning her eyes, but that wasn't all that was making them burn. Turning away from the fire, she walked through the door…

…and into the Crystal Palace. On autopilot, she kept going until finally she saw her house just up ahead. That sight alone almost undid everything Brielle's calming energy had done. She'd asked Senara to stay with her in Bowhar while Senara dealt with all of this, as they all knew the emotional fallout was still to come. But, the Ankou had declined. She needed to be alone.

Making her way inside, she untied her cloak and allowed it to fall from her body before she hung it up on a coat tree near the front door, then headed upstairs. Going directly to the bathroom for a shower, she looked at herself in the mirror, noting the dried blood on her midsection, which had been exposed in Lashyn's outfit. And that, of course, had been what she'd been wearing when…

She stared at it, bringing her fingers to it. It was dry, but even so she could feel a heat emanating from it, and it wasn't just her own body heat. Her gaze drifted up the reflected image of herself until she was looking into the eyes that stared back at her. Many had said they were her best feature, such an unusual color. Right now they were bluer than she'd ever seen them, and she knew it was because of the emotion that was threatening to burst forth.

They say the eyes are the window to the soul, and for Senara, they were the window to her intent, and that was almost more frightening. But right now, they were just haunted.

Looking away, she turned to the shower stall. In her time, baths or dips in the creek were all there was, so now in Duras, she allowed herself to truly enjoy all that time, innovation, and invention had to offer. Her shower was large and glassed in on three sides, the fourth wall polished stone slabs. It was a shower worthy of any household north of the twentieth century.

She stepped into the glassed-in cubicle and turned the water on as hot as she could take it. Lifting her face to the spray, she sighed in pleasure as she felt a bit of her stress melt away. She'd been doing missions for Ankou for years, centuries, and she'd had some that were relatively easy, some that were amusing, and some that were hard and heartbreaking.

But this one…

The tears hit her hard and fast, making her double over with the impact. Her sobs echoed all around her in the closed space as she fell back against the smooth stone wall and slid down to sit hard on the stall floor. She buried her face in her hands as she pulled her knees up, the tears nowhere near stopping. Her sorrow simply swirled down the drain with the water and Kazia's blood.

She wasn't sure how long she sat there, curled up in the corner of her shower, but eventually the tears ran dry and her skin was beginning to prune, yet she hadn't washed a single thing. Sniffling, she uncurled herself and climbed back to her feet. She needed to get on with her shower, and honestly, she needed to get on with her life and her duty. She'd done what she'd needed to do, and it was over.

✺✺✺✺

It had been a long night, filled with nightmarish images and the moment in the training arena over and over again. Before the sun had even risen, Senara had woken up crying. Angry with herself, she'd finally decided to just get up. Dressed in loose cotton pants and a tank top, she was in the kitchen making coffee when there was a knock at her door.

"Come in!" she called, not taking her eyes off the water being poured into the coffee maker.

The front door was opened and then softly closed before footfalls headed back to the kitchen. A moment later, Willem appeared. Not surprised in the least, she kept doing what she was doing.

"Coffee?" she asked quietly.

"Definitely." He went to her cabinet where she kept her mugs and grabbed two before walking to the table to set them and himself down.

Finishing what she needed to do, Senara blew out a breath and ran a hand through her drying hair, another shower taken to ease her emotions that morning. The coffee maker sputtered to life as she leaned back against the counter, arms hugged over her chest.

She met his gaze, brown eyes so open and warm. She knew hers were as guarded as her body language was in that moment. In so many ways he was exactly who she needed to talk to—thus why he was there, she knew—but at the same time, she didn't want to talk to anyone.

"What would you like to know?" he asked softly.

She smirked, reaching over to the sink and the dishrag slung over the sink divider there. She rinsed it and began to wipe down the counters and coffee maker, even as it gurgled along its journey to make the hot, fragrant brew.

As much as she was the kind of woman who looked you in the eye and pinned you to the spot if need be, she just couldn't. She needed to keep emotional and physical distance. Cleaning was a great distraction for just such a thing.

Looking at Willem, such a dear friend and colleague for so many years, she knew he'd been through it, and she knew he was willing to take her on the journey he had been forced to take. A journey *she'd* forced *Kazia* to take.

She wiped up where she'd spilled a little water while filling the coffee maker's reservoir. "Where is she?" she asked so softly, she wasn't sure if he'd be able to hear her.

"Still in detox," he responded.

"Why could she not have gone through that while alive?" she asked, her back to him.

"Because detox is the soul shedding the grievous injuries of the life it just led, Senara. She is no longer attached to the life she was forced to live now. Even you, born so many hundreds of years ago, you are still attached to that life and all that happened during it, because you are alive."

She was quiet for a moment as she absorbed what he'd said. Some of this she'd heard before, but now it had such a deeper meaning to her. She knew, deep inside, that Kazia would never have survived had she lived. Ironically, they had to kill her—no, *she'd* had to kill her—in order for her soul to survive. But would Senara's?

"Damn it," she muttered again, a tear plopping on the counter she'd just wiped down. "No," she said when she felt Willem grab her in a gentle hold. "Let go of—"

"Shh," he said, turning her to face him and pulling her against his chest.

Her tears intensified when she realized he didn't

have a heartbeat as her head rested against his chest. In Duras, Ryarch, and Bowhar, it mattered not whether a being was living or dead, as they were really only living or dead according to the earth-plane realm.

Even so, a living person still functioned as such, including a heart that beat within their body. The heart of the dead did not. Some things just didn't change, regardless of your realm. She cried as he gently rocked her, completely unable to stop.

"Damn it," she sobbed, laughing at herself. "Why can I not stop?"

She felt the pressure of his cheek rest against the top of her head. "Because you care," he said softly. "No matter how much you want to tell yourself you don't."

Senara smiled but said nothing to that. "Is she okay?" she asked at length, giving him a little squeeze to let him know she was moving out of his arms.

He left a kiss on her head and backed away. "She will be." He leaned back against an adjacent counter to where Senara moved back to the coffee maker, which was about done. "What she is going through right now is not easy, but paramount."

Nodding, Senara used the dishrag to wipe at her eyes and face. She let out a long, slow breath. "Is she in pain?" she asked, sparing him a glance.

"Not the kind of pain you're worried about," he said, pushing away from the counter to grab the mugs off the table and place them on the counter for her to pour in the brew. "But," he warned, a brow raised in emphasis. "The other kind of pain is just beginning, and she must go through it."

Senara glanced over at him. "What other kind of pain?"

"The pain of facing herself and all the whys."

He looked her dead in the eye. "Worst pain there is, Senara."

She had to look away, able to still see so much in his own. She poured the two mugs of coffee, sliding his over to him before she placed the carafe back on the hot plate. They were quiet as they sat at the table, cream and sugar provided. Preparing her coffee the way she liked it, Senara considered what he'd said.

"Does she hate me?" she finally asked. "Or will she, once all is said and done?"

He shrugged, setting the spoon he'd been given down on the saucer she'd left there for that purpose.

"Entirely her choice," he said softly, testing his coffee. He took a small sip before lowering the mug back to the table to add a bit more cream. "But I very much doubt it." He spared her a glance. "She was already dying, Senara."

Senara sipped her own coffee, allowing the creamy sweetness to warm her system as she swallowed it down. "Is there anything I can or should do?"

He studied her for a moment, something in his eyes that she couldn't quite read. Finally, he smiled. "Be there if she comes to you for questions or anything else. She has never known true freedom before, my friend. She will be very lost in its vastness."

Those words hit her hard. She had never even considered that. Taking another sip, she set her mug down as she sat back in her chair. "Will she stay in Yewa?"

"Again," he said. "Her choice."

"What made you come here to Duras, rather than stay in Yewa?" She'd never asked him that before. Yes, she'd known since she'd met him that he was "dead," but it hadn't mattered. It meant nothing in their world, and it gave him a very specific skillset for their missions. So, again, it never much crossed her mind.

"Very easy answer," he said with a big, bright smile. "I wanted to see the sun."

Midnight eyebrows rose. "There is no sun in Yewa?"

He shook his head. "Perpetual night, but it's that kind of night that is warm, welcoming, and calming. It speaks directly to the soul." His smile widened. "The kind of night where you feel safe taking a walk with a friend and baring your secrets, knowing they're safe in the darkness. Know what I mean?"

"I do." She wrapped her hands around the warmth of the mug, looking into the creamy depths. She glanced up at him at the softness of her name upon his lips.

"She'll be okay," he assured.

※ ※ ※ ※

Three days after the final cleanup in Rome, the team sat around Macha's quarters in Bowhar. Senara didn't want to be there, but when called, you came. She stood back against the wall, arms crossed over her chest and booted feet in a wide, almost challenging stance. Not one person had walked up to her or spoken to her.

The look in her eyes said it all: *Stay the fuck away from me.*

"So," Ankou said, standing next to Macha, her huge raven perched upon her right shoulder. "I have called you all in here because Macha has heard some grave news."

Senara did her damnedest to not react. All she could think of was, what if Kazia hadn't made it? Was that possible? The absolute only way anyone would even know she'd heard his words were if they noticed the quickening of her pulse in her throat.

He looked at Macha to give her the floor to tell her news. The goddess looked at each one there, a direct look in the eyes before moving on to the next. She paused at Senara for a moment longer than she had the others before looking to the group at large.

"We have word that Bahutha has a group of his death cult in Brittany. They have been spotted now on three different occasions, unsuccessfully trying to abduct children."

Soft reactions could be heard from gasps to outright, *What?* Senara continued to listen. They still didn't know the whole of it with Kazia, other than that Bahutha was involved in what was happening to her. But, even with the little she did know, she hated the bastard so was quick to listen.

"They have yet to be successful," the Druid goddess continued. "But do not kid yourself. It is a matter of time."

"Why children?" Jabari asked, pulling his wife a bit closer to his side.

"Because," Brielle said softly. "A child, particularly girls, are extremely potent at two different times in their lives." She held up a hand and ticked off on her fingers with each explanation. "One, when they're around nine or ten. This is because her young body begins to change, hormones begin the process of puberty. She is extremely powerful with this buildup of energy, making her like a loaded gun. And two," she concluded. "Her first bleed. She is no longer a loaded gun, but a loaded cannon of energy at that time." She met everyone's eyes. "If she has gifts, she can be quite dangerous. It not, she still is incredibly valuable to a parasite like Bahutha."

The room grew quiet as everyone absorbed what they'd just been told. Senara felt nauseous.

Swallowing and clearing her throat, she asked, "What will they do with them? If they succeed?"

Brielle met her gaze and held it. "In Bahutha's name, which means the intent will be loosed for the power to go to him, they will be sacrificed."

Chapter Twenty

Kazia's body let loose again, another stream of oily blackness leaving her mouth and leaving her feeling weak and exhausted. As she watched, falling from her hands and knees to her side panting, she saw that blackness morph into an image, as if played on a screen across the darkness that was the floor, just like the others.

This one was of her father. Well, the father she'd known, anyway. She crawled over to it, watching as he was berating a seven-year-old Kazia for giving him the wrong tool. Wide hazel eyes watched as the girl cowered in the corner, hands curled up against her own chest. He stormed away from her and, as the little girl was beginning to uncurl herself, he returned, the silent browbeating beginning all over again.

The image began to fade, leaving behind the blackness that had come from her body and brought it forth, Kazia's eyes closed. She fell back to her side and curled up into the fetal position. She lay in darkness, though it was comforting, as if a blanket of warmth and protection. She was naked, the floor beneath her not cold, not hot, just…*there.*

Her face was the very image of pain as she felt another one coming. Like a cat trying to work up a hairball, her body began to spasm. Again, she pulled herself to her hands and knees with her head and sweaty bangs hanging. Her entire body was racked as the largest bit yet of the oily blackness was expelled from her body. It seemed to take forever as it flowed from her lips. It hurt so bad that she was left with tears running down her cheeks as she spit the last of the bitter bile from her mouth.

The black puddle on the floor eased to life, and there she saw her mother, her very, very beloved mother.

Maia lay in the marital bed, gasping for air. Her face was pale and gaunt, and as she struggled to breathe, her sunken eyes opened. Kazia pushed to her knees again to look down into that face that she missed with everything in her. She looked into those eyes, knowing they had been looking at a fourteen-year-old Kazia before they were staring into eternity.

The sobs were ripped from Kazia's throat, already raw from so many emotions pulled from her with every bitter, black memory. It felt like her very soul had liquefied and was oozing from her. This last one, which faded away, taking her mother with it, was the worst. Again, she fell to her side, unable to hold herself up anymore.

She cried, oh how she cried. It also occurred to her that she was crying for her mother's death for the first time. She hadn't been allowed to, at the threat of a good beating from her father. So, she'd pushed it down. She'd pushed it *all* down.

Now, here it was, all around her in a smelly, bitter, black, and oily reminder of her life. She had never felt so exhausted before, nor had she ever felt so totally empty. She felt dirty, uncertain, and weak, just like a newborn colt.

Rolling to her back, she slid her legs straight and her arms and hands flopped out beside her. She was as open and vulnerable as it got: naked, alone, and with nothing to protect herself anymore. Her armor of indifference was gone.

Before that thought could go any further, the softest light began to glow above her, a dim light of white. A smile edged onto her lips, though she had no idea why. A moment later, a very soft and warm drizzle began to fall. Her eyes closed and mouth opened, needing the moisture, the warmth, and life it was bringing to her. Her skin, which had started to grow cold and rigid, began to soften, warm.

Slowly she sat up, though her head didn't feel quite fully attached to her shoulders as it bobbed a bit, unsteady. Noticing something, she saw the blackness that had come from her body was slowly beginning to be washed away by the gentle spray.

Fascinated, she carefully pushed to her feet, that newborn colt trying to learn how to use unsteady legs.

Looking down, she watched as it began to swirl at her feet, the thick, mucus-like substance evaporating into black smoke before it was sucked down into an unseen drain, gone. With each inch that disappeared, she felt her body gaining strength, steadiness, yet still so much uncertainty.

Looking up, she felt that the mist-like water had focused over her into a harder, yet still gentle spray. Like a spotlight, it poured down over her, a rainstorm meant for one. It plastered her hair to her head and ran down over her body. She reached up and pushed her hair back away from her face and lifted it to the spray.

She paused, sniffing the air. She smelled a fresh, clean scent, almost like the water itself was mixed with the cleanest-smelling soaps or shampoos. She smiled, unable to help it as she raised her face to the water again and just let the warmth fall over her.

Holding her arms out, palms up, she reveled in it.

It was like a billion soft, gentle hands massaging every inch of her body. A long, languid groan escaped her lips, surprising her as she hadn't remembered giving herself permission to emote verbally.

Again opening her mouth, she allowed the water to flow inside. It was the sweetest, most refreshing water she'd ever tasted. She felt her body coming alive as it flowed through her system, caressed her from the inside.

"Like this! Yes!" Maia giggled like a little girl as she led a grinning eleven-year-old Kazia around the kitchen in a dance. Her giggles echoed in Kazia's mind...

"Well done, soldier!" Her squadron leader walked up to her and slapped her on the shoulder. A man who had barely even bothered to look her way a month ago now looked at her with pride. "Well done."...

"This," he said, his eyes, always so hard, filled with the twinkle of a proud father. "This is a fine blade, Kazia."...

"I know you," she whispered, though she didn't know why she said it, the words just kind of falling out of her mouth. And, the strangest part was, her instincts told her it had nothing to do with their time together in that random bedroom in Mona's house.

She nodded. "You do," she said softly, her hand moving to cup Kazia's cheek. Her thumb caressed the side of the gladiatrix's face...

"Forgive me," Kazia said. Her Brittonic wasn't terrible, but she wouldn't call herself fluent. She'd

learned enough over the past year to communicate with the locals, though she understood it better than she spoke it. "What?"

"The rain is coming down harder," the woman said, indicating the weeping skies above. She had her hands wrapped around Kazia's forearm. "Come."...

She gasped, literally having to take a step back as that last one hit her so hard. She blinked several times, trying to suss out why that had had such a massive impact. Who was that? Why had she made her feel—

Whirling around, she saw one of the fighters, his arm moving like a piston into a huddled figure, the one that had been screaming. With one final loud gasp, the screaming stopped and so did his arm.

Tears came to her eyes as she stared into a painful yesterday. Shaking her head, she swallowed. "No," she whispered.

There was so much blood that the color of her garment was no longer visible. The body was limp as she cradled it up into her lap. With gentle, bloodstained fingers, Kazia brushed the mass of hair back. A loud keening sound left her lips when she saw the pale face, sweet brown eyes heavily hooded and staring off into a place where Kazia could not join her...and they blinked.

Gasping again, Kazia was startled back to the reality of standing beneath the water. The pale, blood-splattered face was still before her mind's eye. She saw the sweet brown eyes, half-hooded in death, again blink. She felt emotional pricks at the backs of her eyes as the gentle water falling down upon her own body began to wash the blood away from that pale face. The long, dark brown hair that had been matted with blood and dirt, long, shiny, and clean.

A smile spread upon beautiful, full lips as the full body of the woman slowly appeared out of the shadows. A tear slipped out of Kazia's eye, sliding down her face and off her chin to mingle with the water overhead. A second tear followed, then a third, and finally, she was full-on crying.

The woman walked over to her, looking up at her with so much understanding before she reached up and cupped Kazia's cheek. There was so much unsaid between them before she took Kazia into her arms, holding the sobbing woman tightly to her. Reality hitting her finally that she was being held by her greatest guilt, she crushed the smaller woman against her as they stood in the warm rain-like water.

"I'm sorry," Kazia sobbed into the hug. "So, so sorry."

Ione said nothing, simply held her. As they stood there, Kazia literally felt like her heart was being removed from her chest, so heavy from unending pain and fear. As she was held by this wonderful woman, she felt the hole that was left being filled with something she'd never known before—hope.

After several minutes, Ione pulled away just enough to look up into Kazia's face. The young woman looked so beautiful, healthy, and *alive.*

"Come on," she said, taking Kazia's hand in hers. "Let's get you dressed and settled."

Saying nothing, Kazia allowed herself to be led out from beneath the water and into the darkness, which immediately began to ease into the soft firelight from a fireplace, which lit a small room. There was furniture there of the sort she'd never seen before: big pieces all covered in material with big, fat cushions. She looked to the smaller woman, who grinned.

"Couch," Ione said, hand resting on the back of the larger piece. "And," she added, pointing to the smaller matching one. "Chair."

She tugged on Kazia's hand, which she still held as she moved through that room and into a bedroom. The bedroom was closer to what made sense to her with a simple bed, but there was a tall wood thing with knobs going all the way down it, like buttons. She'd seen similar pieces in the wealthy homes in Rome. She assumed this one held clothing also.

Ione dropped her hand when they reached the bed. A small pile of folded clothing lay atop the made bed.

"Ankou brought these for you," she explained, placing a hand on the top garment.

"Ankou?" Kazia asked, noticing that Ione was dry, and for that matter, so was she.

Ione's smile was bright. "Yes. He's the one who met you," she explained. Her face took on an overly serious expression. "You know, black cloak, skeleton man." Her smile returned. "He thought you'd be comfortable in these."

Kazia glanced down at the garments, four in total. "Why did he give them to you? Who is he?"

"Ankou is God of the Underworld, Kazia. He brings us home." She indicated the bedroom they stood in. "This is Yewa." She took both of Kazia's hands in her own as she gave her the sweetest of smiles. "And he gave them to me because I waited for you." She squeezed the hands she held lightly. "I'm going back,

back to a time when I can be a woman and truly find my place, on my own and without a man." Her smile was heartbreakingly beautiful. "Know what it's truly like to just be me."

"Going back," Kazia said dumbly, so much in her head and very confused.

Ione nodded. "Reborn. But, like I said, I wanted to be here for you, to welcome you home."

Though there was still so much she didn't understand, Kazia felt relief wash through her in a wave unlike anything she'd ever felt before. She took the smaller woman into her arms, and for a long time, they just held each other. It was a reconnection of two souls who had been through hell in the last moments of Ione's life.

"Thank you," Kazia whispered into the hug. "But where is Hades?" she asked softly. "Is this the Elysian Fields?"

Ione gave her a squeeze and released her. "You would be going there if you were Greek, Kazia," she explained softly, taking the first garment off the pile and shaking it loose of its neat bonds to reveal a garment that was a light color. The bedroom's only light source was that from the fire in the other room. So, it was difficult to tell exactly what color anything was. She met Kazia's eyes. "You are not."

Now more confused than ever, Kazia could only stare. She looked at the garment, which looked to be a shirt. It had no sleeves but was shaped like a very small version of a tunica. It left the arms and shoulders exposed while covering the torso. That was set aside and another garment was shook loose. These were unlike anything she'd ever seen. They were long and a darker color.

Ione must have seen her confusion as she placed them in front of her own body, holding them at her hips. The two long parts covered her legs. Kazia's eyes shot open. Ione grinned, tossing the garments aside. She grabbed a smaller garment, something that was a little more familiar to her.

"Underwear," Ione said, handing them to her. Kazia took them and pulled them on. The longer version was passed to her. "Pants," was explained. "Button," she said, finger tapping the recognizable closure. "Zipper." Ione demonstrated how it worked.

"Wow," Kazia murmured, taking hold of the pull and moving it back and forth, watching in wonder as the teeth opened, closed, opened, closed. A glance to Ione's bemused eyes and she cleared her throat. "Sorry."

"This," Ione said, holding up another garment. "Trust me when I tell you that it makes life more comfortable." Seeing the confusion in Kazia's eyes, she held it up to Kazia's bared breasts, the garment having two little pockets that seemed to be perfectly sized and shaped for them. She handed the garment to Kazia, who looked it over. "That's called a bra," Ione explained.

"How do I put it on?" Kazia asked, realizing the garment was stretchy. She pulled on it and, eyes wide, watched as it shot across the small room like a slingshot. She looked wide-eyed to a laughing Ione.

It took Ione a full ten seconds before she was able to respond as she tried to get herself together. Finally, wiping the tears of mirth from her eyes, she walked over to the flung garment and picked it up.

Ione handed it to her before removing her own garment she wore to cover her top half. That was when

Kazia finally noticed the clothing Ione wore.

Ione also wore what she'd called pants, though hers were a lighter color and seemed to fit her legs, whereas the one she'd shown Kazia for herself were baggier and seemed to be made of a different material. She had no idea how they'd look when worn, however.

The top she'd been wearing was fitted to her body, the neckline dipping down in a "V" and the sleeves just barely covering her shoulders and the tops of her biceps.

Top removed, Ione also wore one of the so-called bras. It was green and ended just below her small breasts, which were lovingly cupped in the little pockets. The bra fit tightly around her, and the straps that went over her shoulders crisscrossed over her upper back.

"Wow," Kazia murmured again, marveling at this new thing. "Why wear this?" she asked, looking down at the bra she once again held in her hands.

Ione pulled her top back on. "These come in a lot of different forms, but this is called a sports bra, as you can move more freely in it. It's more comfortable but will support you here." She lightly cupped her own breasts over the material of her top. She grinned. "It's a bit of a bear to get into, though."

Kazia raised her eyebrows as she nodded. "What is all this?" she asked, holding up the bra and indicating the other articles of clothing. "Is this just for us? Here in Yewa?"

Ione shook her head, that beautiful smile back in place. In fact, Kazia had truly never seen her look so happy and...*free*. She looked like at any given time she could break out into song, her energy so light.

The woman that Kazia knew—memories slowly

coming back—was a sweet woman, yes, but there had always been an underlying sense of stress or fear. Not this woman. It was intoxicating, and Kazia yearned for that for herself.

"Let's get you dressed."

Kazia allowed herself to essentially be turned into a life-sized doll. The bra was, in fact, quite the joint effort, however.

"You see," Ione explained as she worked. "As you know, there was a time before Britannia, before Greece or Rome. Right?" At Kazia's nod, she continued, holding out the pants for Kazia to step into. "Use my shoulder for balance," she offered. "Anyway, so that's called history. Well, the time of Rome, the time of Greece as you know it, and even the gladiators—"

She stopped when Kazia's head whipped up as she looked at her, surprised to hear that word come from her lips.

"Ankou showed me your life, Kazia," Ione explained softly. "I know where you've been." She lightly cupped Kazia's face with a hand before easing the waistline of the pants into place.

Kazia looked down at herself, her legs disappearing into the abyss that was the pants. She leaned over a bit to see her bare feet sticking out the other end. Her gaze returned to Ione's hands as they secured the button and pulled up the zipper.

"How does that feel?" she asked, looking up into Kazia's gaze.

Taking a moment to really feel the pants, she gave her a grin. "It feels weird to be so covered."

Ione gave her a sad smile as she grabbed the thing Ione had called a tank top. "Arms through here, head through here," she explained. "This," she said, indicating a little mark on the inside of the back part. "Goes in back."

Nodding in understanding, Kazia eased the garment over her head and Ione tugged it down over her bra-clad breasts until it covered all of her torso. Completely. Nothing showing. Nothing. She felt emotion rising as she adjusted her shoulders and arms, which were bare.

"What is it, Kazia?" Ione asked gently, hands resting on Kazia's tank-top-clad sides.

Kazia turned her head in shame when a tear escaped. She reached up and wiped it away. "Um," she managed, feeling a bit overwhelmed. Taking a deep breath, she turned back to look at the other woman. "Why am I so covered? Did I do something wrong?"

Ione shook her head slowly. "No," she said softly. "It's because you're a human being, worthy of the respect you deserve." She leaned up and left a kiss to Kazia's cheek. "Nobody can tell you how to dress again. Ankou just started with these so you could be covered and, hopefully, comfortable." She tugged lightly on the hem of the fitted tank top. "But after you get some sleep, we can go and you can pick out whatever you want. Or, if you want to run around naked. Whatever." She shrugged. "It's all up to you."

Looking down for a moment, Kazia swallowed hard, then let out a long, shaky breath. "I don't think I want to be naked ever again," she said quietly.

Ione took her in another hug, just holding her. "It's all up to you now."

Chapter Twenty-One

Slowly and blissfully, Kazia eased up out of the darkness into wakefulness. Her eyes opened and she was lying on her right side on an incredibly comfortable bed, blankets and sheets tucked around her. She wasn't cold, she wasn't hot, she just...*was*. Blinking a few times, she saw from the one window in the small bedroom that it was dark out. Still night? A huge, beautiful full moon smiled down upon the land.

Looking at that bright light for a moment, she smiled. It was so comforting. Selene, the moon was called in her motherland. She took to the skies when the sun retreated. But this...this felt different. It didn't feel like the gods shining light down upon the land to help a day continue, or to help farmers tend their crops or their orchards into the night. No, this felt like a comforting, watchful eye to ensure all was well. A beacon of welcome.

With a long, contented sigh, Kazia looked away and took in the bedroom. It was as she remembered it: dresser, as she learned it was called, with her clothing folded neatly atop it. She also saw the mirror that was mounted to the wall, which reflected the bed and the lone figure lying in it.

Kazia studied that figure, looking into the face, the eyes, and the crazy bed head that was shaggy, dark brown hair. Kazia saw something in her own eyes that she'd never seen before, and for just a moment it startled her.

She saw peace.

Studying those eyes for a long moment, not really recognizing the woman behind them, she saw not only peace, but also contentment and curiosity. That really surprised her. In her life, when she had it, curiosity could get her killed or punished, so it was pushed down in place of duty and orders and survival.

Looking away, she turned to her back and sat up, the covers falling to her waist. Ione had given her clothing to sleep in, a simple white top she'd called a T-shirt and extremely comfortable bottoms she'd called boxers. She brought her hands up and ran them through the crazy mop that was her hair. She needed a haircut. Maybe Ione had a knife she could borrow.

As if she'd heard her name in Kazia's thoughts, suddenly the other woman stepped up to the open bedroom door. She was so beautiful, Kazia thought. Again in her jeans and a casual women's T-shirt, her hair was pulled back in what Kazia had learned was called a ponytail.

She just looked so utterly fresh and young and happy. Kazia smiled just seeing that incredible natural beauty she had, amplified by the radiant light within.

"Good morning," Ione said with a welcoming smile. "I thought I heard you moving around."

Kazia looked at her current position, seated in the bed. "I'm awake," she said. "And I have sat up. So, I suppose it's a start." They shared a smile before Kazia indicated the window and moonlit darkness beyond. "Is it late?"

"In the day, yes," Ione grinned at Kazia's confusion. "It's always nighttime here, Kazia. It's that wonderful, quiet and peaceful time when it's just mellow and…" She shrugged. "I don't know. Just quiet."

Nodding, Kazia could agree with that, from the little she knew. "Was I sleeping long?" she asked, looking back to her friend, who entered the room and sat on the edge of the bed.

"Three weeks."

Kazia's eyes popped open. "What?"

The look in Ione's eyes was so soft and filled with understanding compassion. She reached over and placed a warm hand over one of the warrior's.

"It's completely normal," she assured. "The living say about the dead that now they're resting in peace. They're not wrong," she said, shaking her head. "You're still detoxing, Kazia. It's a process. Your soul went through so much, it, *you* need this time to really be able to let it all go." She squeezed the hand before removing her own. "Let yourself have the time you need. It's not a race, and you'll have many more bouts of these prolonged sleeps. It's your soul shedding all that was and is no longer needed."

Kazia nodded, looking down at her hands, which rested on her blanket-covered legs. "So, now what?" She met Ione's patient gaze again. "And, am I stopping you from going, Ione? I don't want that."

"Don't you worry about that," the other woman said, pushing up from the bed. "And, as for what now, there are some people who are very excited to see you. So," she said, clapping her hands for emphasis. "You are going to get up, get showered—I'll show you how— and then we'll go. Okay?"

A little nervous, Kazia chewed on her bottom lip, but nodded. "Um, I..." She chewed on that lip again, unsure if she should say it.

"What?"

"I'm hungry," she admitted shyly, sparing a

glance to the standing woman.

Ione's grin was large and her eyes filled with mischief. "Then, I guess it's a darn good thing we have a banquet being set up in your honor, huh?" She giggled like a little girl in her excitement. "Come on!"

≈≈≈≈

The shower experience had been amazing and very different than what Ione had told her was called the Shower of Sorrow, when her soul had literally vomited her pain out.

This shower had been in a shower stall, and now, hair slicked back from her face as it dried, she grabbed the neckline of her tank top and, for the fourth time since putting it on, surreptitiously sniffed it.

Ione said her clothing had been "laundered," and now it smelled like she was a walking, talking field of flowers. She had never smelled so good.

"What?" she muttered, noting Ione's amused gaze as they made their way out of the small house, which also had a very small kitchen attached. It was very much like a little bungalow and was cute as could be.

"Nothing at all," Ione responded, that little smile still in place.

The street was filled with the same style of little house, each one tucked into its own little bit of land. She noticed in some lights could be seen through the windows, others were dark. She didn't recognize the style of these houses. She'd been all over the Roman Empire, and of course Greece, but had never seen anything like it.

And the street beyond, the "night" beyond,

was so quiet and still. So peaceful and safe. The big, welcoming moon above glazed everything with a silver sheen like a thin layer of silver. Even the long, shiny dark brown hair that flowed down Ione's back. It was beautiful.

"Is this only for Yewa?" she asked, indicating the bungalows they were passing. "The style? The shower in your house?"

Ione shook her head. "We didn't really get to talk much because you crashed." She playfully nudged Kazia's shoulder with her own. "But I told you there was history before our time," she said, Kazia nodding at the refresher. "Well, Yewa is not just our time, Kazia, or that before us, but *all* of time. Time doesn't end. You and I were in our own time for that lifetime, but Yewa is eternal. So, there are people here who have died in future times, long after a time that we knew." She glanced over at Kazia as they walked. "Make sense?"

Kazia was quiet for a long moment, hands tucked into the incredibly handy things called pockets in her pants, and nodded. "It does." She glanced over at her companion. "What you wear, the jeans and the T-shirt…another time?"

Ione nodded. "Yes. Some people here prefer to dress as they did in their life." She shrugged. "Either they feel more comfortable that way, like it, whatever. But I, for one," she added, pointing at herself with an impish grin on her lips. "Will never wear a damn dress again."

A bark of laughter escaped Kazia's lips, to *her* surprise and obvious delight of Ione. "Sorry," she muttered, sparing a sheepish glance to Ione.

"Why?" Ione turned and walked backward so she faced Kazia. "Be you, Kazia!" She grinned up at her.

"Be free. Laugh, enjoy who you were always meant to be."

"How do you know what and who that is?" Kazia asked softly, truly baffled. She so longed for the very freedom she saw in Ione's every move and every expression. She just had no idea how to go about it.

Moving back in next to her, Ione wrapped her arms around Kazia's. "It takes time," she said. "You'll get there."

⁂

The large building they finally came to was made of stone. Ione explained that it was called a great hall and was something out of what was called the medieval era. Intrigued, she eagerly followed Ione inside to see that it was a huge room, long and with high ceilings veined in stone. Two massive fireplaces burned on either end, the firebox easily large enough to accommodate four grown men standing shoulder to shoulder.

Long wood tables with equally long wood benches—which she was familiar with from her army days—were lined up in three long, neat rows. The center table was lined with every single dish of food imaginable, more being brought out from a swinging door to the right. The two flanking rows of tables were already filled with seated women and men. They were talking, laughing, and, it seemed, just having a wonderful time.

One turned and saw Kazia and Ione enter, and he bellowed, "She's here!"

Eyes growing wide and wanting to go into a defensive posture, Kazia felt a hand to her arm, as if centering her. Swallowing, she stood where she'd stopped and watched as every single person there, young and old, rose from their seats and stood next to the long benches.

They began to applaud, all of them looking at her. There were cat whistles that rent the air shrilly and cheers that echoed in the cavernous space.

Confused, she looked to Ione. "Why are they doing this?"

"It's all for you," Ione said, loud enough to be heard over it all. "All these people," she said, indicating those applauding, "They were there, Kazia. All of us"—she placed her hand on her own chest—"lost our lives that day. *These* are the people you protected and you fought for. They were all overjoyed to hear you were actually one of us the whole time." She smiled. "They wanted to thank you for all you tried to do for them that day and all the time you were there at the garrison."

With this new information, Kazia took in the faces. Though they were dressed in all spectrum of time and bathed, she saw it. She saw the old man she used to help get water from the river for. She saw the woman who had twin baby boys that she'd held one or both of more than once while their mother was pulling laundry from the line.

She had to look away as tears hit her eyes when she saw the little boy, no older than four, who used to run up to her every time she was on patrol and would give her a stone. She never knew why but always took them and picked him up to give him a hug. And as she stood there, trying to wipe away her tears, she felt a tug on the hem of her shirt.

Looking down, she saw him grinning up at her. He had no stone, but he held his arms up, and she immediately picked him up and grinned at him. As if him running up to her had broken the dam, they all made their way over to her, some slapping her on the back, others shaking her hand while many gave her a meaningful hug, which she eagerly returned.

She knew these faces and she'd cared about every damn one of them. These had been good, hardworking people, and they'd been massacred that day. The hardest part of that pill for her to swallow was that more than once she and the army she'd been forced to march with had done the very same thing. But now, these people, once upon a time effectively her captives, tugged her to sit with them, eat with them, and rejoice with them that better days had begun.

How was that possible?

⚜ ⚜ ⚜ ⚜

"Try this, love," an older woman said, placing yet another new food on Kazia's plate.

"So," the man who had been telling yet another story about Kazia said.

She brought up a hand and covered her eyes with an embarrassed groan, making those around her laugh.

"And," he continued, stepping to the outside of the long bench they were all seated at. "I tell you this is true." He put his arms out as though wrapped around a barrel, hands not touching. "Tree," he said, using the finger on one hand to indicate the empty circle his arms made. "This one," he continued, nodding across the table at Kazia, who was looking at him through her fingers. "Says, 'Where you want it?'"

Those around them began to laugh, Kazia groaning again.

"I says, 'Well, uh, how about over there so I can

chop it up?'" His face took on an exaggerated expression of exertion as he slowly lifted his circled arms, replete with sound effects as if uprooting the tree they were wrapped around, then turned to face his left direction with said tree. "'Okay,'" he said, imitating Kazia's voice. "'Tell me if I'm going to trip on anything.'" He lumbered away carrying his tree.

Kazia burst into laughter along with everyone else. "It was not that big!" she protested through her laughter.

The man grinned and returned to his seat, reaching across the table to slap Kazia on the shoulder before sitting.

"In all seriousness," he said. "Though I was telling the truth!" he insisted. "Kazia, you were always so good to me and my wife. Which," he added, nodding to the woman who sat next to him. "For some crazy reason, she's decided she still loves me in Yewa."

"I'm in charge here," she quipped, earning grins and laughter, especially from the women.

He smiled at her, stealing a kiss before turning back to Kazia. "I never forgot that. You were nothin' like I'd ever seen, man or woman. But," he added. "You weren't any more free as a Roman soldier than we were as the conquered locals. Know that meant a heap to all of us, your kindness."

"Hear, hear!" someone exclaimed.

Kazia looked down at her plate, off which she'd eaten more food than she had in her entire life. She couldn't keep the smile off her lips, relief and perhaps even a bit of pride washing through her. She'd cared, damn it.

The huge gathering was coming to a close, people saying their goodbyes or making plans to meet up at another occasion. The man who had been telling whoppers about Kazia's feats of strength at the garrison—admittedly all true—indicated he wanted her to walk with him.

She did, the two heading outside of the great hall. It was so gorgeous outside, insects chirping away in unseen hiding places and a gentle evening breeze ruffling Kazia's hair.

The man, whom Kazia had come to learn was named Brian, glanced over at her. He gave her a wide smile before he clapped an affectionate hand to her shoulder as they walked. He looked to be no older than thirty, beard a bit long but not unkempt. His long, light brown hair was pulled back in a series of braids. It was a style she'd remembered from her time in Britannia, though he was dressed more like Ione, in jeans and a T-shirt.

"You know," he finally said, voice softer as opposed to the loud, exuberant fellow he'd been in the hall, entertaining those around them with his stories. "The last thing I saw that day was you going after them two Roman soldiers." He met her gaze, his blue eyes filled with respect. "I saw what that monster had done to Ione, those soldiers not doing a damn thing to stop him. Saw the whole thing."

His hand fell away from Kazia's shoulder, and he looked away, clearing his throat. It was clear it had affected him deeply. It was her turn to reach out to him, squeezing his shoulder in mutual understanding of the most horrible day of their lives, and frankly, the end for them both.

"I was just about gone myself," Brian continued. "So I couldn't do a damn thing to help her. But you came in, and…" He whistled through his teeth. "I already liked you and respected what I knew you were capable of, but I have never respected another living person like I did you that day, Kazia." He met her gaze. "Still do. Was so glad you made those bastards pay for what they'd allowed to happen to her."

Kazia didn't say anything for a long time, needing a moment to absorb what he'd said, but also her feelings about all of it. She knew she still had a lot of healing and self-forgiveness to deal with for that, but the process had begun.

"That was a horrible day," she finally said. "A horrible, horrible day."

"Look," Brian said, stopping their strolling with a hand to Kazia's arm. "I never really got to know you as a person, and I'd really like to." He grinned. "Especially that whole tree uprooting thing." With a wink he added, "Think my wife would find that sexy."

Kazia grinned and chuckled. "Some things cannot be taught."

Brian laughed. "Well, all serious, Danielle and I want to have you over for supper. To say thank you again, absolutely, but really just to start over and get to know you." He tucked his thumbs in the belt loops of his jeans. "We were all thrilled Ione waited for you, as I knew you'd need that. And honestly," he added with a shrug. "I think she needed that, too. Closure from that day, you know?"

Kazia nodded. "I definitely know."

"But she'll be leaving soon enough, and we just really want you to know you ain't alone, Kazia. You got good people here who care about you. And, we want you in our lives." He looked her in the eyes, his so open and honest. "'Kay?"

She gave him a big smile and held out her hand. When he took it, she gripped his in a firm shake. "Okay."

"Excellent!" He pulled her toward him with their clasped hands as leverage and into a hug. "Welcome home, Kazia," he said, slapping her back with his free hand. "We've all been waitin' on ya."

Chapter Twenty-Two

She met his gaze. "And, she's okay?"

Willem nodded. "She made it through the Shower of Sorrow, hardest part by far. Now, she'll sleep off and on, sometimes for weeks or months at a time."

"How long will this take, for her to fully detox?"

He shrugged, the red streaks of smokelike energy washing over his face before once again leaving him in darkness. "Could take months, it could take years, Senara. Depends on how much she needs." He shrugged again. "She'll have days where she feels amazing, totally free, but then will be hit all over again with something that is nearly crippling." He squeezed her shoulder. "It takes time."

Nodding, Senara squared her shoulders, needing to focus. She was currently wearing the mask of a man, big shoulders, big arms and hands, and the leathery skin true to that of a mariner. She had concerns, so had her blade mounted to her back underneath the mask, easily pulled out as the mask was pulled off.

"Ready?" she asked him. At his nod, barely seen, she stepped through the door...

...and into Brittany along the docks. Willem's surveillance had turned up evidence that it was where Bahutha's cult was largely focusing their hunt. With ships coming in from around Europe, those immigrating to Brittany's shores for a new start, many had children upon them.

Not only that, but with the gateway to Bowhar off

Brittany, many of the blood felt compelled to come this way. And, that was what his goons wanted: the more powerful the blood, the more powerful the energy for Bahutha's plan, still as yet unknown.

"I'm heading out toward the fish market," Willem said inside her head.

Nodding, Senara continued on, her unseen colleague and friend heading off. She could feel the morning sun on the bald head of her mask, wondering how on earth men could take it without a hat or covering of some sort. She wore no cloak, as it didn't make sense for her role. Her guy had just gotten of a fishing ship and, as much as she hated it, smelled every bit the part. Willem had a bit too much fun helping her spritz on some fish oil before they'd left.

She made her way to the waterfront to look for the girl named Enori. She knew Brielle was particularly worried about her. She was the perfect type of victim for the cult—alone, not a soul in the world to notice she was missing.

If the girl was found, Ankou had given Senara permission to ask the girl to accompany her to the Underground for safekeeping until this was over. If she refused, he'd given permission to take her, just to keep her safe, then happily return her wherever she wished to go.

The dark gray eyes of the fisherman swept the area, not seeing Enori or anyone else, for that matter. The waterfront was eerily quiet, in fact. Hands on hips, she turned in a slow circle, taking in a panoramic view of the entire harbor and market beyond. There were people moving about, ships coming in and being unloaded and loaded. There were people in the market buying, selling, and haggling, the dense forest just beyond the market.

But underlying all of the normal was something very *abnormal*. It was a feeling, an almost expectant heaviness in the air. And, as she listened, she could hear something…a hum? No, that wasn't quite right. Her booted toe began to tap softly in rhythm with what she was hearing but mostly feeling. She paid attention to that tapping and realized that it was in time with a heartbeat: *Thump, thump. Thump, thump.*

"What is that?" she whispered. Instantly her gaze fell down to the ground at her feet. She could feel the soft, almost undiscernible beat beneath the leather soles of her boots.

"You all right, lad?"

Senara's mask looked up to see a fisherman standing ten feet from her, a heavy coil of rope held upon his shoulder. "Feel that?" the mask asked, voice gruff.

The fisherman stopped and seemed to take note of his surroundings, eyes drifting randomly as he was clearly using his other senses. Finally, his gaze returned to hers. "Like a rumble," he said, now using his eyes as he looked around, mainly to the docks. "No ship ran inta nothin,'" he muttered in observation.

Senara wasn't sure if she was relieved or not that this ordinary man felt it, too, even if he had a different term to describe it. He'd felt it.

"Storm comin' in," her mask said to the man, storm-colored eyes looking up into the cloudy blue of the morning.

"Aye," the other man said. "Careful today, lad, if'n ye got little ones."

This caught Senara's attention. The head of her mask whipped back in the other man's direction. He studied him for a moment before his large bulk walked in that direction.

"What news?" he asked. "Been out to sail." He nodded toward the ocean beyond the harbor.

The other man heaved his burden a bit higher onto his shoulder, bracing it with both hands as he explained.

"Littlin's begun to go missin,'" the man said, voice lowering and his gaze moving quickly to those on the docks, as if to make sure he wasn't being overheard. "Some," he continued, looking back to the big man standing in front of him, "are sayin' it's Manannán, angry too many fish are bein' taken from his waters and not enough thanks given back." He shook a shaggy head. "Our gods wouldn't do that, lad. I don't believe it."

"Why would they say him?"

"Because it's mostly happenin' round here." The man indicated the docks and market beyond. "Me wife and I made extra offerins to him, but I don't believe it," he said again. "You got little ones, especially girls…" He slapped the mask hard on the shoulder. "Be watchin' over them, lad. Be safe."

"And to you and yorn," the mask offered.

Senara watched the man turn and head back to his task, easing the heavy rope down to the docks before trotting back up the gangplank of the ship he'd apparently just disembarked after it landed ashore.

"Get to the market, now!"

Not asking Willem any questions, Senara turned the hulk of her mask in that direction and took off at a sprint. So used to her own body size and density, it was always difficult to recalibrate in an instant the energy needed to propel a much larger mass than her own.

Adding more fuel to the fire, she sped up when she saw what was happening.

Only so much Willem could do on the earth plane, he was doing his damnedest to stop the man who had the screaming, wiggling girl slung over his shoulder. A woman, face bloodied and on the ground, was screeching for help. Clearly her daughter, as the two were spitting images of each other.

As the man was doing his best to make his way out of the market, items kept "magically" flying at him from booths, sellers staring on stunned, both by what had just happened but also by their wares flying with an invisible hand to hit the man in the head and body to try and slow his steps.

"Take her!" her mask roared to one of those who seemed frozen in stunned inaction. She grabbed the merchant by the front of his shirt and shoved him in the direction of the fleeing man, she following. The seller grabbed the girl, who squealed anew as he ripped her out of the man's hands and tried to hold on to her. He took an elbow in the face from the terrified girl for his troubles.

Knowing the girl was away from him and free, Senara's mask all but tackled the man who had taken her. He fell hard, grunting as his head plowed into the thick post that was part of the construction of one of the market booths at the end of the row. The bastard had almost made it out free and clear, as thick, dense woods lay just steps beyond.

Turning over, the man tried to use the blade of his dagger to stab her, but the mask used a huge fist to deliver a powerful blow to the man's jaw, again knocking his head against that tree-trunk-sized post.

So angry she could slit the man's throat with

the power of her fingernails right there, Senara forced herself to calm so she wouldn't lose her mask. Instead, she grabbed the man by the front of his tunic and yanked him to his feet so hard he nearly fell into the mask, who stood easily six inches taller.

The smaller man looked up at him with huge, terrified brown eyes. "I had no choice!" he exclaimed, blood and a tooth dribbling out of his mouth with his protestation.

"You're comin' with me," the mask said. Looking over his shoulder, Senara saw that the girl had been reunited with her sobbing mother. "Somebody escort the lass home!" he bellowed.

"Let's go before you kill someone," Willem said.

Senara smirked. Not far off from the truth. She was so angry in that moment, she was shaking. Looking back to the man she still held in the iron grip, she shook him, her mask's face within inches of the smaller man's.

"You're comin' with me," he said again. "Fight me, and I gut ya."

⁂

Willem had run ahead to speak to Ankou. A door had been created that went directly to the Underground. But, before taking him through that door, the mask had tied the man's hands and blindfolded him. Once he was contained, Senara's mask led him through the door Ankou had created…

…and into a tunnel. Once inside, the mask removed the blindfold. The man looked around, looking even more terrified than before, finding himself in a very different place than last he'd seen. This, of course, was the point. They were trying to get him to understand that though he may fear the entity he was working for, Bahutha was no match for what he'd stepped in.

The mask used huge hands to turn the man around by his shoulders, nearly sending him face first into the wall of the tunnel before the man stopped himself with his tied hands to the cold stone. Without a word or issue, he began to walk in the direction he was shoved.

The tunnels were lit by torchlight every fifty feet or so, leaving deep pockets of shadow in between. Willem had informed Senara she was to take him to Brielle's chambers in the Underground, so that was where they were headed.

She created doors as they went, the only place where Ankou were able to do that on their own. So much energy flowed through the Underground—what was used to create a door—it could be corralled and utilized. More than once a day Senara wished she had the ability to self-create the energy necessary to do so above ground.

But, alas, that was Ankou's specialty. Sometimes if you asked real nice he'd make one specific to a situation, but not often. Though she understood why he didn't want random doors lying around, it would still be oh-so-helpful.

They were on the last leg of their little journey, and Senara made sure it was a long one. She wanted this idiot to feel he was walking to his own death. Depending on how he behaved, perhaps not too far off the mark.

Just as Brielle, the friendly little Druid Firestarter,

had set up her chamber, as they neared it, torches, one by one, lit around the space. Revealed was a stone chamber with a sleeping nook, bedding folded neatly atop a sleeping pallet tucked within. There was a stone table carved right out of the rock wall and two stone stools carved on either side. Little nooks were also carved out for shelving. Many of Brielle's little pouches of this or that were tucked inside them.

The centerpiece of the room, and certainly for today's visit, was a stone slab seemingly magically balanced upon a narrow stone column. The slab reached to the average man's waist and was plenty large enough for a grown man to lay upon, and one would very soon.

The captive looked around once they'd entered the space, then turned to look at the big, bald man who had followed him inside.

His eyes grew wide, nearly whimpering when Senara's mask dissolved, leaving a very angry woman behind. She glared at him using the full power of her eyes, no doubt the color of flame as the torchlight reflected off the silvery rage. His mouth worked as though he were trying to form words, but none would come forth.

"Sit," she ordered, palm slapping against the smooth, cold stone top of the slab.

When he didn't move, clearly frozen in his fear, she reached behind her and grabbed the grip of her sword. She slowly eased it out of its scabbard, never taking her eyes off him.

Oh boy, she thought when she saw the smoky mist that was beginning to ooze through the solid stone of the chamber wall next to the sleeping nook behind and just to the left of the man's periphery.

His eyes were so riveted on her hand and the blade she was taking her sweet time drawing that he wasn't even aware of the nightmare image that was forming behind him as the smoke began to solidify. The black cloak was solid and visible now, and Senara knew what was hidden within the depths of the deep hood and oversized sleeves.

The man's eyes were jittery as he saw Senara looking past him and no doubt felt the immensity of the energy that now stood tall behind him. With a little mewl of fear, he slowly turned. His entire body stiffened, but it was when that hood was slid back with one quick, fluid movement and the skeleton face was revealed that the man let loose of his bladder.

And when the very face of death itself opened its mouth far wider than would ever be feasible to roar at the little man standing before it, the man let loose a shrill, heart-wrenching scream that Senara honestly had no idea a male's vocal range was capable of. His hair literally blew back from the power of Ankou's rage.

A moment later, the man went down like a ton of bricks, legs collapsing beneath him. Senara looked down at him before she quirked an eyebrow at the being across the stone slab from her who, like a chameleon and their mask, slowly shrank down into the pudgy middle-aged man in his monochromatic outfit of shades of brown.

"If you killed him…" she muttered.

Amused brown eyes met hers. "Then I'll be getting information from him all by my lonesome in Yewa."

She smirked, watching as Ankou used his abilities to lift the man, still out cold, up and onto the stone slab without laying a physical finger on him.

"Goodness," a woman said as she entered the room. "Heard that one all the way in Ryarch."

Senara glanced over to see Macha and Brielle and another of the super Ancients called Arali enter. Arali was the oldest of the supers, a man of the Sumerian peoples. He was around the same height as Brielle yet powerfully built. His skin tone wasn't as dark as Jabari's but was much darker than the paler tone of the women and Ankou. His head was shaved bald, though heavy dark brows set off his intense, deep-set brown eyes.

A purist, Arali still wore the kaunakes of his time. It was essentially a skirt made of a fleece-like material that reached to just below his knees, denoting he had not been royalty, as theirs were worn at a much longer length. He was bare chested, and his feet were encased in the most basic of sandals: leather sole and leather toe loop with ankle strap to keep the shoe in place.

He was an incredibly intense man who rarely left Ryarch, so Senara was stunned to see him with the other two Druids. He looked at Senara, giving her a nod of acknowledgment before turning his focus back to the man who lay upon the stone slab, still out cold. Everyone stepped back to give him his space, including Ankou on the other side.

Arali walked around the slab, taking in the man from every angle. He reached out and touched this part of him or that only for a split second before moving on. Finally, he moved back around until he was where he'd started, at the top of the slab and the man's head.

He placed his hands upon the man's cheeks and closed his eyes as he bowed his head a bit, his forehead above the man's slightly parted lips and Arali's closed mouth above the man's forehead.

He seemed to be feeling for something or trying to sense something, but finally he readjusted himself so his mouth was over the unconscious man's, sealing their lips. The man's chest expanded, almost to the point of looking like it was going to burst, before with a sound like wind whistling through the trees, it was sucked down as Arali's cheeks grew concave, the man's ribs showing through his clothing as he lay still.

Arali's own cheeks puffed out, chipmunk style. As he was doing this, Brielle was making a small fire upon the top of her stone table, chanting softly until it exploded upward into a tall column of fire then whooshed outward until it was a wall of flame against the stone.

She quickly moved out of the way as the Sumerian lifted his head. As if expelling water through pursed lips, a spewed stream of black smoke shot out across the space and against the wall of fire that would act as a "screen."

Similar to what had happened in the cave with Brielle, pictures came to life in those flames. They were taken on a journey through tunnels, all drawn in the inky blackness that was the smoke pulled from the man's body and released by the Sumerian's. Death nooks, much like the one behind all of them, used for sleeping purposes in the Underground.

But what was incredibly disconcerting was when the journey continued past the death nooks, outlines of skeletal dead in each, as the cavernous space filled with grinning skulls. They were stacked upon each other in neat, macabre rows, filling the entirety of the massive space.

The journey moved on past that and down more

turns, left then right then right again and another left before straight ahead. There, at the very end, young girls were tied to each other, arm around arm, around a massive bonfire, an entire circle of them.

With a *whoosh,* black flames shot out from the bonfire, the orange flames of Brielle's own firewall melting through the image until there was nothing but the original small fire she'd created upon the tabletop.

Senara could only stare. She was stunned and felt shell-shocked. Looking to Brielle, she saw a look of focused determination on her beautiful face that Senara had never seen before. Her normal calm was gone. She was ready to do battle.

They all were.

Chapter Twenty-Three

The quartet—though only three seen—made their way through the dense forest that lay beyond the docks and market near Brittany's harbor. After Arali had sucked the darkness out of the man that Bahutha had steadily been feeding him, Ankou and Macha grilled him for every single bit of knowledge and information he possessed.

He'd talked mostly freely, though it was clear he was scared to death. Truth was, it wasn't clear if he was scared of the two gods facing him down or the one he was betraying.

Now, he was leading the way to the mouth of the cave where he claimed he and the rest of the "chosen" were staying. They hunkered down there and awaited orders from Bahutha. It was also where the children were being kept.

They were all little girls, he'd explained. Ten of them, though the plan was for more than twenty. Fistful of shirt in her hand, Senara had warned him if *any* of those little girls had been harmed in *any* way, she'd be collecting scrotums.

Alas, he'd assured her that Bahutha had threatened the men with worse, as the purity of the girls was the point. Time would tell, she supposed. For now, he was on a very tight leash, and he knew it. One lie, one false move or one misdirection, and he'd be holding his Adam's apple.

She could feel the fear coming off him as he led the way.

Her sword was drawn and ready as they hurried along a path, beaten to clear by wildlife and booted feet. Finally, the cave's mouth came into view. It was a small entrance, a grown man nearly bent over at the waist to enter. Senara stopped his progress, again taking him by a handful of the front of his shirt. Wide brown eyes met hers.

"You best be leading us the right way," she murmured, her icy gaze freezing him to the spot. "Understand?"

He nodded vigorously. "Aye," he whispered.

Shoving him away from her with disgust, he barely caught himself on a tree before he did a face-plant in the vegetation. Senara absolutely despised this weak little man and everything he stood for with Bahutha. She had a debt to settle with the God of Chaos on behalf of Kazia, and she intended to collect in full.

Again, she grabbed the man, this time by his scruff. "You go after me," she said.

She had no idea where they were heading, and the last thing they needed was for their captive, who assumedly knew where to go, to take off once he was through. She glanced over her shoulder at Brielle, catching her eye.

The Druid nodded, clearly understanding her thoughts. She knew her friend felt the exact same way she did on all this and was just as passionately committed to getting those girls out, especially since they had a suspicion Enori was with them.

Senara knew that, for whatever reason, Brielle had a specific bond with that girl. And with the knowledge that she, too, was being held for horrific reasons, Brielle was even more determined.

Though Brielle was beautiful, soft-spoken, and

came off as very sweet, which she was, it was a fool who took her nature for weakness. She'd light a person on fire like a torch with a wave of her hand and watch them burn before she let them hurt anyone she cared about or who was unable to defend themselves.

Bending down, Senara was all senses as she ducked into the cave opening. The outer one opened into a bit of a small antechamber with a much higher ceiling and wider entrance into the innards. She stood out of the way but ducked down again to be seen by Brielle. She waved them in.

Once the other two were in, all able to stand fully erect, Brielle brushed the hood of her dark gray cloak back and brought up her right hand. Opening the fingers, a small incandescent orb sat upon her palm. It was roughly two inches in diameter, but in the darkness of the tunnel system the man had told them about, it was plenty to give them enough light without making themselves a target like a torch would. Plus, it could be easily hidden should they need to go dark.

The orb was handed off to Senara, who held it in her left hand, her sword gripped within her right. A second orb appeared, this one Brielle keeping hold of. The man looked between the two women with wide, stunned eyes. Senara smirked at him.

"You chose to back the wrong horse, buddy," she muttered.

The orb in her hand felt similar to a bubble from a child's bubble wand just before it popped. The gentle luminescent glow could be extinguished in a heartbeat with the simple closing of her fist, yet it was much heartier than it would seem, as neither wind nor blowing on it would extinguish its brilliance.

She focused on what lay beyond the larger

entrance, which she led the way through. From what their captive had said, he was part of a sect of self-styled Bahutha guards that numbered twenty.

In other words, a group of thugs who couldn't succeed at anything else and needed to feel a bit of control. And with Bahutha being the ultimate in manipulation and finding self-serving uses for the human, it was a beautiful and symbiotic partnership.

The tunnel they were heading into was long and rough-cut. Several areas had a low ceiling or extremely narrow walkway. Neither woman very large, both had little extra clearance. How on earth did any of these men easily pass through here?

One good thing, Senara supposed, was that it formed a great bottleneck to keep intruders, like themselves, slowed down. She waited until she knew the other two had also gotten through the narrow chasm. Brielle was bringing up the rear, so the man was out first. He leaned over to speak quietly in Senara's ear.

"Just past the bend to the right up ahead, we'll reach the first of the little caves where we all sleep," he told her.

"How many are in here at any given time?" she asked in return.

Shrugging, he shook his head. "It depends on what our Lord needs us to do."

She nodded, catching Brielle's gaze again before continuing on. She nearly jumped out of her skin when suddenly Willem's voice sounded in her head.

"There are four men in the caves," he told her. "Two asleep, and the other two are eating."

"Are they all together?" she asked softly.

"The two sleeping aren't, the two eating are. And, I've found the girls."

"And...?" She was almost afraid of the answer.

"They're okay. Terrified, but okay. They're being held together in a jail-type thing."

Senara's eyes fell closed for a moment before she let out a long, relieved breath and paused. Looking back to Brielle, she caught her eye again. She held up two fingers and pantomimed sleeping, then two more fingers and pantomimed eating. At Brielle's nod of understanding, Senara turned back around and continued on.

Sure enough, just around the bend was a small cave-like room. It was pitch-black inside, but from what Senara could see with her little orb, one man was curled up on his side, covered by a blanket as he slept on a bed pallet upon the stone floor. A sword lay on the floor very close to his hand. Several other pallets were in the room, some rolled up and the blanket folded atop it while others looked as if the person had thrown the blanket off them when they'd gotten up and walked away.

There were enough bed pallets in there for ten inhabitants. So, she assumed this was sleeping man number one. Turning to Brielle, she lifted a finger to indicate this. Grabbing their captive, she brought him close to her face.

"Keep your mouth shut and she will not hurt him. Say a word and alert him, you and he die." At the vigorous nod from him, Senara looked to Brielle, who moved to stand at the entrance to the cave.

She lightly clapped her hands together, the orb vanishing. When she pulled them apart again, a cat's cradle of fire spread out between them, connected to each palm. Throwing her hands wider apart, it expanded until it was the size of the crude doorway into the cave.

With steady and careful movements, she placed it in the doorway, lips moving the entire time as she silently chanted the words for the result she was looking for.

Never tiring of watching the Druid work, Senara's eyes were wide in awe. The fire frame in place, Brielle dropped her hands and turned to the two who looked on. Her beautiful features danced in shadow and light as the inch-thick lines of fire danced and sparked.

"He will not hear nor see what happens beyond this border," she explained. "Should he wake, he will not be able to leave this room but will not be harmed."

The man swallowed and nodded, looking on in horrified awe. "Aye."

"One down, three to go," Senara murmured before turning and heading onward again.

The light of the fire gate lit the way for a bit, allowing Senara to see farther down than the light orb. She saw a fork in the tunnel coming. She reached out with her senses beyond her eyes and ears. She realized that the heartbeat she'd felt beneath her feet that day on the waterfront she was feeling again. It was in the air, and though silent, it reverberated through her body.

Stopping, she looked both ways, her attention drawn to the right-hand tunnel. Gasping, it hit her that depending on how far it stretched out, that tunnel would be heading beneath the market and toward Bowhar. It couldn't be possible, could it?

"The girls are that way," the man offered, his finger pointing to the tunnel Senara was so drawn to.

She looked at him, studying his face for any sign of deception. Seeing none, she looked past him to see Brielle already looking at her. The two had an entire conversation in the span of three heartbeats, agreeing.

Brielle walked to the entrance of the other tunnel to the left and, with a *whoosh* left a fire burning that filled the entire archway. The man's eyes nearly popped out of his head, the flames reflected in their shock.

He looked to Brielle. "Will they burn to death?" he gasped.

"Not if they don't touch the fire," she quipped.

Smirking, Senara continued down the right tunnel. Everything was buzzing inside her, and she had no idea why. It felt like she was walking toward an immense amount of energy, like an electrified gate. Her palm was sweating as it held the grip of her sword. She adjusted her fingers, the little orb in her other palm leading the way.

"I hear you guys," Willem said. "I'm at the bend that's coming up in about one hundred feet."

"All right," Senara whispered in return, still not trusting to be too loud. The tunnel they were in was narrower than the previous ones. It felt claustrophobic, and she had to take several deep breaths to not let her anxiety kick in. "How far down are the girls?"

"Not far past the bend," Willem assured.

As promised, they reached the bend, and she felt a cold breeze brush across her face and knew it was Willem, letting her know he was there. They continued on, her friend next to her. Though she couldn't see him of course, she could feel him. It didn't help that he dropped the temperature about twenty degrees wherever he was on the earth plane. And, with it already being cooler in the underground depths, she could see her breath.

As they made their way farther down this tunnel, which was indeed headed right toward Bowhar, she could hear soft crying and other little voices trying to comfort. Her anger grew with each step. It looked like directly up ahead was a dead end, the glow of the orb in her hand showing the rough stone of the wall, little pockets of shadow forming in the pockmarked surface from time and erosion.

She gasped, feeling completely nauseous when she saw the wood already built for the bonfire, right there at the end where the tunnel widened a bit. It was exactly as had been shown in the little presentation Arali offered that day in Brielle's chamber in the Underground. It was large and sturdy, ready for the intended fate of the girls.

Looking to her left, she saw iron bars that formed the door. The little whimpers and voices were just beyond, and when the light of her orb was noticed, they grew louder, the fear from these babies absolutely palpable.

Feeling a touch to her arm, Senara turned and saw Brielle next to her. The Druid said nothing, simply gently pushed her aside and stepped in front of the bars.

She raised a hand as if to wave, but instantly the cries quieted. "Time to go, my sweets," she said softly. She glanced back to Senara, as the iron door was locked.

Stepping forward again, Senara didn't look into the black maw beyond the bars, as she knew she'd gut the man next to her if she saw those terrified little faces looking back at her. Instead, she felt for the tumblers in the lock with her mind, concentrating on sending a little burst of energy to each one until, with a loud metallic click, the lock disengaged.

Senara pulled the bars open, Brielle immediately stepping in once more. "Come to me, my babies," she said softly, using that tone that lulled a body into complete calm and obedience. They didn't need a terrified little girl taking off in uncontrolled terror.

Within moments, ten little girls, who were all filthy and looked to be in the range of eight to ten years old, swarmed around her. It reminded Senara of a mother duck and all her ducklings gathering. And yes, one of them was little Enori.

She looked up at Senara, and something passed between them in that moment. Yes, this child would be something great someday, Senara thought. She could feel the power emanating off her like a pulse.

Senara realized that the intensity of energy she'd felt was the combined power of these little girls as well as whatever lay beyond that stone wall at tunnel's end. She could feel it in her bones, and it filled her with a sense of awe and foreboding.

Something caught her eye. Her head whipped in the direction of the bonfire structure and saw… something…walking toward the wall at the end of the tunnel. It was like a colorless humanoid shape. She only noticed it because the rough stone of the wall shimmered a bit within the confines. As it got closer to the wall, which on the other side seemed to Senara to be the source of that strange heartbeat she felt, the figure began to glow very dimly.

It was just the outline of that humanoid shape, as if one of Brielle's little orbs had been used as glowing chalk to trace the figure. From size and shape, she realized it was Willem. She took a step in that direction, unable to take her eyes off him. He walked toward the wall as if in a daze.

"Willem?" she called to him. He didn't respond or react in any way. A sense of dread began to fill her as she took another step. "Willem? What's wrong?" And, what strange power was making him glow and visible on the earth plane?

"Oh no," their captive hissed. "Oh no!"

Senara's head whipped back to look at him. He stood on the other side of Brielle and the little girls who surrounded her. Huge, terrified eyes looked from woman to woman, then to Willem.

"He knows we're here," he whispered harshly. "He knows we're here!" He turned and sprinted off into the darkness, frantic footfalls heard echoing off the stone.

Senara's first instinct was to go after him, but it didn't matter now. She had the feeling they were dealing with something far bigger than that little bastard. Besides, he'd done his job. She turned back to Willem in time to see him walk up to and right through the wall.

"Willem!" She ran around the piled wood and to the wall beyond, hands slapping against the very solid stone. She looked everywhere, looking for maybe a hidden door, even an Ankou door. Nothing.

"He is collecting them."

Surprised to hear the sweet little voice, Senara glanced over her shoulder to see Enori looking at her from where she still stood by Brielle. "What?"

"He is collecting them," Enori said again.

"Who, sweetheart?" Brielle asked, her fingers trailing over long, matted, and filthy light blond hair.

Enori looked up at her. "The bad man."

Senara slowly walked back over to them, her gaze never leaving Enori. "Collecting what?" she asked.

Enori looked back to her. "The dead."

Chapter Twenty-Four

Senara's gaze whipped up from Enori's cryptic words when she heard something. Feet. *Lots* of feet. "We've got to go, now!"

About to take off, she stood there, transfixed. Brielle brought her arms up, hands out and open wide as she tilted her head back and closed her eyes. The ground around her and around the girls began to glow in that same thin line of fire that the fire gate in the doorway had been. Except, it began to rise.

Before it got too high, Brielle stepped over the growing fence of fire and turned to face the girls. She didn't lower her hands until the top rail of the fire fence was above the tallest girl's head. Finished, she dropped her hands.

"My sweets," she said softly to them. "This fire will not harm you but will harm anyone who tries to get to you. You need to stay together, as this will stay with you as we get out of here." With that, she looked to Senara. "Let's go."

Knowing that Brielle needed to stay close to the girls, even in their protective ring, Senara took off. The good thing was, with that mobile fire protection following her, it lit her way. At this point it made no difference if they were seen or not; the men knew they were there, and from what their captive had said, Bahutha did, too.

Sure enough, three men ran out of the shadows down the tunnel at her. One was armed with a sword, the other two with axes. She sent a bowling ball of energy at the frontrunner, sending him flying back into his two comrades. The one farthest back hadn't been knocked down, so she took him on. His sword clashed into hers. A good swordsman, he was able to keep up.

"Don't kill him!" Brielle yelled out as she ran toward them. "Don't give Bahutha any more!"

Oh, right. Heeding the warning, she redoubled her efforts, sending him backward in the tunnel as he tried to fend off her aggressive and powerful attack. Meanwhile, she heard what sounded like a crack of thunder reverberate throughout the tunnel and a man scream, then a thud, sounding like a body falling to the ground.

"My eyes!" he screamed.

Senara winced inwardly, as she'd seen Brielle use that tactic before. She knew there were scorch marks where his eyes had once been, rendering him blind for the rest of his days. Down one, and she was about to literally knock this guy out. He scurried back farther and farther, now using two hands on his grip as he tried to keep up. Finally, she used the pommel of her sword to crack him in the forehead.

Down he went. Turning, she saw the girls reaching them, so relieved to see them. She gave them a brilliant smile before turning her blade to the final man, who was about to swing his axe at her. His hand and the axe with it went with one swift slice, leaving him staring at the bleeding stump with wide, shocked eyes. His screams were deafening as he fell to his knee, cradling his arm.

No time to worry about him, Senara ran on, Brielle shepherding the girls past the carnage and following. They reached the bend where they'd initially met Willem, which Senara had to keep out of her mind for the moment. She had no time to dwell or worry about that. She had to get them all out alive.

They were about to reach the end of this tunnel, which would lead to the main one at the end of the "fork," when she heard more running footfalls. From what she could see, they hadn't yet gone through the narrow, bottleneck portion of the tunnel. Turning to Brielle, she nodded at the girls following.

"You stay with them," she said. "I am going to surprise them through that narrow bit."

Brielle nodded. "All right."

Without another word, Senara took off and eased herself into that space, where a person had to glide along with their back against the wall. She could no longer see what was coming from the benefit of the protective fire ring, nor could she chance using an orb, which was long gone from the fighting anyway.

Standing there in the dark, she listened. She could hear her heart pounding in her chest, so she took several deep breaths to try to calm it. Wouldn't do for her to have a heart attack right there and Brielle have to drag her behind back to Bowhar along with ten nine-year-olds.

Closing her eyes, she reached out, separating each step, in her mind seeing how many men there were based on those. At least eight.

"Damn it," she whispered.

Looking back the other way, she could see the glow way down the tunnel from Brielle's fire. There was no way she was taking the Druid from those girls. Fire ring or not, she was all they had.

Chewing on her bottom lip, she looked back the other way. No choice, she tightened her grip on her blade and, with the roar of the warrior, she launched herself out of that chasm, sending a massive blast of energy into the well-armed men running her way.

All of them stopped, some sent flying backward into the others farther back. The torch one of them had been carrying landed on the ground, the fire still burning, shedding a bit of ghoulish light and shadow on the situation. Others hugged the wall, hands covering their heads until it passed. By that point, she was already in action.

Some of them were no match for her and they were easily cut down, but others were proving to be a challenge. In this moment, if they died, they died. She had to get her and those behind her past these bastards.

"Brielle!" she yelled out, still blocking every advance by the man who was currently in front of her. "Go now!"

Hoping like hell she'd been heard, Senara cried out when she took an elbow to the mouth. Instantly she tasted blood but kept going. Another man was jumping in to join with the first. She got in a good kick to the second man's groin, which dropped him temporarily to his knee.

Teeth gritted, Senara gave it all she had when finally, as though a dragon had been loosed in the tunnels, a massive wave of fire shot out from that chasm.

Just barely seeing it come in time, Senara grabbed the man she was fighting in a bear hug, turning his back to the tongue of flame so she was protected between his body and the wall. The screams were horrendous as the other men ignited. Within that stream of fire was Brielle and the girls, all running for their lives.

Beyond relieved, Senara's eyes fell closed for just

a moment before she shoved as hard as she could, the man she'd been fighting falling back into the tail end of the blaze, his pants catching.

Hurt and bleeding, Senara ran as hard as she could, feeling as though she were chasing the tail of a comet. She saw the larger entrance, the antechamber beyond lighting up like a firebox as Brielle and her train entered.

Relief was Senara's last thought before her foot was grabbed and she was brought down so hard that her head smacked against the stone floor. She blinked rapidly as she saw stars and little birdies. She only had about three seconds to think about that before she realized what was happening.

Flopping over to her back, she used powerful legs to send the man leaning over her flying backward. Another man crawled up to her. His hair was still smoking, half his face blackened. The look in his one good eye was pure murder. He was wheezing; obviously the damage went beyond skin deep with him.

Raising a dagger, he was about to bring it down to her chest when she sent him off her with an energy blast. He hit the wall and slid down. She figured he was probably dead, attacking her with his last bit of life.

Scrambling to her feet, she saw most of the men were still burning, bodies charred beyond recognition. Her head hurting so badly from her fall that she wanted to throw up, she took a moment to catch her breath before turning to head out. But, just before she could do that, she felt her entire body slow and then stop. It was as if she were made of molasses. Even just to breathe, her chest was heavy.

She staggered backward as she felt as if gravity itself was pulling at her, tugging at her legs to buckle.

Opening her mouth, she couldn't speak, couldn't scream, and could barely think. Listless, she fell to one knee, head teetering on her shoulders like a bobblehead. It was then that she saw it.

Oozing out of all the men on the floor, all clearly dead, was a black mist. It was oozing out of their mouths and nostrils, slowly billowing into the air and making it hazy. It was all around her, and it was the same smoke-type thing that Arali had pulled from the man's body.

It had no smell but was cool as it brushed against her face and over her arms like a lover's caress. It reminded her of the energy in the Crystal Palace, though this left her feeling decidedly empty. Her mind lost all focus, and her emotions were just...flat.

Finally, her legs gave out totally, and she fell to her side with a grunt. She knew it hurt, but her brain wouldn't even focus on that. Instead, she rolled to her back, staring up at the ceiling of the tunnel through the haze. She knew her head hurt, and she knew her hip hurt from where she'd just fallen. She knew her arm was bleeding, and she knew she needed to get out of there.

But...what? But, what?

There was a presence beside her now. She couldn't even turn her head to see who it was. That was okay, he did it for her. A cool touch to her chin and she was looking over at a man kneeling next to her. He wore a dark brown cloak, hood pushed back. His light blue eyes were so dull, she thought. Lifeless. Kind of how she felt.

His fingers caressed the side of her face, those dull blue eyes studying her features before they wandered down to look at her breasts and her body.

"So beautiful," he said. His hand trailed down from her face and over her throat to cup her left breast. "Always wondered what it would be like to have breasts," he murmured, gaze flicking back to Senara's. "A most sensuous body part. Maybe I'll have to try that next time," he murmured, as if to himself.

She wanted to tell him…tell him… Tell him what? Why would she tell him anything, again?

She could only stare dumbly at him. Soon enough the hand was removed from her breast and returned to her face. Her cheek was cupped, and he readjusted his body so he was on his knees next to her. Moving to hover his face over hers, he looked deeply into her eyes.

"So beautiful," he said, again almost as if to himself.

Lowering his face, his other hand came up so he had both sides of her face cupped in his hands. He pressed his lips to hers and, tightening his hold, he sucked so hard that her head arched back on the cold stone floor. She couldn't breathe, as it felt like a fire hose had been placed in her mouth and turned on, but in reverse.

A massive rushing sound filled her ears, like a tornado had just been loosed inside her head. She tried to lift her arms, move her legs, anything to get him off her, but her body refused to comply. She felt doped, drugged, and now, smothered. The heel of her left boot limply thudded against the floor before everything went black.

Chapter Twenty-Five

It was dark. It was very dark. She had no idea where she was, so stayed put for a moment, hoping her eyes would adjust or her ears would adjust, something. She was standing, she knew that. Reaching out, she felt around until she could feel a wall, a door, anything. Her hand did come into contact with something, and it was cold and smooth in parts and rough in others.

Stone? She slowly knelt down, eyes as wide as they'd go as she tried to pierce through the darkness, which was so complete. Yes, at her feet, stone. This was largely smooth as if worn that way by thousands of feet treading upon it. Standing back erect, she took a careful step, waiting for her toe to nudge something. It came into contact with nothing, so she took a second step, equally as careful.

Her arms flew out for balance as her third step resulted in a dropped foot, landing on another hard surface. Stairs? Again reaching down, yes, it felt like stairs. She used the heel of her foot to keep track of the back of the previous step as she lowered herself to the third step and the fourth. Finally, she was on solid ground again. That is to say, there were no more steps in the immediate vicinity.

She took very small steps forward until her toe did tap against something hard. Reaching out, she gasped when she realized what she was touching was something soft. Feeling around, she felt the softness of a garment, a shirt. Then, beneath that shirt was the pectoral muscles of a man. Her hand whipped away as if it had been burned.

"I'm sorry," she gasped.

The man said nothing, nor did he move or seem to react in any way. Confused, she reached out again. Same thing, soft shirt, defined pectoral beneath. She slapped lightly, no response. Her hand slid up to feel a throat and an unmoving Adam's apple. Up farther, the face, which needed a bit of a shave. Nothing.

Her hand moved out a bit and delivered a slap. Not enough to cause pain but to get some sort of response, even if just the slight shaking of the head. Nothing. With featherlight touches, her fingers found his eyes. They were open, and even with the touches to his eyelashes, nothing. She also realized when placing her hand before his nose and mouth, there was no breath.

Shuddering physically and verbally, she staggered back and into something else soft. Whirling around, again her hands came into contact with a standing clothed human. This one was a woman, and when her left hand accidentally cupped a breast, nothing. No reaction, the nipple didn't harden from contact, no gasp of indignant surprise. Nothing.

Suddenly, she felt completely closed in, as if these still figures were moving without her knowing, closing in on her, suffocating her. Panic began to settle in, and she pushed at the woman, who did not move, did not fall, nor did she step back to regain her balance.

Panic full-on, she tried to shove her way through these...people, ping-ponging her way from one to the other and back again.

Nearly desperate now, she clawed her way through the silent throngs and the inky blackness. It was so quiet, so dark, she could almost hear the silence. She could almost feel the complete darkness, darker than the grave.

Tears ran down her cheeks and her breathing was near panting now. Everywhere she went, another person, another body, another body part grabbed, hit, or squeezed as she tried to get out, get away.

Kazia.

She gasped, frozen in place. She blinked several times as she tried to see if she'd actually heard that or if it was just in her mind. She used the shoulder of her shirt to wipe at her tears. She—

Kazia.

"Hello?"

Kazia.

She whirled around, as she swore it was coming from somewhere behind her. She strained every sense she had, trying to listen for movement, breathing, anything!

Kazia.

"I'm here. Who are you? Where are you?"

She cried out when a hand rested on the back of her neck and, about to turn around, a second hand found its way to her face, holding her steady as soft lips pressed to her own. She was startled but then relaxed as there was something familiar about those lips. Something comforting and something remembered.

She sighed into the returned kiss, relieved. But then, she realized she tasted something. What was it... Blood. She tasted blood.

She pulled her mouth away and turned her head. Her hand came up to her lips and she felt blood dribbling down her chin from her mouth. Stupidly, she looked down at her fingers, even though she couldn't see them at all.

Suddenly, with a loud clack, a light was turned

on, like a spotlight. The blinding light shone down on the woman standing before her, blood all down her chin and onto her neck. Gasping, she took a step back to see the woman's torso was covered in blood. Her body began to fall, and it was all Kazia could do to catch her before she hit the floor.

She pulled the woman up into her lap, her eyes taking in the incredible damage done to her torso. The tears began anew as her gaze trailed up to the face. Instead of the expected sightless brown eyes, she saw blue-tinted silver eyes looking back at her.

"Help me," the woman whispered, a bloodstained hand reaching up to cup the side of Kazia's neck. "Help me."

"No!" Gasping for air, Kazia shoved the covers away as she desperately tried to get away from…

Panting and eyes wide, she looked around as she was on hands and knees on the bed. A figure hurried into the room and to the bed. She was but a silhouette against the firelight coming from the other room, but immediately her presence was comforting. She sat on the edge of the bed, her face coming into focus as Kazia calmed.

"It's okay," Ione said softly. "Shh." She ran her fingers lightly through Kazia's hair before she cupped the side of her head. "It's okay."

Taking several deep breaths, Kazia tried to get herself to calm and her heart to stop racing. She found it so incredibly strange that, though her heart no longer beat, it still reacted.

She looked around, noting she'd nearly destroyed the bed. Falling back to her butt, she and Ione got the covers back onto the bed and in place before Kazia was urged to lie back.

"Come here," Ione said, lifting the covers and scooting beneath them fully dressed. She held out an arm, indicating Kazia should move up to snuggle in against her.

Not the first time she'd woken from some horrible nightmare or memory, Kazia gave her a sheepish look before doing as bade. She laid her head on Ione's shoulder tentatively, worried she'd hurt her.

"Oh, come here," Ione said, sounding amused even if understanding, pulling her in against her. Once Kazia got settled, the smaller woman again ran her fingers absently through shaggy, dark strands. "Want to talk about it?" she asked softly

Did she? Kazia tried to remember what had happened. Finally, she swallowed and spoke. "I was in this place. It was so dark. You know, the kind of dark you can almost smell, almost taste."

Ione nodded. "Okay."

"There were all these people there. Just standing in rows. They didn't move, like they were in a trance or something. I couldn't get away from them. Then finally…" Her voice hitched on the last word as she saw it again. "So much blood," she whispered, the tears coming back.

Ione said nothing, simply held her for a long time until Kazia began to calm. "I know it's hard," she finally whispered. "Do you know who the people were? Maybe those you killed in battle? Or maybe the Colosseum?"

Sniffling, Kazia used the sheet to wipe at her eyes and cheeks. "I don't know," she finally said. "Probably. But," she said, sniffling again before setting back against Ione's shoulder. "The one at the end. The one who was so bloody. She kept calling my name, asking for my help." She smirked. "That was after she kissed me."

"Kissed you?" Ione said, surprise in her voice.

"Yes." Kazia smirked again. "Only me, right? In the middle of a soul-purging nightmare, a beautiful woman shows up." Her smile was small at the little chuckle she heard.

"Well," Ione said, a bit of playfulness in her tone. "You did have your way with the ladies, you know." She was quiet for a moment, then said, "Can I tell you something?"

"Of course you can." Truth was, Kazia was relieved for a change in subject. She was badly shaken by that dream or whatever it had been.

"I have worked through pretty much everything, now. Finally, my death. Which," she added in a gentle tone. "That is usually the last to come. It's not easy."

Kazia said nothing for a moment. She hadn't been told how she died and had no memory of it. Early on, Ione told her she would not be told, that it had to come to her when she was ready.

"Um, I look forward to it?" was all she could manage.

Ione chuckled, resting her head against that which rested on her shoulder. "Anyway, so the last thing I need to do before I go is tell you this. You were the only person in that lifetime that made me feel special, made me feel beautiful, and made me feel I was worth anything." She left a kiss on Kazia's forehead. "Thank you for that," she whispered against the soft skin.

Kazia lifted her head, bracing herself on a forearm as she looked down at the woman who looked up at her. In the many, many weeks she'd been in Yewa—or was it months, now?—she and Ione had not discussed where their relationship had been headed, nor what they'd done in the baths that last night.

She felt that it was pretty much mutually understood that they had been two women who had desperately needed to be seen for who and what they were. Because of that, they'd been drawn to the other, a bond forming that had literally lasted beyond death.

She smiled, bringing up a hand and gently tucking some long dark strands behind one of Ione's ears.

"You are one of the most beautiful souls I've ever known, Ione," she said softly. "And I suspect that I will *ever* know. You deserved so much better than you got, and even though I am going to miss you so much, I am so glad you're going back." She cupped her face with her hand, giving her an encouraging smile. "You deserve all the happiness that you can possibly get."

"You know," Ione murmured, looking into Kazia's eyes as if into her very soul. "I think in another world you and I would have had a real chance." She reached up and stroked Kazia's cheek and jaw with her fingertips.

"I do, too."

They shared a smile before Ione lifted her head, lightly pressing her lips against Kazia's. They remained that way for a moment, reacquainting themselves with the other woman's touch. Another press, this one a bit more firm. Kazia followed her as Ione's head rested back on the pillow.

Their lips began to move together, slow, testing, gentle. For Kazia, it was so healing to know that Ione was all right, despite the fact she'd been staying in her house since the day she'd finally finished up in the Shower of Sorrow.

During their time together, it had never once been uncomfortable, nor expectant. The air between them had never been heavy or filled with the need that had begun to build between them at the end in Britannia.

And now, she knew in the depths of her soul that this wasn't about sex or lust. In fact, she felt none of the things that would normally go along with such a thing. She felt a deep love for this woman and a deep caring that she knew she'd always carry for her.

It wasn't exactly just a "friend" kind of love, but it wasn't exactly romantic love, either. Perhaps, she thought, more of a first love sort of thing. That person you'd always have in your heart no matter what, though they weren't meant for you in the long term.

Finally, the kiss came to a natural and beautiful end, and Ione pulled her into a tight and warm hug.

"I'll always love you, Kazia," Ione murmured into the hug.

Kazia's smile was filled with so much peace at those words. "I'll always love you, too," she whispered, leaving a firm kiss to the side of Ione's head.

❧ ❧ ❧ ❧

They walked through the space, Kazia looking around. Her hands were tucked into the pockets of her baggy trousers, which she'd decided she really liked. She and Ione had gone "shopping," and she'd grabbed a few other types of clothing to try, but overall she'd stuck to what had been provided for her that first day. She did, however, finally get a pair of boots. She'd seen some of the men wearing those in Britannia and had always wanted a pair. In Rome, that wasn't going to happen.

Now, her booted steps thudded dully on the wide plank flooring. This was a very small little house with a downstairs and an upstairs. She wasn't sure she needed the upstairs, but she'd agreed to allow Ione to show her different styles and eras. This one, Ione had explained, was what was called a two-story cottage. It was made of rock and in many ways reminded her of Britannia.

The second floor in this house was a loft, so basically large enough for her bedroom. The downstairs had a living room with a really nice fireplace. She'd found at Ione's place that she really liked that. It also had a kitchen and bathroom with her beloved shower. She walked over to one of the three windows in the loft and looked down at the wide-open expanse beyond the cottage.

She hadn't wanted to live close to others, needing to really learn what it meant to be on her own with all her own choices. Yet, she would have the full freedom and ability to be part of others' lives whenever she wished. Ione had said it was the best of both worlds.

"It's so quiet here," she said.

Looking over her shoulder, she saw her friend, who leaned against a wall out of Kazia's way yet was there for support or to answer any questions Kazia may have. She was still learning how everything worked.

Kazia was still realizing that she and she alone had the right to decide. It was a definite learning curve for her to not defer to everything Ione said or suggested, as that's what she knew. The smaller woman had been incredibly patient with her, asking Kazia's opinion on everything.

She would give the warrior a look that cried bullshit when Kazia tried to give her an *I don't know* or *I don't care.*

"That's one thing you said you wanted," Ione reminded her.

Kazia nodded. Turning away from the window, she walked to the safety railing that ran along the length of the loft and looked down over everything on the first floor again. "I can't get over the fact that you don't need coins here." She met Ione's amused gaze.

"Nope." Ione pushed off the wall and headed to the steep stairs, Kazia following. "In Yewa and Duras, there's plenty for everyone. And," she added. "If you got to Bowhar, where you deal with humans, you'll learn the system there. I've not been there, but I know it works more like the earth plane than either Yewa or Duras does."

Kazia considered this as she made her way down after Ione. "I'm not sure about this Duras place yet."

"There are some who never leave Yewa again, Kazia," Ione said, reaching the main floor and walking over to the fireplace to take a seat on the wide hearth. "You don't have to leave here if you don't want to. Or," she added, resting her arms on her thighs. "You can live here and visit there, shop there, whatever." Her smile was brilliant. "Choices."

"I know," Kazia grumbled good-naturedly. "And, you've been there?" She glanced her way before she wandered to the back door in the kitchen, which was only separated from the living room by what Ione called a cooking island.

"I have. But I knew I wasn't staying here, so I didn't really spend much time there. While I waited for you, I worked on a lot of preparation for my next turn." Her smile was so excited. "All about the history!"

"Are you nervous?" Kazia asked, walking back to

the living room and sitting next to her on the hearth, the stone cold beneath her behind.

Ione gave her a shy smile, a smile Kazia hadn't seen since she'd been in Yewa. The Ione she'd come to know now was so filled with life and seemed so happy and filled with self-assurance. For her to look like this now, Kazia felt the need to give her the support that Ione had given endlessly and selflessly to her during her profound journey of healing.

Scooting over a bit on the rough, cold stone they sat upon, she wrapped her arm around the smaller woman's shoulders. Ione's head rested against Kazia's shoulder.

"No idea where or when you're going in time, but I think you're going to do amazing," Kazia said softly. "You are so smart, so clever and loving. Your determination and curiosity is your greatest asset."

"Thank you," Ione murmured. "There's so much I want to do. So much I want to experience."

"Like what?"

"Well," Ione said, "Love. Real, true, and deep love. *Passionate* love," she added.

"And this time," Kazia said. "You'll be able to be yourself and find that amazing woman and love her openly and honestly."

Ione nodded before she lifted her head, looking at Kazia. "You, too." She lightly poked her in the tank-top-covered chest. "She's here, you know."

Kazia shook her head. "I've had enough of that to last me ten lifetimes."

Ione gave her a sad smile and shook her head. "No. What you had was forced sex, Kazia. Not love. Love is more than that. I hear sex with a woman is amazing," she said with a saucy grin. "And as much as

I look forward to experiencing that in its time, there's so much more." She looked deeply into Kazia's eyes. "You have a soul cord, Kazia."

Dark eyebrows drew. "What's that?"

"It connects you to her, no matter what." Those soulful brown eyes studied her again, digging into places that Kazia was afraid to know what they'd find. "Trust me."

Kazia felt very sad all of a   sudden and couldn't continue to look into those eyes. Instead, Kazia looked down at her lap. "I don't have anything left to give, Ione." She shook her head. "I just don't."

Ione rested her head against Kazia's shoulder again and let out a long, contented sigh. "You will," she murmured. "I promise."

Chapter Twenty-Six

The scampering of Hamish's excited feet could be heard all over the small cottage. "Don't get in trouble, lad!" Brian grunted as he and Kazia carried the dresser very carefully and a bit awkwardly up the steep and narrow stairs to the loft.

Kazia grinned at him over the heavy piece of furniture as she backed her way up to the top of the stairs, her feet securely on the floor of the loft. With a grunt of exertion, she heaved the dresser up and over until it, too, was on the floor of the loft, no longer on the stairs.

She felt eyes on her and looked to see Brian still standing on the stairs, hands still out where they'd been bracing the dresser, which was no longer there, his mouth open.

"What?"

Brian said nothing, just shook his head "Uh, should I go get more?" He thumbed the direction of the front door.

Bursting into laughter, Kazia waved him up. "Help me."

As the two got the dresser into place, they heard Hamish giggling as he scampered to the front door where Ione and Danielle were coming in carrying boxes filled with the dishes Kazia had picked out for herself.

First time she'd ever done anything like that and though it may have taken nearly a full day to do it, she got it done. She was damn proud of herself for all she'd done, the progress she'd made, and how freeing it truly was.

"Okay," she said, slapping the man who had become a true friend to her, along with his wife, on the shoulder. "Now for the bed."

"How 'bout this," he suggested as they headed to the stairs. "I'll go grab the headboard and you can grab the rest." His laughter filled the entire cottage at the look on her face.

Three hours later, everything was moved in, and the group had eaten. Now, a fire was going in the fireplace. Brian and Danielle—affectionately called Dani—were cuddled together on the couch with Hamish curled up in Dani's lap. On the matching love seat, Kazia and Ione sat, the smaller woman cuddled into Kazia's side.

Kazia absolutely loved how comfortable it was between them. She truly felt like Ione was her best friend, a special relationship of pure caring like she'd never known could even exist.

"So," Ione was saying. "Hamish"—she glanced up at Kazia—"the little four-year-old who ran up to you every day, was killed in the attack." She looked back to Dani and Brian. "But his parents were somehow spared."

Dani nodded, a soft smile upon her lips as she absently ran her fingers through the boy's short blond hair. He was fully conked out in her arms. "Aye."

"And, your own baby also survived," Ione continued.

Brian nodded, sadness passing briefly through his eyes. "Bittersweet feelin,'" he said. "Knowin' he's out there. But," he added, tone brightening. "Now we get to raise this little guy, and his parents in the earth plane are raisin' *our* boy." His smile was filled with a beautiful peace. "How it works when wrongs are righted. Even though," he added, looking down at the sleeping boy in his wife's arms. "Not always easy to recognize that right away."

Kazia looked away as she brought up the hand that wasn't resting on Ione's other shoulder. She wiped at the tear that had appeared out of nowhere. One thing she had found was her emotions were so close to the surface so often, now. She once asked Ione if something had gone wrong in the process in the Shower of Sorrow.

In response, Ione had given her the sweetest look and the sweetest hug.

"No. That's how it's supposed to be, Kazia," she'd explained.

Kazia had been a bit bemused at the fact that it had taken her heart to *stop* working for it to *start* working. Now, she smiled at her emotion as she looked at the little wet spot on her fingertip. It took her a few moments, eyes blinking rapidly as she felt more emotion threatening to leak out.

Laughing at herself, she shook her head. "Sorry." Looking to her lap, she finally felt she could speak. She looked to the little family sitting across and to the left of her. "I think it's really wonderful."

Brian leaned over and placed his hand on her knee. His gaze bored into hers, so much understanding in his. No, Kazia was not a man, but she'd spent her entire lifetime learning from, working with, and fighting against them. She understood them in a way that she was just now learning to understand her own gender.

In that moment, something passed between the

two, "man to man," as it were. It was an understanding and almost permission from Brian for Kazia to just be herself. And, most importantly, it was encouragement to *feel.*

⁂

Ione had offered to stay with her this first night or take her back to her own place, but Kazia was determined to face this on her own. She had to get her sea legs under her. Ione had been the most incredible person to bring her through the most difficult and profound experience of her life, but it was time for her to lean on herself.

The after-dinner mess had been cleaned up and goodbyes had been said. Hamish had even, yet again, nearly squeezed Kazia's head off her shoulders with one of his wonderful hugs. Now, she was alone in the little cottage.

The fire was still going in the fireplace, which she stood in front of. Hands tucked into the pockets of her trousers, she stared into the flames, which had far more of a silvery glow than the orange she was used to on the earth plane.

Everything in Yewa seemed to be kissed by the moonlight, inside and out. Initially it was a bit disconcerting, but now it was beautiful. And, as she looked at those silvery flames, her mind tossed in a bluish hue to them.

That took her aback for a moment. She knew that color. Where from? Reaching up, she used her fingers to brush her entirely too shaggy bangs out of her eyes.

Eyes... She saw them, the most unusual and beautiful eyes she'd ever seen. Almost like precious jewels, so beautiful and seemingly translucent. Who was that? Who did they belong to? She could see the eyes but could not see the face. The harder she tried, the farther away it got. Finally, she decided to stop. Like so much, she knew—well, hoped—it would come to her in time.

Turning away from the fire, she headed to the bathroom area to get ready for bed. She looked into the mirror above the pedestal sink, taking in her reflection. She wasn't sure how old she'd been when she'd died, as she'd long ago lost track of time once she'd been sold from the Roman army.

She thought it had been about two years, her time in a cage and then the Colosseum, but wasn't positive. If that was true, then she was twenty or so. Far too young to die. But, the irony was, that was pretty par for the course for a gladiator. A brutal existence and so often a brutal death. Had *that* been how she'd died?

Kazia turned her face this way and that, noting the sculpted features, proud jaw, and high cheekbones. She trailed her fingers over them, feeling the soft skin, which no longer held the deep tan she had in life. From the age of fifteen, forced into the Roman military and her life spent mostly outside. Then, forced into the arena and topless most of the time, even her torso had been dark.

With that in mind, she reached down and grabbed the hem of her tank top, tugging the garment up and over her head. Her gaze fell to that torso and the sports bra that now secured her breasts snugly inside. Ione had been right—definitely more comfortable to have the support. Tossing the tank top aside, she removed her bra, too.

With the rebirth, as it were, her tanned skin was

now the shade it always should have been, undamaged by the sun. The scars left by blisters from horribly sunburned skin no longer freckled her shoulders or forehead.

The tip of her nose no longer had the constant darker brown hue that had come from it being sunburned over and over again and finally the redness turning to a permanent slightly darker brown than the rest of her face. No doubt from the profound damage to the layers of skin.

The scar that had been just beneath her left breast from a spear she'd taken in the arena was also gone. That one had hurt, and frankly she'd thought that was the end for her. But ultimately they'd patched her back together, even though she'd had to miss two matches for that one. She looked at her arms, running the hand of one along the skin-covered muscle of the other. That she had not lost in death.

In life, it had baffled her father while she'd been growing up in Greece. How was it that, seemingly without effort, she'd developed such a sculpted body? The strength and power of her body had seemed to stun and disgust him in fairly equal measure. As much as he'd made very consistent use of her attributes in the physical labor of his profession, he'd ridiculed her for not being "normal."

The irony was never lost on her that, despite being forced into the military, it was the only place where her physique had given her acceptance, as she could do what the men could and, oftentimes, beyond.

Her fingers moved to her torso, avoiding her breasts. Ione had been the only woman who had ever looked at her like she *was* a woman and not just an object to provide entertainment or pleasure. She had no idea how she felt about her femaleness. It was part of her—she understood and accepted that—just had no real idea what to do with it.

So, her fingers moved on to her stomach. She could see and feel the muscle groups that made up her abdominals, fingertips tracing the definition. Though unseen in the baggy trousers she still wore, she knew her butt, thighs, hamstrings, and calves all shared the same definition.

The human body could be developed, she knew that. But she also knew her particular muscle structure wasn't common, didn't seem to be built in the normal way. Her hand slapped against the taught stomach as she met her own eyes again in the mirror. What was behind it? One of the soldiers she'd fought beside had once suggested she was part goddess.

This, of course, was not true. But there *had* to be something…*more*. Her body was essentially an example of the perfect female specimen, yet she had the strength and power of two men. By the sheer physiological makeup of the male, the weakest among them were stronger than the strongest female.

Not Kazia. Why? And then there was her fighting prowess and natural ability with any weapon put into her hands. Again, why? She'd never questioned any of this during her life. She'd just utilized the gifts she'd been given to help her survive another day. Now, she had so many questions

Ione told her that Ankou would visit her when she was ready, and he held all the answers. She looked forward to that day and wondered what it would take for her to finally "be ready."

For tonight, she decided she'd pondered enough. There would be plenty of time for that. Now, she wanted to wash her face and brush her teeth, then try out her brand-new bed. *Her* bed. *Her* bedroom. *Her* home. *Her* new start.

❧❧❧❧

The day had come, and Ione had showed up at Kazia's house, as she'd said she had a gift for her. So now they stood in her living room, the ever-present fire crackling in her fireplace. Looking very nervous and a bit shy, Ione handed over something wrapped in cloth. It very much reminded Kazia of their time in Britannia. And, as soon as she unwrapped the item inside, she understood why.

A basket. It was about the size of a large cereal bowl, all handwoven to perfection. She held it in her hands, so much rushing through her in that moment. She swallowed—hard—and looked to the other woman for explanation.

"I wanted to make that for you while I still had the know-how," Ione explained. "No doubt that will all be gone, memory erased so I can fill it back up with a whole new life of skills, knowledge, memories, and experiences."

Kazia could feel the emotion coming off Ione, even as her warm brown eyes remained dry. She had a feeling they wouldn't remain so for long.

"I didn't make one of my huge ones for you, as you don't really need that or have a lot of room for it." Ione smiled. "But I wanted to leave you with something that was made while I still remember you." The last word hitched as her eyes began to well.

Kazia gently set the basket aside and gathered the smaller woman into her arms. "This will be one of my most cherished possessions," she murmured into the dark hair tucked just beneath her chin. "Thank you." She smiled when she felt that dark head nod. "You will go on and do wonderful things in the twenty-first century." She smiled. "Can't even imagine the things you'll see."

"I'll send you a postcard," Ione murmured.

Kazia chuckled. "My wish for you," she whispered, growing serious, "is to become all that you wish to be. All that your brilliant mind can lead you to be. And that you'll finally have the love you so deserve, Ione. Good parents, siblings, and a life partner who gives you all you dream of."

She felt the woman in her arms start a bit as Kazia's own attention was drawn to the front of her house. Ione was leaving from there. It was the sound of clopping horse hooves and the creaking of a carriage.

Kazia squeezed her eyes closed, holding back her own tears, as Ione didn't need that. Instead, she squeezed her tightly before releasing her from the hug.

Ione took a long, deep breath as she stepped back from her. She smiled up at Kazia before leaning up and leaving a soft kiss on her lips.

"Here we go." She took a deep breath then hold of Kazia's hand. "Come with? See me off."

"Sure."

Hand in hand, the two left Kazia's cottage. She was surprised Ione still held on to her, but she suspected it was because she was literally trying to *hold on* to her. Where she was about to go had to be incredibly daunting, and she was completely alone in this. There was literally not another soul who could join her, unless she'd be part of a multiple birth situation, which she was not.

Parked just beyond the path up to Kazia's door was a beautiful carriage, which looked as though it had just driven out of the nineteenth century. It was ornate and stunning in its Victorian-era design and embellishments, with its two-horse team pulling it. A uniformed coachman sat in his place, reigns in hand. He said nothing, nor did he climb down to open the door.

The pair stepped up to the beautiful vehicle, and Kazia pulled open the door for her. Inside were two facing bench seats, the padded seating covered in rich velvet, as was the padded interior, with delicate stencil work in gold upon the wood ceiling and walls.

Kazia ducked her head in to check it all out. Looking back to Ione, she raised her eyebrows. "Fancy!"

Ione smiled. "Hey, I was given the choice, and I wanted to go in style."

"As you should."

She grabbed the smaller woman again, hugging her so hard she lifted her off her feet, earning a little squeal of surprise. Finally, she lowered her back to stand on the ground. With the gentle care of holding the most breakable egg, Kazia cupped Ione's face. She left a lingering kiss on her lips.

"Go get 'em, tiger," she whispered against them.

Ione smiled, her gaze studying Kazia's face as if trying to memorize it. She brushed the taller woman's cheek with the backs of her fingers before turning and stepping up into the carriage, which jostled under her weight until she got settled on the front-facing seat.

They shared one final smile before Kazia stepped back, her hands easing the door into place, the window now separating them.

Taking another step back when she heard the

coachman click his tongue, she watched as the carriage began to move, raising her hand to return the final wave from the woman inside. With silent tears lazily trailing down her cheeks, Kazia watched as the carriage moved forward until it was out of sight and she could no longer hear the clopping of the horses' hooves.

Epilogue

Senara lay on the ground on her back, one leg straight, the other slightly bent, her arms out at her sides. Her sword wasn't far from her right hand, the blade still smudged with the blood and gore of the fight. Her lips were slightly parted. Her eyes were open, staring sightlessly up at the ceiling of the cave-like blue-tinted chips of ice: beautiful in color but no life behind them.

Then, as though a dagger's tip had slashed the light blue, the color began to bleed out of the iris and flood into the white of the eye and across the pinpoint that was the pupil, darkening as it covered the entire surface of the eye until the light blue became coal black.

A loud gasp escaped parted lips before the inky blackness rushed back toward the pupil, as if sucked through a straw, leaving blue-tinted chips of ice behind.

To be continued in Book Two of Ancients—*The Found*

If you liked this book...

Share a review with your friends or post a review on your favorite site like Amazon, Goodreads, Barnes and Noble, or anywhere you purchased the book. Or perhaps share a posting on your social media sites and help spread the word.

Join the Sapphire Newsletter and keep up with all your favorite authors.

Did we mention you get a free book for joining our team?

sign-up at - www.sapphirebooks.com

Check out Kim's other books.

1049 Club - ISBN - 978-1-939062-97-0

Almost two hundred souls, one plane, six survivors, endless heartbreak.
When flight 1049, headed from Buffalo, NY tc Italy falls from the sky, a firestorm of drama, pain, angst and sorrow ensues. Can an author, a business owner, a teenager, good ol' boy, veterinarian and ruthless lawyer survive? Better yet, can those left behind?

1049 Club is a story of survival, love, deep regret and miracles. Can the living make peace with the
presumed dead? Can the presumed dead make peace with the lives and loves they thought they had before?

Blinded – ISBN – 978-1-943353-53-8

After a horrible explosion sends local television news reporter, Burton Blinde reeling both physically and emotionally, she walks away from her life and the dream job she was about to start at a major news network.

For six long years she hides out in a small mountain town, working at the local library, though is haunted by the life she had, including mysterious messages and gifts she was receiving before her life was turned upside down, a veritable bread crumb trail leading to the unknown.
Unable to resist, Burton begins to follow the clues, which will lead her into the darkest places of human nature that she may not be able to return from.

Damaged - ISBN - 978-1-939062-45-1

Family. A group of people you are related to by blood or love.

Nora Schaeffer has come home to her family after twenty years working around the world as a photographer for National Geographic. She's welcomed into the open arms of her father and siblings.

Family. A group of people who support you, lift you up when you fall.

Shannon, the youngest of the four Schaeffer siblings, has vanished, leaving her five-year-old daughter, Bella, terrified and alone. To help find Shannon, Nora has no choice but to turn to the dark-haired specter who has haunted her for twenty years. Along the way, she finds her own long-dead heart and uncovers chilling family secrets beyond imagination.

Family. A group of people who will stick together to hide the rotten soul at its core at any cost.

Who will live? Who will die? Who will be the most damaged? And who will learn to love again?

The Gift - ISBN - 978-1-948232-47-0

The dead do speak. You just have to listen. Homicide Detective Catania "Nia" d'Giovanni is the only daughter in a large Italian family of six children. The backbone—a position not applied for nor wanted—she continues to create new glue to hold the dysfunctional group together.

For Nia, family time feels more like herding cats than spending time with her brothers and feisty, aging parents.

Her heart has always been in her career with the Pueblo Police Department, especially since it will never be okay with her very Catholic mother to openly give her heart to any woman, until she meets a secretive waitress who has her at, Can I take your order?

And then it begins…

Three murders that are so gruesome, so horrible, they rock the small town to its core. Nia and her partner Oscar are left to piece together a deadly puzzle to find the key to unlock the monster they hunt.

Or, are they the hunted?

As they dissect the murder scenes where not one shred of evidence is left behind, more bodies begin to show up, each cleaner than the last, the shadowy specter that is the killer vanishing without a trace, making the woman Nia loves disappear right along with it.

When there is no evidence to follow, Nia must trust her instincts…or, is she being guided?

The Plan – ISBN – 978-1-948232-43-2

As the dark days of the Dust Bowl came to an end, the midsection of the United States tried to rebuild and revitalize. In the small, dusty farming town of, Brooke View, Colorado, teenager, Eleanor Landry and her mother were dealing with her father, a self-appointment fire and brimstone preacher to his congregation of two. A plan to survive.

As the dark era of the robber baron comes to an end, giants of industry and innovation emerged with fabulous fortunes manifested in the mansions that dotted the landscape across the country. Lysette Landon, the teen daughter of the wealthiest family in Brooke View, was everything a good, proper girl of privilege should be. Only problem was, she wasn't dreaming of finding a young man to raise a family with. A plan to be free.

One look, one touch, all plans are off.

Secrets deeper and darker than the grave would bring Eleanor and Lysette together, their families connected by a web of lies and broken promises. A plan to escape.

Be careful because, life has other plans…

The Traveler Book One: The Hunted - ISBN - 978-1-948232-91-3

A story so epic one book can't contain it. BOOK ONE:

1977: In the era between flower power and the yuppie, Sonia Lucas is a young wife and mother, just starting out in life. Without warning, a strange presence and dark force enters her life, clouds building…

1917: …and a storm brewing as the world reeled from the horrific events of World War I just before it was ravaged by a Spanish flu epidemic that would kill millions. Sephora Lloyd is a 16 year old girl lost in the responsibilities of an adult world helping to support herself and her mother. A beautiful young nun-in-training enters her life, bringing love and hope with her. That is, until a force bigger than either of them threatens everything Sephora holds dear.

Four women - three deaths - two words - one house
THE HUNTED

The Traveler Book Two: The Hunter - ISBN - 978-1-948232-93-7

A story so epic one book can't contain it. BOOK TWO:

1890: In the dying days of the Old West, Sally Little runs her booming brothel with the passion and tenacity the business of sex requires. Savvy and indulgent, there's one itch Sally can't let herself scratch. Afraid of hurting the woman she loves, she instead unleashes...

Present Day: ...her renovation crew and fixer upper TV show on a dilapidated mansion that has known nothing but death since a murder there in 1977. Samantha Leyton sees ratings gold in bringing the sagging old house to life, but instead she discovers only she has the power to unlock the mystery that hunted four women across time, leaving death and destruction in its wake. Can she release her sisters who came before her and finally be granted the gift of love that is stronger than any evil?

Four women - Three deaths - two words - one house THE HUNTER